Revenge
of
the Evil
Librarian

Revenge
of the Evil
Librarian

Michelle Knudsen

CANDLEWICK PRESS

First edition 2017

Library of Congress Catalog Card Number 2016951636
ISBN 978-0-7636-8828-8

16 17 18 19 20 21 BVG 10 9 8 7 6 5 4 3 2 1

Printed in Berryville, VA, U.S.A.

This book was typeset in Chaparral Pro.

Candlewick Press
99 Dover Street
Somerville, Massachusetts 02144

visit us at www.candlewick.com

For Brent Felker,
who is the kind of friend I'd like to be someday

Chapter | 01

Italian class is not what it used to be.

I am thinking this as I watch Signor O'Flannigan list our summer vocabulary words on the board. Signor O'Flannigan is young and enthusiastic and very, very nice. He flashes his sunny smile constantly and never yells at anyone and will talk to you in English outside of class without giving you a hard time about it. He is different from Signor De Luca (may he rest in peace) in pretty much every possible way. Almost everyone loves him.

But almost everyone has no idea what really happened to Signor De Luca. They don't even know he's dead. They especially don't know that the reason he's dead is because he was trying to help us defeat the evil librarian who was taking over the school and bewitching my beloved best friend.

They don't know that he would still be alive right now if Ryan and I had never gone to him for help. Which is something

I keep trying not to think about, but it's not easy. His memory is like a grouchy Italian dagger permanently embedded in my heart.

Today, incidentally, is the next-to-last day of school. (Tomorrow is a half day, consisting only of homeroom and an assembly, and therefore barely exists.) It's cute that Signor O'Flannigan is trying to teach a final class. No one is paying any attention to him.

Annie, the aforementioned beloved best friend, is sitting next to me, not only here and alive but also free from the influence of any demonic love spells. (I know that generally goes without saying about people, but Annie is a special case.) She is doodling in her notebook and daydreaming about her not-very-secret love interest. She's drawing little hearts and flowers and various intertwined versions of the initials *A* and *W*. (His name is William. He's in third-period statistics with her, and she talks about him a lot. A LOT. It's adorable.)

One row over and two rows up from where I am sitting, the lovely Ryan Halsey is also here and alive. He is also now my boyfriend (!!!) which perhaps I may have neglected to mention thus far. He is not very subtly playing a game on his phone. I forgive him for doing this instead of sending me sexy messages or turning around to give me affectionate looks or using this time to write me a sonnet or something because I am a really awesome girlfriend.

I am observing the people I love in this room and basking in their continued here-and-aliveness, and feeling so relieved that none of us are consorts to horrible demons for all eternity. I know I maybe seem to be fixated on the whole still-here-and-alive thing, but it was a big question for a while there in the fall. We all almost died. *Everyone in the whole school almost died.*

Annie was the only one in danger of becoming a demon consort, though. Well, other than Aaron, but he is old and does not go to our school and is not someone I care about. Plus, he *wanted* to be a demon consort, so there really wasn't a downside for him. Oh, and Danielle, but that was very sudden and brief and hardly counts. Plus I don't really like her all that much. Although I'm still glad she wasn't killed or made a demon consort.

It is possible that, out of context, none of this makes any sense at all.

Let us review:

During the fall semester, a ridiculously attractive but also very, very evil demon (Mr. Gabriel) set up shop in our high school as the new librarian and tried to steal away my best friend to be his demonic child bride. He killed some teachers, including poor Signor De Luca and our super-nice principal, and sucked out parts of a lot of kids' souls or life forces or whatever, but in the end I totally vanquished him. Well, with some help. Some very welcome help, like from Ryan, and some less-welcome-but-still-necessary help, like from the demoness who temporarily posed as our replacement Italian teacher.

The help from the demoness was tricky because it required me to make a promise to return to the demon world twice more at times of her choosing. Because it turns out I have some innate demon resistance that she can borrow to use against other demons if I let her. (The rather insulting technical term for the kind of human I am is *super-roach*. Or at least that's the rough translation of the unpronounceable demon word.) It's kind of complicated, I guess. But the short version is that I let her borrow my resistance the first time to help her become queen of the demons, and in return she gave me some (highly questionable) magic items that (nevertheless) helped me to kick Mr. Gabriel's evil ass and save Annie from him forever.

No one else actually knows about the thing where I have to return twice more to the demon world. Except the demoness, obviously. And the aforementioned Aaron, who used to be the guy who ran the esoteric bookstore and who later, sort of thanks to me, achieved his (highly questionable) lifelong dream of becoming the demoness's consort and going to live with her in fiery bliss until the end of time. He doesn't matter. The people who do matter—Annie, Ryan, Leticia, Diane—have no idea. Actually Leticia and Diane have no clue about any of the demon stuff at all. They just thought I was going through the usual tech-week stress during the time leading up to our *Sweeney Todd* fall musical production. Which I was, of course. There was just also a lot of extra stress involving multiple demons and Annie going temporarily crazy and many complicated and confusing feelings regarding Ryan, who confessed his growing affection for me right before I stabbed him with a magic protractor so I could get sucked into a vortex to the underworld.

But! All the stuff with Ryan worked out in the end. Did I mention that he is now my boyfriend? Also, he has forgiven me for said stabbing and for almost dying in order to save Annie. And for some lying that happened, since we agreed no more lying from now on. And so no more lying. Except about the two-more-trips-to-the-demon-world thing. But that's an old lie, not a new one, and so the rule does not apply.

Okay — enough about all the demon stuff. I don't want to dwell on bad things. The bad things are over now. Now is the time of happiness and joy across the land.

Exhibit A: Annie is not a demon bride! Also, she is alive and well and beginning to have a non-demony real-life love connection with an actual human boy.

Exhibit B: Ryan Halsey is my boyfriend!

Exhibit C: In exactly eight days, I will be getting on a bus with Ryan to go to Allengate, the theater camp he has been attending nearly every summer of his entire life. This is because (a) he got his parents to talk to my parents about how great the camp is, and (b) thanks to Mr. Henry's glowing recommendation and my set-design notes and sketches for *Sweeney Todd,* I was accepted into the camp's highly competitive set-design track, which means I will get to be set designer on one of the shows going up during each three-week session. I will be there for three sessions, and so that is three entire shows I get to design sets for, and I am incredibly excited about this. They even have mock Tony Awards at the end of each session, and I am going to win all of the set-design awards, because that is the kind of goal I like to have.

And while I am designing sets and winning awards, I will get to spend the *whole summer* with Ryan. Up in the woods somewhere. And I will get to watch him be amazing in whatever shows he gets into while I am being amazing designing the sets for whatever shows I get assigned to, which will maybe hopefully even be the *same* shows, and it is going to be the best summer ever in the history of summers.

When the bell rings, Signor O'Flannigan calls out some kind of have-a-good-summer-but-also-keep-practicing-your-Italian nonsense, but I'm not listening because (a) that's just silly, and (b) I'm too busy watching Ryan slide out of his chair and turn and walk toward me. It's rather a breathtaking sight. Even after all this time.

It's funny; in some ways I feel like I've known him forever, and in other ways he is still a big beautiful frustrating mystery. He's the only one who really understands (almost) everything that happened. We have shared experiences that no one else can even begin to imagine. And we've only gotten closer since then, even without the threat of horrible death to accelerate our connection. But I can still hardly ever tell what he's thinking. And he still makes me feel ridiculous and light-headed a lot of the time. Like right now. I've watched him get out of his chair at the end of Italian approximately forty-six times this semester, and you'd think I'd be over it, but I'm not. He is both strong and graceful, like a leopard or a ninja, and he kind of slides up and out and turns in one lovely fluid motion. And then he gives me one of those lopsided half smiles, and I have learned to remain sitting until after that part.

Once the smiling happens and I've adjusted, I can get up, too. And then he comes right up to me, which, I know, is normal, because he's my boyfriend and everything, but there is still a tiny part of the old Cyn lurking in the back of my brain who can't help shrieking with excitement that Ryan Halsey is standing RIGHT THERE. I tell the old Cyn to get a grip, but she just can't.

"Last Italian class of the year," Ryan says, shaking his head in mock sadness. "Are you sad? Do you need a hug?"

"I'm devastated. Please hug me."

He does. My legs forget to hold me up for a second, but they remember eventually.

"See ya later, lovebirds," Annie says, squeezing past us. This is her current favorite thing to call us. She has penned multiple drawings of Ryan and me as lovestruck ornithurae. I have some of them in my room. Others had to be destroyed, because, my God, that girl has an obscene imagination.

"See you at lunch," I say from against Ryan's shoulder.

"See you tonight," Ryan says to her, turning both of us awkwardly around because he's still hugging me. "Are you bringing William?"

I punch him as well as I can while still in the hug because he has been warned that the whole William thing is a very new and delicate situation. Annie glances away. "I — maybe. I haven't asked him yet. But yeah, maybe. I mean, that would probably be fun, right?"

"Ask him," I command, snaking a hand free to point at her. "You promised."

"Okay, okay," she says, backing toward the door. Then she flashes me a quick smile. "Probably." And then she's gone.

Reluctantly, I say to Ryan, "If you don't let me go, I'm never going to make it to English on time."

"It's the last day. No one will care."

"And you'll be late for Schwartzman. *He'll* care."

"Hmm."

"And I will see you later."

"But that's later. I like now." He squeezes me a little tighter. See? These are the things that make me love him.

"I like now, too," I say, trying and failing to get free. And not really minding, obviously. But he really will get in trouble if he's late. Even on the last day. "But . . ."

Finally he sighs, which, on the inhale, presses his lovely chest momentarily even tighter against mine, then lets me go.

"Oh, all right." He gives me a steely look. "I want more of that later."

"If I must."

"You must."

"Okay, then." I feel myself grinning in that ludicrous helpless way I do when I look at him for too long. It's such a relief not to have to try to hide it. He grins back, which only makes me grin more, and so I push past him and out the door before we get stuck in some kind of endless grinning black hole that no one can ever escape.

I'm still grinning when I get to my next class, even though I'm a few seconds after the bell. And even when I finally get my face to stop, the grinning continues on the inside. I know, I know: I'm ridiculous. Whatever. There's nothing I can do about it, and, honestly, I'm just too happy to care.

At lunch, Leticia and Diane and Annie are already at our usual table when I arrive.

Leticia begins to sing the Miss America song as I approach.

I give her a quizzical look as I sit down, and she shrugs. "It just felt right. I went with it. I'm sure there was some Sondheim song or other I could have chosen, but you know I don't know crap about musical theater."

"True," I say. "I don't mind being sung the Miss America song. Does this mean I have to devote my reign to bringing about world peace?"

"Or ending world hunger," Diane says.

"Or reversing climate change," Annie puts in.

"I'm exhausted already. I'm just going to eat my lunch."

"Good idea," Leticia says. She looks down and contemplates her own lunch. I look, too, and then put my sandwich down without taking a bite.

"What is that?" I ask.

Diane leans in. "L is only eating things that are green this week."

"Oh," Annie and I say in unison.

Leticia's lunch consists of sliced green peppers, a spinach salad with edamame and asparagus, a tiny (green) Tupperware container of guacamole, and some green Jell-O. None of us says a word as, after a minute, she goes for the Jell-O first.

"Anyway," Diane says finally, "do you guys want to come over before the party later? We can all leave from my house together."

"Sure," Annie says. "I can never get ready at my house without one of the siblings trying to 'help' me."

"Good," Leticia says to Annie. "Maybe our combined forces can prevent you-know-who from wearing something utterly inappropriate."

"You can try," Diane says, winking at L. She looks at me. "Cyn?"

"Absolutely. I need to get my Annie and Leticia and Diane time in before I leave for camp."

Annie pouts. "I still can't believe you're leaving for the whole summer. The *whole summer*. Who does that?"

"Future Broadway backstage megastars, that's who," Leticia says. She reaches over and pats Annie's hand. "Don't worry. We'll keep you company. If you're not too busy with sweet, sweet William."

Annie turns a highly amusing shade of scarlet. "Will you guys quit it? He's not — I'm not —"

"Yeah, yeah," I say. "Did you ask him yet?"

"About tonight?" Diane asks in alarm. "You mean you didn't ask him already?"

"No," Annie moans. "I can't. I want him to come, but I can't just walk up to him and say, 'Hey, want to come to a party with me?'"

"Yes, you can!" Diane and Leticia and I insist together.

Suddenly Diane looks up and then uses both feet to kick all of us under the table. We all turn to follow her gaze.

William is walking toward us. Leticia and Diane smile brightly at him. Annie seems to be trying to melt into the floor.

I watch him approach. William is super cute in a very slightly nerdy kind of way. Hipster glasses, plaid shirt, dark skin, and light-brown eyes. But he's got a little bit of a swagger, and there's something in his smile that is definitely not textbook angel. Like he's ninety percent sweetness and light and ten percent the opposite, but in all the best ways.

I think he's perfect for Annie.

I think she thinks so, too. Which is why she's so terrified.

"Hi, there," Leticia says when he reaches our table.

"Hey," William says, looking around to address all of us. Then he looks at Annie. "Can I talk to you for a minute?"

Annie nods and gets up without making a sound, following him over to the side of the cafeteria.

We stare shamelessly.

"Can you hear anything?" I ask.

"Nope," Diane says. "Too far. And my lipreading sucks."

"Their body language is good," Leticia says. "See how he's leaning in? I wish Annie would uncross her arms, though. It sends the wrong signal. Ooh! Uncrossed! Good girl. Now touch his hand. Touch it! Touch it!"

Diane lays her hand on L's arm. "I don't think she can actually hear you, honey."

"I know. I'm trying to send messages to her unconscious. It worked with the arms uncrossing."

We continue to watch them. He smiles, she smiles, *he* touches *her* hand, and then he walks away. Annie watches him go, a beatific smile still on her face.

Finally she comes back to us and sits down.

"Well?" Leticia says. "What happened?"

Annie's smile gets even bigger. She's having trouble looking at us. "He asked me to go to the party tonight. I didn't even know he was friends with Sarah."

"Yay!" Leticia shouts, loud enough for people at neighboring tables to look over. We all shush her.

"Yay," she says more quietly. "Although I still wish you'd asked him first. You need to take charge of your own destiny, girl!"

"Okay, okay," I say. "One step at a time. The important thing is that Annie is going to the party with William."

"Yes," Diane agrees. "Is he going to pick you up? Did you tell him to come to my house? Do you know what you're going to wear?"

"Do you own any eye shadow?" Leticia asks.

Annie looks at me helplessly. I put a protective arm around her. "No more questions, please. All will be revealed in the fullness of time. For now, everyone eats her lunch and is happy. Except you, L. I know you can't possibly be happy while eating that lunch."

"Shut up. It's a thing I read about. It's supposed to be super healthy."

"Green Jell-O?" Diane asks.

"Did you not hear me say shut up? What are you eating, dead fish in thick, slimy, white, disgusting sauce? Again?"

Annie puts her head on my shoulder as L&D continue their not-an-actual-argument, sounding even more like an old married couple than they used to. Their longtime best-friendship transformed into something more over the past few months, which surprised nobody, although I suspect there are more than a few disappointed teenage boys scattered about as collateral damage.

I pet Annie's soft brown curls. "It's going to be okay," I tell her. "He likes you. You like him. This is good. I promise."

"Okay," she says. "I trust you. You'd know if he was a . . . you know. Right?"

"Right," I say. It is not the first time she has asked me this question. One of the almost certainly unintentional gifts the evil librarian left me with was the ongoing ability to see if someone is a demon in disguise. Demons, to my enhanced eyes, have a glowing red halo kind of thing above their heads. William is entirely halo free.

I haven't seen any red halos since I returned from rescuing Annie from the demon world.

And that is the way I would like it to stay forever, please.

Except for those two return trips, I guess, since that would be hard to pull off. But I am still not thinking about those. It could be years before the demoness calls on me again. It could be never if she forgets that humans only live for like eighty to a hundred years, if we're lucky. Sometimes at night, when I can't sleep, I comfort myself with the idea that I'll probably be dead long before she thinks to call in her remaining favors.

Later, we go to Sarah Patel's annual end-of-the-school-year party. (Earlier, we went to Diane's, and Annie let us tell her what to wear and also let us put just a little extra eye makeup on her, and Diane did not let us tell her what to wear, and when William came to pick Annie up, we refrained from shouting lewd suggestions out the window at them.)

And now I am snuggled on a couch with Ryan, nestled

under his perfectly muscled upper arm, watching the party go on around us. Everyone is slightly manic with pre-summer energy. The seniors are talking about where they're going to college, and the few freshmen Sarah invited are mostly haunting the fringes of the room, not really knowing how to act or whom to talk to. The sophomores and juniors are more relaxed; most of us have done this before, and it's nice to not be nervous about being young and new and also not be distracted by being about to graduate and start whole new lives in possibly faraway places.

But it is the start of my last week before camp, which has me nervous in all kinds of other ways. I've never gone away for the summer before. I'm excited, of course, but also I know I'll miss Diane and Leticia and especially Annie. They promised to write and send care packages, but that will not be the same as actually getting to see them and talk to them. This is one of those camps where you have to surrender your cell phone when you get there, and laptops and tablets are not allowed. I guess that's so we can get the "full summer camp" experience, like they did in the old days, or whatever. But it means I won't even be able to talk to Annie on the phone. I'm sure once I'm there I'll get caught up in the shows and everything else, and it won't be so bad. Ryan loves this place like crazy, and that alone makes it something worth experiencing. And the idea of spending the whole summer immersed in musical theater is like some kind of magical dream. I know it will be great. It will.

But I keep feeling more and more uneasy.

All night long, I keep thinking I see something out of the

corner of my eye, only to turn my head to find nothing out of the ordinary. Just people having a good time at a party.

I catch a glimpse of Annie and William, who have not left each other's side for a second all night as far as I can tell, sitting on the floor in a corner, their heads close together as they talk.

I see Leticia and Diane dancing together through the door into the next room, laughing and holding hands.

I see random other people from my classes, some theater kids, some of Ryan's friends whom I've met over the past few months, some kids I only know vaguely from the hallways or study hall or wherever else. The few strangers don't seem at all out of place; just other kids that I never happened to have a class with or pass often enough in the hall to recognize. Nothing is wrong. Everything is fine. But I can't stop turning my head trying to see . . . something.

"Why are you all twitchy?" Ryan asks, his question tickling my ear as he leans close to be heard over the music. I am tempted to pretend not to hear him so he will lean even closer, but I'm too distracted by . . . whatever keeps distracting me.

"I don't know. Something . . . feels weird. I keep thinking I see something."

I feel his body tense where I'm leaning against it. "See what?" Just like me, there is some part of him that will always be waiting for another demon to appear.

Always.

I shake my head, frustrated. "I don't know." I look at him and smile weakly. "It's probably nothing. It's definitely nothing. I'm just having end-of-the-year hallucinations or something."

"Oh, right. Those. Of course."

"It doesn't matter." I try to make this true. "Whatever it is, it's nothing. I'm probably just tired. And excited. Only one more week before camp!"

"Okay," Ryan says. "But you'll tell me if . . . you know."

"Of course!" I elbow him for asking such a stupid question. Even though I suppose he has some tiny justification for wanting to remind me of the rules of disclosure. "But it's not anything like that."

"Okay." He smiles at me, and that helps a lot to make me forget whatever else might be going on in the room.

"Okay," I say, smiling back.

Then he pulls me closer and kisses me, and the rest of the room no longer has any significance whatsoever.

This is good, Old Cyn reminds me from somewhere in the back of my brain. *Everything is good. Everyone is alive and happy and good and this is going to be the best summer ever. Theater camp! All summer! Ryan Halsey is your BOYFRIEND!*

Yes, I know. Now shut up. I'm busy.

I focus my attention back on the kissing.

Oh my God the kissing.

I will never get tired of this.

It is going to be the best summer ever.

Chapter | 02

The best summer ever begins ridiculously early.

My alarm screams at me from the darkness, and I feel around for the snooze button.

"Cyn?" my mom calls from somewhere in the ridiculous early darkness. Like she was lurking outside my room just waiting for this signal. "You up?"

"Uhhh," I groan in response. Why does the stupid bus have to leave so early?

She heartlessly flips on my light, forcing me to burrow more deeply into my covers. "Let's go," she says. "Ryan's parents will be here in an hour."

I crawl half-conscious to the shower. The hot water and the aggressively energetic scent of my tangerine bodywash work their magic, and wakefulness slowly descends upon me. I am washed and clothed and downstairs with my enormous duffel in time to grab an English muffin and some orange juice before we hear the horn outside.

"Have a great summer, sweetie," my dad says, getting up from the table to envelop me in a giant dad hug. We already said our real good-byes last night, but ever since the "chemical leak" at the school in the fall, he has been making an effort to hug me a lot. I don't mind, really.

"Don't forget to write," my mom says with a not-quite-ironic smile. She hugged me last night, too, but I think that was enough for both of us. We're not really huggers. Of each other, I mean.

I smile back at her. "I won't."

And then Ryan is at the door, offering to carry my duffel because he is awesome and it is freaking heavy. He is smiley and excited. Like a puppy. A tall, sexy puppy. I try to shake off my lingering grouchiness at the early hour for his sake.

In the backseat of the car, I lean my head on his shoulder and half listen to the radio and his parents' occasional conversation. It's not only this early morning that's got me so tired; I've been exhausted all week. Some of it is because of many late nights with Annie and Leticia and Diane, but some of it is because of the relentless baseless uneasiness that still hasn't gone away. I still keep looking around for . . . something. It happens all the time when I'm awake, and my sleep is filled with demony nightmares that I can't quite remember when I wake up. I'm sure it's just anxiety about leaving my friends for the summer manifesting in wonky ways. It has to be. I focus on believing that once we get up there I'll be able to relax and have a good time.

Ryan gets his own parental hugs when they drop us off at the bus stop. They don't leave, exactly, but they go park in a spot in the parking lot and stay in the car and pretend not to be there, like all the other parents. There are a bunch of kids already waiting. Ryan knows nearly all of them, and he introduces me as his girlfriend to everyone, which cheers me up immensely.

"You waking up finally?" he asks after all the introductions are over, giving me a little squeeze.

"Yes, sorry. It's just been a weirdly long week. And I haven't been sleeping so great."

He kisses the top of my head. "It's going to be a great summer. You'll see."

I squeeze him back. "I know."

The bus arrives, and we all stack our duffels in the storage compartment and then climb aboard. The bus makes a few more stops and then heads for the hills. Chatter on the bus ranges from catching up on the past year to speculation about what the shows will be this summer.

"They're way overdue for *Candide*," a guy Ryan introduced as Craig says for about the fifth time. He's sitting across the aisle from us.

"Craig, you are the *only one* who likes *Candide*," someone calls from another seat. "None of us are going to hope for that with you."

Craig seems undeterred. "It's a great show. You just don't know how to appreciate it properly."

"What do you guys have against *Candide*?" I ask Ryan.

"Oh, nothing," he says back. "Craig's just been obsessed

with that show since birth, so we like to give him a hard time about it. Someday they really will do *Candide,* and we'll all be happy for him."

Not everyone is there for musical theater; there are straight plays as well, although I don't pay as much attention to the speculation on those. But no one seems to have any real information — it's all guesses and rumors and wishes. They'll announce the list tonight. And then tomorrow are auditions, and by the end of the day, everyone will know what show they're in. The audition equivalent for the set designers happened when we sent in our applications, but we won't find out the shows and our assignments until the same time everyone else does.

At some point I must doze off, because suddenly Ryan is shaking me gently awake. "Come on, sleepyhead. We're here!"

We stand and file off the bus. Through the windows I can see a crowd of other campers waiting to see who disembarks. Ryan jumps down ahead of me, and before he has taken three steps, someone streaks out of the crowd and tackles him to the ground. For a second my heart stops, but then I see that he is laughing, and I relax. Someone he knows. Obviously. Besides, I'm pretty sure a full-body tackle in broad daylight in front of scores of witnesses isn't most demons' style.

And then I see that the tackler is a tall, pretty, blond girl who has completely wrapped herself around him in her enthusiasm, and I stop relaxing.

Someone gives me a polite nudge from behind. I step off the bus and walk over to where some girl is sitting on top of my boyfriend.

"Hi!" I say brightly.

Ryan disentangles himself, climbs back to his feet, and smiles at me. "Cyn, this is Jules. She's been coming here as long as I have, so we've known each other pretty much forever." Then he turns to the girl. "Jules, this is my girlfriend, Cyn."

For the briefest moment, her smile seems to falter just a tiny bit. But then she reaches out to shake my hand. "Hi, Cyn! Welcome to paradise. You're going to love it, I promise."

"That's what Ryan keeps telling me."

"Well, he's right. What bunk are you in? Do you know yet?"

I look at Ryan helplessly, and he comes to my rescue. "Those people with the clipboards have the bunk info. They'll tell you where to go." He pulls my duffel from the storage compartment onto the ground and then hefts his own onto his shoulder. "Go on and get settled. I'll see you at the big gathering before dinner tonight."

Then he kisses me on my head again (it's less charming this time) and walks off. With Jules.

I make myself stop watching them walking away together and try to figure out what I'm supposed to do now. Other kids are swarming around me, grabbing duffels, hugging friends, squealing and shouting. There are a few other confused-looking idiots like me, too. I turn in place, trying to locate these alleged clipboard-holding entities. As I scan the crowd, I suddenly see a flash of red.

Demon-halo red.

This time my heart stops for more than a second. Everything seems to stop. I am alone in the universe with my horrible fear, trying to see where the demon is.

But now it's gone.

I stare around more wildly, but I don't see it again.

Probably because it was just your imagination, moron, my brain tells me. My brain is still grouchy and tired, apparently.

Was it my imagination? That would be nice to believe. I *am* still tired. And disoriented. And annoyed at the whole Jules thing even though I'm sure she is a perfectly nice person and there's nothing at all to be worried about there even though she has apparently been Ryan's summer BFF for practically his entire life and he never actually mentioned her until today. Not one time in all his gushing about camp over the past few months. Not one time ever.

I finally spot a college-age-looking girl holding a clip-board and drag my duffel in that direction. It was my imagination. I'm going to go with that. Because why would there be demons at camp? There would not be. That's just ridiculous.

"Name?"

"Cynthia Rothschild."

The girl flips through her pages. "You are in . . . bunk six." She looks me up and down. "First time?"

I love that it's so obvious.

"Yes."

She smiles reassuringly. "I know it seems crazy right now, and it's weird when almost everyone else knows one another already, but you'll pick it up fast. And there's another new girl in your bunk — her name's Susan."

"Thanks," I say with real gratefulness. It hadn't even occurred to me that everyone else in my whole bunk might already be lifelong friends. In fact, I hadn't really given much thought to whom I might be living with. All of my thought had been focused on Ryan and musical theater. Which are both totally thought-worthy, of course. But I probably should have left a little for all the other details of camp.

I manage to get my duffel into some semblance of a fireman's carry and trudge off in the direction she indicated.

The campus is pretty much as expected. I mean I'd seen pictures and stuff, and I had a general image in my head of square wooden cabiny things for the bunks, which are basically what they are. The boys and girls are housed on opposite sides of the campus, to prevent after-hours fraternizing, although of course that happens anyway, according to Ryan. There's a lake somewhere that I can't see from here, and a lot of trees, and a cluster of buildings in the middle, and few farther-off buildings in various directions that I assume are the performance spaces. All of the bunks have helpful numbers painted on them, and I locate number 6 without too much trouble.

Inside, it's kind of rustic but not dirty or anything. There are five sets of bunk beds and two regular beds, and several of them are already claimed by piles of stuff. Six girls are standing in the center of the room, chattering excitedly. They all turn to look at me when I walk in.

"Um. Hi," I say to the room in general.

"Hey," they respond nearly in unison. One of the girls adds, "You can take any bunk you want that doesn't already have stuff on it."

"Thanks." After a quick survey of what's available, I settle on one of the bottom bunks at the far end. I am fully aware that some part of me is probably choosing that because it's most like a cave that I can hide in, but I don't care. Besides, I can't change my mind now. I'd look stupid.

The girl who told me to take any bunk I wanted walks over. "I'm Hana. There's shelves and stuff that we all kind of share along the wall that you can use for your things, and you can keep some bathroom stuff on the counter in there if you want. There's room."

"Thanks," I say again. "I'm Cyn."

She nods and indicates the other girls, who are still talking, "That's Amina, Lisa R., Lisa P., Sasha, and Caroline," she says, pointing at each one. "Hey, guys, this is Cyn," she adds, a little louder.

There is a chorus of "Hi, Cyn" and some repetitions of names, and then another couple of girls walk in and everyone erupts into excited squeals. I focus on unpacking and making my bed.

By the time the announcement comes over the loudspeaker to gather at Hines Hall (the center building/gymnasium, where a lot of social activities happen), the rest of the girls have arrived. I am introduced to all of them but only remember one or two of their names. Susan turns out to be a painfully shy girl who doesn't speak much but nevertheless seems to want to attach herself to me as the only other new person. I follow Hana and the others out with my silent new appendage looking fearfully around beside me.

The noise and movement is almost overwhelming when we first enter the packed hall. I search for Ryan (not for anything else, certainly not for flashes of demony red) and find him after a minute in the middle of a group that, of course, also contains Jules. I consider trying to shake Susan, but that seems unnecessarily cruel, so I just let her tag along with me. The other girls from our bunk have melted into the crowd, looking for more old friends.

Jules sees me first and points me out to Ryan. He turns and gives me a delicious Ryan-smile that instantly makes me feel better about being new and clueless and everything else. Well, almost everything else. I think about maybe telling him about the halo. But then I remember that I already decided it was only my imagination, and he seems so happy right now, and I really don't want to ruin it.

I am introduced to about ten more new people whose names I instantly forget. I introduce Susan in turn, who mumbles hello and tries to burrow more deeply into my side. I must draw the line at this, because right now the only person I want touching me is Ryan. Luckily, just then the camp director steps up to the front of the room, and everyone begins settling down on the floor. Ryan pulls me down to sit with him, and I snuggle between his legs, leaning back against his chest. Susan seems to realize at last that she is not actually connected to my body in any literal sense and sits down a few inches away. Some of Ryan's friends attempt to be friendly to her, which is really nice of them.

The camp director's name is Steven. He is cheered loudly by everyone in the room, so I assume he is generally well liked. Unless everyone is just excited that he is about to announce the shows and are just cheering for that. I ask Ryan.

"Both," he says. "He's a pretty decent guy, but mostly right now everyone is thinking about the show list."

Steven says some general welcome-y stuff and then gets down to business. He clearly knows his audience.

"All right. I know what you're all waiting for, so I'm going to shut up now and turn this over to the directors, who will each come up and announce their shows. We'll start with Upper Camp first."

The hush that falls over the crowd is nearly frightening in its total and complete perfection. And at that moment I suddenly realize: all of these people love theater. I am in a room filled with people who love it as much as I do. Somehow it didn't quite hit me until this second. Right now, no one here can think about anything other than wanting to know what the shows are. Ryan tightens his arms around me, and I finally let myself relax and really appreciate the fact that I am here.

And then the first director, a twentyish guy with multiple visible piercings, steps forward and after a dramatic pause shouts out, *"West Side Story!"* and everyone goes nuts, and I love every single person in the room almost more than I can stand.

The other Upper Camp directors (all college students enrolled in various theater programs, Ryan explains) come up one by one, and the crowd continues to be nearly as enthusiastic for each one (which is only fair; it's hard to top *West Side Story*). The other musicals are *How to Succeed in Business Without Really Trying, Brigadoon, The Scarlet Pimpernel,* and *Aftermass,* which is the brand-new original musical written by one of the campers for the contest they hold every year.

The straight plays (not that I *really* care) are *A Midsummer Night's Dream* and the female version of *The Odd Couple*.

Ryan is beside himself about *The Scarlet Pimpernel*.

"Oh, my God," he says. He says it several times. "Oh my God oh my God oh my God."

This is a side of him I have not previously seen. He actually cannot sit still; he is wiggling around in excitement, drumming his feet against the floor and rocking me from side to side.

I turn around to look at him. "*Scarlet Pimpernel*? Really?"

He stares at me. "Do you not know that one? It's amazing. One of my favorites. I mean my favorite favorites. I mean like of all time."

"It didn't last long on Broadway."

"That's because people are idiots. The music is amazing."

"What part would you want?"

He looks at me like this is the most ridiculous question ever. "Chauvelin! I've always wanted to play him."

I can only look back at him. *"Really?"*

"Yes!" It is clear that he cannot quite believe I am even questioning this.

"I had to read that book in English last year. Isn't he a horrible, disgusting old man with no redeeming qualities whatsoever?"

Ryan sighs in exasperation. "That's the book. The show is different. Chauvelin is awesome. 'Falcon in the Dive' is one of the best songs in the entire history of musical theater."

"Um. Okay."

"I'm serious."

"Okay! I believe you."

Just then Jules scoots over and ruffles Ryan's hair like he's her five-year-old brother. "I know someone must be excited about *The Scarlet Pimpernel!*"

Why does she know this about him when I don't?

Ryan grins at her, and she grins back. I don't want to watch that going on, so I lean over toward Susan. "What do you think of the show list?" I ask her.

She shrugs. "They're good."

"Are you here for backstage?" I ask her. Hoping not, because I would kind of rather not have her on whatever show I'm working on.

She shakes her head. "Orchestra. Violin."

"Oh!" Good. "I didn't realize. That's great!"

She shrugs again. "Yeah. I've never played for theater before, though. My parents thought it would be good for me."

Huh. "Oh. Well, they're probably right. I mean, you like theater, right?"

She shrugs again. "It's okay."

I would like to leave this conversation now. I peek back at Ryan and Jules to make sure the grinning has stopped. Then I make myself ask, "Which show are you hoping for, Jules?"

"Oh, *Scarlet Pimpernel* for me, too. I want Marguerite."

Of course.

"Well, um, break a leg tomorrow!"

"Thanks!" She flashes me a beautiful smile. I am starting to hate her just a little.

The directors go on to announce the Middle and Lower Camp shows, but we pay less attention, since those are for the younger kids and we won't get to see them, anyway. Some of

Ryan's friends have siblings in those shows, though, so there are a few excited reactions to several of the selections, even so.

Finally, the gathering breaks up into a slow migration to the dining hall, where I am introduced to the magic of camp food (not so bad, really). I sit with Ryan and his friends, and Susan, and try to remember more names. All the singers are talking about audition songs. Susan mostly just looks down at her food.

"What show are you hoping for, Cyn?" Ryan asks suddenly. "I just realized you never said."

I'd been thinking about this. Part of me wants to be involved in whatever show Ryan is in, because then I'll get to see him more. But a larger part of me, the part that's not just thinking with its romance-y parts, wants the original show. Because it's totally new. I'd get to design the set from scratch without trying to match or not match or consider at all whatever previous set designs have been used. I know the chances of some camper-written show being good enough to continue on to Broadway someday are, let us say, pretty slim . . . but even so, I'd be the first one to ever design a set for it. Even if I'm also the last.

"I want the new show," I tell him. "You know I'd love to do whatever show you're in —"

He cuts me off, shaking his head. "No, you need to do the best thing for you — that's what this is all about. And we'll still see each other plenty, no matter what shows we're in. I think that would be great. I hope you get it."

"Thanks." I smile at him. "And I hope you get what's his name."

"Chauvelin!"

"Right. That guy."

"It's getting very hard not to break up with you right now."

"Okay, okay. I am sure I will come around to appreciating *The Scarlet Pimpernel* once I see how awesome it is."

"You better."

"I will!"

"Hmph."

Usually there is some kind of evening activity after dinner (Ryan explains), but tonight is left open so that everyone can just catch up with friends and get settled or practice audition songs or whatever else they want to do. Ryan grabs my hand and pulls me toward one of the doors. "Come with me, young lady."

I call a hurried good-bye to Susan, who looks slightly terrified to be left alone, but I am not going to feel bad about it, because (a) it is not my job to walk her through every step of her camp experience, and (b) it will be good for her to practice standing on her own two feet, and (c) I appear to be about to have some actual alone time with Ryan, and I'm sorry, but that trumps keeping the new girl company by, like, a million.

We emerge into the darkness and he leads me toward the boys' side of camp. Girls are not technically allowed in the boys' cabins, so I wait outside while Ryan runs into his bunk to "get something." It's a little chilly now that the sun's down but not really uncomfortable. It smells good here — like, well, nature. Trees and rocks and dirt and fresh air and all of that good stuff. I look up and am startled by the number of stars I can see scattered across the sky.

Ryan comes back out and takes my hand again.

"What did you get? And where are we going?"

His eyes smile at me in the dark. "You'll see."

He leads me up a long path toward one of the performance spaces. I haven't learned all their names yet. It's one of the larger ones, and it sits dark and silent in the middle of all the nature. We duck in through one of the openings along the side and walk back to the last row of seats. Instead of actually sitting in the seats, though, Ryan sits down on the floor behind the last row, in a small aisle tucked between the seats and the back far wall of the building. There is just enough starlight coming in through the open windows to see by. I sit too and look at him expectantly.

From his pocket he produces an elderly but apparently still functional mp3 player and two pairs of earbuds.

"Hey, that's contraband!"

"No, it's not, Hawaii Five-O. We're allowed to have music. They just don't want everyone on their phones or computers all the time." He hands me one of the sets of earbuds, and I see that he's already got a splitter plugged into his device.

"Oh, thank God," I say. "I mean, I brought one, too, but I thought I was going to have to sneak it under the covers at night or something."

"Nope. No sneaking required."

"What are we listening to?"

"We are going to address this incomprehensible issue of you never having heard *The Scarlet Pimpernel*."

"The whole thing? Won't that keep us out past curfew? I don't want to get kicked out my first night."

He laughs. "Trust me, it takes a lot more than that to get kicked out. But no, not the whole thing. Just a few songs. The best ones. Starting with the best one of all." He cues up "Falcon in the Dive."

It begins with some weird talk-singing and I give him the side-eye, but he shakes his head at me. "Just keep listening."

So I do.

I can hear instantly that the voice part is right for him. And as the song continues, I can tell that Chauvelin is like a lot of the parts he's drawn to: a person driven to some deeply felt goal that may or may not be understandable to anyone else around him. I barely remember the plot of the book and have no idea whether it's remotely the same in the musical, but that doesn't even matter right now. The song is full of passion and longing and desire, rising and falling and soaring with the emotion of the singer (Terrence Mann; I'd know his voice anywhere), and it gives me very delightful chills to think of Ryan singing it.

When the song ends, he pauses the playback before another song can start, and looks at me. "So?"

His eyes are fixed on mine, and I'm shocked to realize he's nervous. Nervous I won't like it? Nervous I won't see what he loves so much about it? That I won't understand?

"It's beautiful," I say. And I mean it. I had no idea. I can't believe I've never heard the music from this show before.

"There's more," he says, looking down to cue up another song. "I won't make you listen to the whole thing, I swear, just a few more. Some of Marguerite's songs are gorgeous, and there's this trio . . ." He trails off, scrolling.

32

I ignore the part about Marguerite, which would only make me think of Jules, and instead just lean forward and kiss his sweet, gorgeous face. He turns toward me, and I kiss him again, this time on the mouth.

"What was that for?" he asks afterward.

"Nothing," I say. "Just felt like it."

He smiles and returns to finding the next song. I sit back against the wall and watch him. Loving that he's so excited. About musical theater! I mean, I know this about him, obviously, but I don't usually take the time to reflect and appreciate it. None of my really close friends have ever been into theater the way I am. They come to shows to support me, and they're excited for me when happy theater-y things happen, but being excited *for* me is not quite the same as being excited *with* me.

Ryan's excitement is both purely his own and something super important that he wants to share with me. I *love* that we can be excited about this stuff together. And I really do love seeing him so happy. He's the sexiest happy puppy ever.

And he's your boyfriend! Old Cyn whisper-shouts from the back of my brain.

Yes, I know. Shut up.

But yeah, he is.

He catches me grinning before I can stop.

"What?"

"Nothing. Just . . . happy."

He smiles back at me in the starlight.

"Yeah. Me, too."

Chapter | 03

Auditions begin right after breakfast the next morning. Orchestra and set people get a few hours free while all the acting and singing types wait anxiously for their turn in Schulman and Santorini theaters, respectively. All the musical directors watch all the musical auditions, and then callbacks for each show are held separately. Same for the plays.

Susan and I are sitting outside one of the craft buildings, watching the musical audition line. She's loosened up a bit since yesterday. She now allows several inches between us when we walk around together. Ryan's friends were apparently relentlessly kind to her last night after we left, which must have helped a lot.

"I don't know how they do it," she says. "Just walk up there and sing in front of everyone."

"Well, you play in front of everyone, don't you? It's the same thing."

She shakes her head. "It's different. And anyway, usually I'm playing with a whole orchestra."

"Didn't you have to play alone to get into camp?"

"Well, yeah. But it's still different. I didn't have to get up on a stage or anything."

I'm waiting for Ryan and Jules to finish their auditions. Well, I'm waiting for Ryan, but he and Jules are clearly in the habit of doing everything together at camp, and so by necessity I am waiting for her, too. When they finally appear and start walking toward us, I focus on smiling and not thinking about how easy and perfect they look together.

"Wow, they look really perfect together, don't they?" Susan asks. She glances at me, then, seeing my expression, quickly adds, "I mean, if he weren't your boyfriend. I'm just saying they look like they belong together, that's all. Like, visually."

I don't say anything. I just let her run down and hope that the negative reinforcement of my nonresponse encourages her to think more carefully before she speaks in the future. It doesn't help that she's right, of course. Jules has that same glowing happy energy that Ryan does, like the world is just a giant amusement park and they can't wait to try out all the rides. It's a quality I love in Ryan. I don't love it as much in Jules. I wish she were grouchier, or more cynical, or maybe just a little less attractive.

Or a lot less attractive. That would be okay, too.

"So? How'd it go?" I ask when they arrive.

"He nailed it, of course," Jules says, doing that annoying hair-ruffling thing again. "I was right after him and could hear him through the door."

"You nailed it, too," Ryan says, smiling at her. "Of course."

"Great!" I say, too loudly. Out of the corner of my eye I see Susan flinch slightly. "When do the callback lists go up?"

"They post them during lunch," Jules says. "Then callbacks go on all afternoon, and the cast lists go up tonight!"

They both get called back for a few different roles, including Chauvelin and Marguerite. Ryan spends the time between lunch and his callback times practicing all the Chauvelin parts he thinks they might ask him to sing. I listen and remind him that he's awesome as often as he needs me to. Then he runs off to the first callback.

It's a weird long day of waiting. I'm eager for the lists to go up that night, too, since that's when I'll find out what show I've got, but in the meantime there's nothing to do but wish the auditioners broken legs and wander around with Susan. I do take advantage of the free time to go to the computer lab and send Annie and Leticia and Diane an update of what's happening at camp so far. After today the computer lab is only open at particular times, and Ryan's told me there's always a line of people waiting to get their technology fix. So I warn the girls that (a) the chances of me being online when they might be are very slim, and therefore (b) they should actually check their e-mail, since that is the way I will probably have to contact them. I sigh and try not to miss my phone. At least e-mail is quicker than, like, actual physical mail.

Although I remind them that I wouldn't mind getting some of that, too.

I dedicate a large portion of my message to talking about Jules. Because I'm still trying to work out how Ryan completely failed to mention her, despite their obvious closeness. Also, I know I can count on Annie, Leticia, and Diane to tell me what I want to hear about all the things that must be wrong with her and how Ryan would never even look at another girl because he has me and I'm so great and everything.

I do also tell them the rest of my first impressions about camp, and the girls in my bunk, including Susan, who is (of course) sitting at the computer next to me. And I tell them about the shows, and which ones all of us are hoping for.

Obviously, I am hoping Jules gets her second choice instead of her first so that she and Ryan won't be spending hours together every day at rehearsal. But in the way of things going just how you'd expect, they both get the parts they want.

Happily, I also got my first choice. So there is much group celebrating at the canteen after dinner, and everyone goes to bed excited for everything to start the next day. Except Susan, who doesn't really seem to get excited about things. But she's in the orchestra of *West Side Story,* so everyone else is excited on her behalf.

Because: *West Side Story.* I mean, come on.

In the morning, our bunk is buzzing with first-day-of-rehearsal fervor. All of the other bunk 6 girls are performers, and they are all relatively pleased with their show assignments, although not everyone got their first choices. Hana is in the chorus of *Scarlet Pimpernel*. When I mentioned last night that my boyfriend (!) was cast as Chauvelin, ten pairs of eyes turned to stare at me incredulously.

"Ryan Halsey is your boyfriend?" they asked in screechy harmony.

I keep forgetting that everyone here knows him.

They hadn't really seemed to know what to talk to me about before now, since they don't quite get the appeal of backstage track, but this gave them plenty of conversational material. It's not so much that they suddenly find me more interesting; it's just that now there's an obvious entry point for discussion. They want to know what he's like back home, what he was like in *Sweeney* (when I tell them that's how we got to know each other; I leave out our other shared, demon-related activities), what he's like in the kissing department (that was just Lisa P., who is very nosy). None of them seem to know him very well, they just know who he is, like everyone here knows the people who tend to get cast as leads again and again.

"I thought he and Jules Frisk were together," Amina says.

"Nope," I say quickly. And firmly. "They're just friends."

"Huh," she says. "They look so good together, though. And they spend like all day together, every summer."

Not this summer! I want to shout at her, but I just smile. I am happy and secure in my relationship. I will not be threatened by everyone else's apparent certainty that Ryan and Jules belong together. Because if they really belonged together, they would have gotten together by now. And that has not happened. And Ryan is with me. So everyone should probably just shut up.

Today is a little like the first day of school. People have chosen their T-shirts and tank tops with care. Breakfast is brief and high-energy. I give Ryan a quick kiss good-bye and watch him head off toward the Colosseum (what they call the theater where *Scarlet Pimpernel* will be performed) with Jules and some of their friends. Hana gives me a tiny wave as she trots off after them.

Sasha is in *Aftermass* with me. She's got a part, but since none of us know anything about the show yet, she has no idea whether it's the lead or the smallest non-chorus part or something in between. She wanted Marguerite but seems to feel no animosity at losing out to Jules. "She's amazing," Sasha had said with all apparent sincerity. "You should have heard her at callbacks. Oh, my God. That's going to be an amazing show." (Sasha likes to use the word *amazing*.)

As we leave the dining hall, Sasha fills me in on the gossip she heard this morning. "So there are these two girls, Darleen and Celia? And they *hate* each other. I mean, like, they've got this lifelong blood-feud thing happening — it's crazy. Generally the powers that be try to keep them out of the same shows, just for everyone's health and safety, you know? But for some reason, this year they're both in our show. Something is totally going to happen. And we'll be there to see it. It's going to be amazing."

Our show is in Blake, out past the music buildings. We join

a growing procession of campers headed in the same direction. I expected to be nervous, at least a little, but I'm not. I'm just excited. I don't have to perform, after all; today I just get to watch and listen and take in all the initial information that I will then begin to sort through and use to create my wonderful set design. Later, once there is something on the line, I will start to be nervous, I'm sure.

We reach the theater and head inside. The counselor/director is sitting in a metal folding chair on the stage, talking with a teenager in another folding chair next to him. Probably the writer/composer, I imagine. He's turned away from me at first, but when he looks away from the director for a second to glance out at the theater, I see that he is rather easy on the eyes, in a buttoned-up kind of way. Dark, slightly longish hair, blue eyes behind black plastic eyeglass frames, cheekbones to die for.

Hey, I may have a boyfriend, but that doesn't mean I can't appreciate some delicious eye candy when it presents itself.

The cast is directed to sit in the audience, those with named parts in the first two rows, chorus behind them in vocal sections. Backstage/technical-track kids are directed to another section. Sasha bids me farewell and heads toward her designated area. I take a breath and head up the stage steps to introduce myself to the director and the writer.

Before I can open my mouth, the director gives me an exasperated look. "Did you not hear the instructions? No one should be onstage right now other than Peter and myself. Are you either of those two people?"

I blink, taken aback. "But —"

"Do you not *know* whether you are performance or backstage track? Do you need me to find your name on the list?"

Awesome. The director is an asshole.

I will admit I had not foreseen this exciting development.

I raise my hands in surrender and turn back for the steps. The camper — Peter, I assume — reaches out a hand to stop me. "Are you Cynthia? Set designer?"

I turn back, warily. "Yes. I just thought I should introduce myself. But I can certainly do that later."

"No, no. I'm glad you came up. I'm Peter. I'm really looking forward to working with you, Cynthia." The director sighs loudly and rolls his eyes but doesn't say anything else. I decide it's safe to respond.

"Cyn, please." I smile at him, trying to communicate my gratefulness for his civility and general contrast to the asshole. "And likewise."

He smiles back, and there is something very much notbuttoned-up in that smile. "Nice to meet you, Cyn. Let's get together after the sing-through and we can start talking ideas, all right?"

"Sounds good. Thanks, Peter."

I head down to the backstage section and take a seat, deliberately not looking back at the director at any point. At least the *writer* is a decent human being. In addition to being super cute. Not that I care. I'm just being thorough in my description. And it looks like he can hold his own against the director, so that's good. It never occurred to me to worry about the director being so unpleasant. Valuable reminder, I suppose. Liking musical theater does not automatically make one a nice person. I suddenly realize how much I've been spoiled by dear Mr. Henry back home.

Once the rest of the cast and crew arrive and find their correct places to sit, the director stands up and welcomes everyone, managing to sound sincere. Maybe he can at least *act* nice when he feels like it. It is theater camp, after all. While a girl who appears to be his deputized assistant hands out the scores, he tells us how excited we should be to be working on a brand-new show and how lucky we are to have him for our director. (Okay, he doesn't exactly say that second part, but it's very clearly implied.) He says we're going to just jump right into the sing-through right after the writer/composer says a *few* words.

Everyone turns politely to Peter, who stands up and walks to the front of the stage.

"Hey, guys," he says in a not quite shy but completely adorable understated way, and I can tell his contrast to the director's self-assured arrogance (which comes across even when he's acting nice) instantly wins over the entire theater. "I thought it would help to give you a quick idea of what the show's about before we get started. Some of this is written up in the front of your scores, along with full descriptions of all the characters, but basically, *Aftermass* is a postapocalyptic thriller/romance/adventure about the enduring power of love in the shadow of the end of the world."

Now, this is not generally a statement that a lot of people could pull off with a straight face, let alone without eliciting a bunch of eye rolling and awkward titters and seat shifting from those hearing it, but Peter manages to do just that. The only response is one of palpable quiet excitement, and as he goes on to describe the basic outline of the plot, everyone is clearly and enthusiastically on board. Including me. And I'm not usually a postapocalyptic kind of girl. The story focuses on a handful of survivors thrown together after a mysterious world-ending disaster, and the two main characters have conflicting ideas about how to carve out a new life for themselves and the others in their little group. It's part love story, part horror story, part ghost story, with some exciting-sounding fight scenes and soul-wrenching difficult choices to be made and a lot of other things that I personally happen to love in my musical theater.

"I'll stop talking now and turn things back over to Michael," Peter says, giving the group a final charming smile. He doesn't look at Michael (who, by the way, never actually bothered to introduce himself, presumably assuming everyone already knew who he was), but somehow I can tell that Peter knows how antsy the director is to take back over. His timing is perfect; he's been brief enough that Michael really can't object, but he's milking it just enough to make the director squirm. "I'll just say this one last thing: I cannot *wait* to see what you guys do with this show. Thank you so much for helping me bring it to life."

Everyone cheers and applauds at this, and Peter ducks his head in semi-embarrassed thanks as he retakes his seat. Michael gets up with an air of tolerant beneficence, like a dinner host who's let the visiting elderly relative hold forth at the table just a bit longer than courtesy dictates, but he has to wait a few seconds for the cheering to die down before he can begin speaking again.

"All right, then," he says. "Let's get started." He nods to the accompanist, who nods back and then begins to play the overture on the piano.

We all listen.

Waiting.

Hoping.

And the overture is really, really good.

After just a few notes, people start looking around at one another, wide eyes communicating how impressed they are. Before now, I hadn't quite allowed myself to dwell on the fact that the show might not be any good. I mean of course you'd expect whoever won the competition to have created something really great, but, well, you never really know. Plus, what if the people judging the contest just had horrible taste? But this music is . . . incredible.

I sneak a glance at Peter up on the stage. He's looking at the pianist, not out at the audience, but it's plain from his expression that he can tell how everyone is reacting. I know that feeling — that moment of sharing something you've created, believing in your heart that it's good, but still, in that second of actually revealing it to others, you can't help but be a little terrified that it's not. Peter's face shows that barely contained joy/relief/satisfaction of having your heart's original opinion confirmed by the ones you most hoped would do so.

There is more enthusiastic applause after the overture, and then the sing-through begins. I'm always in awe of people who can look at music and lyrics in a score that they've never seen or heard before and just sing it. I can't sing worth a damn even when I know the song by heart. The singing isn't perfect, by any means, and once or twice Peter or Michael or the accompanist (Leon) jumps in to help someone who's struggling, but overall the cast is really great. Sasha's part turns out to be a cool one — she's the ghost of the hero's best friend, who was secretly in love with the hero's sister but never had the courage to act on it while she was alive. (And now that she's a ghost, no one else in the cast can see or hear her, so she finally confesses everything, but no one knows except the other ghosts.) Her songs are a little funny and a little tragic, and Sasha's voice is perfect — kind of tart and sweet with something a bit 1940s girl Friday about it.

Darleen and Celia both have fairly large supporting roles. I can tell who's who because there's a copy of the cast list tucked inside the front cover of the score. Both girls have great voices and their parts are about the same size, which is probably good in the avoiding-trouble department. Neither of them immediately seems to be an aggressive lunatic or raging diva; I'll have to ask Sasha for more of their backstory.

The sing-through takes nearly the entire morning rehearsal period, but it feels like it flies by in a second. The show is that good. Postapocalyptic America and ghosts and battles and love scenes and death scenes and big dance numbers are all beginning to swirl around in very exciting ways in my head as I start to think about what the stage might look like through all of this. I don't want to get too attached to any ideas until I have a chance to talk to Peter, though. I believe the final say is mine, but obviously I want to create something that he's going to love as well. And ideally Michael, too, although I could probably live with myself if he didn't.

Michael declares that we'll take a short break and then use the rest of the time before lunch to start work on the first big chorus number. Peter is instantly besieged by adoring fans. I wait, smiling, watching his obvious pleasure as they tell him how much they love the show. Michael is also watching, with less smiling. I don't really know what his deal is yet. He can't not want people to be excited, and he must understand that in this particular case, with the show having been written by one of the campers, everyone is going to be very interested in the author. But I suspect he's used to a certain amount of director-worship and is maybe worried that Peter is going to steal the spotlight entirely.

Suddenly there is some unhappy-sounding shouting from some of the girls in Peter's fan group. At first I can't even see what's happening, and then I hear "Hey, watch it!" just before Celia goes tumbling off the edge of the stage. There's a collective gasp and then several people run over to help her. Peter hasn't moved; he seems transfixed by this sudden explosion of violent activity.

Darleen is standing on the stage just above Celia. "I *told* her to move over," she says calmly to no one in particular. "It's not my fault she fell."

"The hell it's not," Celia says back, launching herself up toward the other girl amid a confusion of shouts from assorted friends and onlookers. Everyone has stopped whatever else he or she was doing at this point and is just watching the drama unfold. Michael strides purposefully toward them, looking somewhat pleased to have a way in which to demonstrate his authority.

Interesting as all of this is, something else catches my eye and draws it away from Michael's advance upon the fray. I thought, for a second . . .

There.

A flash of red. The you-know-what kind of red. The kind I swore I didn't see and would not see, not here, because *demons do not go to theater camp.* They just do not. Because that would be ludicrous. And so not fair.

Except apparently I was mistaken about that.

Everyone else is drifting over toward the fight, and Michael is trying to sort out what happened, and Celia is crying now, and someone is saying that her ankle is totally sprained and that Darleen is going to be sorry and it doesn't matter what happened last night at dinner, but I only register this in a far-off, unimportant kind of way.

My attention is arrested by the demon halo that has flickered into solidity and remains clearly visible, denying me any opportunity to reconvince myself that I don't see it.

Nope. No denying it. There it is.

Right above Peter's head.

Chapter | 04

My feet are moving before I can even really think about it. I bound up the steps toward Peter.

He turns and sees me coming. Starts to smile, then sees my face, and his expression freezes. His eyes flick up. The halo disappears.

"Too late," I tell him, grabbing his arm. I drag him backward, into the wings and deeper backstage. Back to where set construction will be happening. Except it won't be. Not now. Because . . . because . . .

"Are you kidding me? Are you seriously freaking kidding me?" I push him away, and he stumbles, catching himself on the wall.

"Cyn, what—"

"You're a demon!"

"What? No!"

I just look at him.

"Well, okay. Yes. But it's not what you think!"

"How can it possibly not be what I think?"

"It's not, I swear. I'm not —" He looks around, lowering his voice. "I'm not evil."

I laugh, but it's not remotely funny. I cannot believe this is happening.

"All demons are evil. It's part of the definition."

He shakes his head. "No, it's not. Really. Lots of demons are evil, but there are plenty of us who don't want anything to do with the whole demon-throne-maim-and-destroy-torture-humans-and-feed-on-their-souls way of life. Well, okay, maybe not *plenty*, but definitely a whole bunch. Or, well . . . a few, anyway."

I wait.

"No, that's it. I'm sticking with a few."

"I don't believe you."

"No, really, I think *a few* is pretty accurate."

"I mean," I say through clenched teeth, "I don't believe that you're not evil."

"Oh." He seems to think about this for a minute. "Well, I'm just going to have to convince you." He smiles his charming smile at me.

"Don't you smile at me! You are not nearly as charming as you think you are."

His smile broadens. "Oh, yes, I am. Don't lie. I'm pretty charming."

"Not anymore," I say, trying to avoid looking directly at him. The smile is kind of distracting. "Not now that I know what you are."

That makes me think of something.

"How did you hide it, anyway? The halo."

"Oh, that," he says. "It's pretty easy, really. It's just that normally there's no reason to. But I knew that you were able to see them, so I masked it. It just takes a little concentration. But I guess I got distracted for a minute and let it reappear." He peers out toward the theater. "I wonder what's happening out there. Did Darleen really just totally push Celia off the stage?"

"Hey! Focus."

"Sorry. What were we talking about?"

"You were about to explain what the hell you are doing here."

He squints at me. "Are you sure? I don't remember that."

"Yes."

"Oh, fine." He glances away, and I swear he is starting to look the tiniest bit embarrassed. "I don't really know where to start."

"Just pick somewhere and start talking."

He sighs. "Okay. Soooo . . . remember that time you came to the demon world to rescue your friend?"

I'm still so in shock about what's happening right now, I can't even muster the scathing response that question deserves. "Uh, yeah."

"So, I was there, watching the battle. I mean, everyone was there, so maybe that's obvious."

"Were you one of the ones who tried to eat me?"

"No!" He actually makes a face, like a three-year-old being ordered to take a bite of some much-hated vegetable. "I told you, that's not my thing. No, I was rooting for you. It was so exciting! The show, the dramatic rescue, John Gabriel almost killing you at the end there . . . I was riveted."

"I'm so glad it was entertaining."

"Anyway, when the new queen sent you and your human friends back through to your own world, I . . . hitched a ride."

He stops like this is the end of the explanation. We look at each other for a few seconds.

"And then you decided to go to theater camp?" I ask, finally.

"Well, no. Not right away. I didn't even know there was such a thing! But once I heard about it . . ."

"Where did you hear about it?"

"From Ryan. Same as you."

My mind spins for a minute as I try to find the sense in what he is saying. "You talked to *Ryan*?"

He laughs. "No, silly. I was tethered to you, so I was, uh, nearby. When he was telling you about it."

I decide the time has come to sit down. I lower myself shakily to the floor, my back against the wall. After a second, Peter sits down beside me.

"Please tell me you haven't been invisibly watching me for the past seven and a half months. Because it kind of sounds like that's what you're saying."

"No, no," he says reassuringly. "Not the whole time. Just sometimes. It took a while to build up enough strength to regain a full physical form, and then I had to contact Hector . . ."

"Hector?"

"My current, uh, assistant. My contact in the human world. He's been feeding me musical theater stuff for years.

But he doesn't live anywhere near you, and I couldn't go outside the tether range . . ."

I hold up a hand to stop him.

"Please explain about the tether."

He explains. Allegedly, because he wasn't strong enough to build an actual portal like Mr. Gabriel did into our high school, and because he didn't want to be tied to a single location, and because he only had a few seconds to make his decision and hitch his ride, Peter had to anchor himself to either me, Annie, or Danielle Hornick as we were sent back home from the demon world. (He chose me.) And then he had to stay within a certain distance of me at all times, because that is the nature of the tether thing, apparently.

"I had to stay pretty close to you at the beginning, but once I gained some strength, I could stretch it out a bit. But the maximum distance is only about 1.63 miles, so I could never go very far."

"So you just . . . just . . . kind of loitered around the neighborhood?"

"I kept busy!" he says rather defensively. "Trust me, it's not easy to establish an identity and fill out all the forms for camp and stuff when you don't have parents or a bank account or an actual address. Hector does his best, but he's not the sharpest crayon in the box. Loyal to a fault, though, which is ultimately more important in the long run."

I lean my head back against the wall. Not happening. This. Can. Not. Be. Happening.

"I thought maybe you'd be sympathetic, since your best friend had dated a demon," he says.

My head stops leaning and whips toward him again. "Annie was not *dating* a demon! She was coerced into a severely unhealthy relationship by magical means and then abducted in a manner requiring dramatic rescue, remember?"

"Okay. Bad choice of words, sorry. But I thought, some-how . . . you would understand. I mean, sure, mostly I was hoping you just wouldn't find out until I was ready. But if you did find out, I was hoping you would understand. Plus, we have the whole shared passion for musical theater thing! I know all the demons had been going on about *Sweeney Todd,* but they only like it because of the killing and cannibalism. I love *Sweeney* for the music and the drama and everything else. Like you! You were the perfect ally. I was sure of it. And then, later on, I heard Ryan talking about theater camp, and I realized that's exactly what I wanted. A chance to get my start."

I am still trying to find the sense. Trying and failing. "Your start in what?"

He looks at me like he can't understand the question. "In show business! What do you think I'm doing here?"

"I have no idea what you're doing here! I assume it has something to do with killing people and sucking out their souls and trying to make my life miserable!"

He throws up his hands. "Why aren't you listening to me? I have no interest in killing people and sucking out their souls! I just want to create quality musical theater!"

I can only stare at him. I may have lost all hope of finding the sense, ever.

"What? Demons aren't allowed to appreciate the arts?"

"No!"

"That's . . . that's racist!"

"It's not racist. You're not of a race. You're not even human!"

"Well, then, it's just demonist."

"Exactly!"

He sighs and puts a hand to his forehead like I'm giving him a headache. Like *I'm* giving *him* a headache.

"Look," he says. "For longer than you have been alive, I have lived in the demon world on a secret diet of smuggled-in old-timey ballads and jazz standards and eventually every single bit of musical theater I could get my hands on. I've consorted with countless humans who have helped get me in to see everything on and Off and Off-Off and Off-Off-Off Broadway it was possible to see, and I have waited and waited and waited for the right circumstances to occur that would allow me to escape to your world forever so I could become a part of that experience for real. You were a dream come true for me, Cyn. Not only my ticket out but someone else who loved theater like I did! Someone who could maybe help me get on my feet once I got here. But there wasn't time to discuss it, there wasn't time to ask your permission, and there certainly wasn't time to explain. I saw my chance, and I took it."

"Okay," I say after a minute. "Okay, fine. You saw your chance, and you took it, and then you spied on me and my boyfriend for a while, and now here you are. Mission accomplished, yeah? So now you can take yourself off into the world and disappear and never make me have to see you again."

He shakes his head. "I can't. Also, I won't, but I can't anyway. I'm still connected to you. I might need your help to break the tether. But I'm also not leaving. I need this chance. This contest gets national attention every year. Producers will see my work. It's how I'm going to start my Broadway career."

"But . . . but . . . you're a *demon*. You have demony magic and stuff, right? You don't need this chance. You can just go insert yourself onto Broadway anytime you want, can't you?"

"I don't want it that way. I want to make it on my own. And I can! I'm really good! I just need to get my start."

Another idea occurs to me. "You cheated to get into camp, didn't you?"

"What? No! Well, okay. Yes. But I would have gotten in anyway. My show was totally better than any of the other submissions. I just had to make sure."

I push myself back onto my feet.

Peter is up in an instant beside me. "Where are you going?"

"I need . . . I need to think. Somewhere where you are not."

He nods. "Okay. Okay, sure. Just . . . just don't do anything hasty, okay? I know it doesn't seem like it now, but this can be a good thing. I promise. I can help you! I know you have to go back to the demon world two more times. . . . I can help you prepare! Give you inside information, whatever you need."

I am in the process of walking away, but I stop and turn back to face him, shaken. "How do you know about that?" Definitely not from eavesdropping on me and Ryan, since Ryan doesn't know anything about it.

"Aaron," he says, shrugging.

"*Aaron?* Bookstore Aaron? The demon queen's consort Aaron?"

Fucking Aaron.

Peter nods again. "Oh, my *God*, that guy's a talker. He'll go on and on forever if you let him. But he's a good source of intel."

"How — when did you even talk to him? If you left when I did . . ."

"Oh, I've known Aaron for a while. We used to talk sometimes before he came down — trading information, shooting the breeze, you know — and he's the one who told me about you in the first place. Otherwise I'd never have even gone to the arena for the demon-throne battle; it's not like I have a particular interest in watching other demons rip one another to shreds. But I knew you were helping the demoness, and Aaron had told me all about you and Ryan and Annie, and I had to see what was going to happen. We've kept in touch since then, too. I figured he'd have more information about you, and it's always good to keep a contact back home, just in case."

I have officially reached my limit.

"Okay. I'm going to walk away now." I pivot on my heels and resume my away-from-here course.

He waves as I turn away and then talks at my back. "Sure, that's fine. Take all the time you need. We can talk about set stuff later. Or tomorrow, you know, whenever."

This time I keep walking. I don't know if morning rehearsal is technically over, but I don't care. I need to find Ryan.

I head across campus to the Colosseum. There are a few other campers here and there, so it must at least be close enough to the end of the period that some groups have already been let out. I shouldn't be too conspicuous in my wandering around.

I can hear voices as I approach, winding my way up the gradual hill to the top of the path. It's not one of the songs Ryan played for me, but it's definitely of the same flavor. The Colosseum is an open-sided theater, a big black platform with a roof and some walls around the backstage area but not around the audience, which is filled with long benches instead of individual seats. So I don't even have to try to sneak inside; it's easy to just walk up and peer past the outer supports. The principals are sitting onstage in folding chairs (clearly this director doesn't feel the same need as Michael to keep himself above everyone else). The chorus is in the first few rows of the audience, and I can see other campers moving around at the far edge of the stage, who I assume are the backstage track group. The music stops as I reach the outer rows of benches, and the director starts to talk. It sounds like he's beginning to wrap things up.

Ryan and Jules are sitting next to each other, and it breaks my heart a little to see the perfect way they coexist up there on the stage. Like they were put there together on purpose for everyone's aesthetic appreciation. As I watch, the director says something that makes everyone laugh, and Jules leans her head on Ryan's shoulder for a second while she's laughing. He pats the top of her head, kind of like I might do if Annie were laughing so hard she had to lean on my shoulder . . . but also not like that at all.

I believe him that they're just friends. I do.

But.

People start shuffling to their feet. I linger outside, watching campers file past. The director has a few last words with the principals before setting them loose, so they all walk out more or less together. Ryan sees me and flashes me a gorgeous surprised smile.

"Hey, Cyn! What are you doing here? Get out early?" Then he takes in my expression.

"I need to talk to you." I think it's clear that I mean *just you*, but Jules doesn't seem to take the hint.

"Everything okay?" she asks.

"Yeah," I lie, trying not to sound as impatient as I am for her to leave. "I just need to talk to Ryan about something." *So please go away now.*

She still doesn't seem to get it.

"We'll catch up to you at lunch," Ryan tells her, which finally gets the message through.

"Oh. Okay, sure. See you in a bit."

She heads down the path, jogging to catch up with some of the other kids. I think I see her look back once, but I can't really bring myself to care if her feelings were hurt.

"What's going on?" Ryan asks. "Did something . . . happen?"

"Yes," I say simply.

"Crap." He sits heavily on the edge of the outermost bench. After a second, he looks up at me. "Are you sure?" He is nearly pleading.

"Oh, yeah. I'm sure." I sit down next to him and give him the short version. Not that there's really a long version at this point. "The guy who won the camper writing/composing contest? He's a demon. He's able to mask his halo, although not if he forgets to concentrate on it, which is how I found out. He followed me home from the demon world, apparently. To do musical theater."

Ryan takes this in stride, as much as one can.

"What does he want? Did he . . . did he try to hurt you?"

"No. Nothing like that. And as for what he wants . . ." I let out a long, slow breath. "Well, that's the thing. He swears he doesn't want anything. I mean other than to do his show and eventually have some kind of Broadway career. He says he's not evil."

"Ha." There is nothing laughlike about that syllable the way Ryan says it. I feel like he is trying very hard not to freak out right now. His previous run-ins with demons have not been very pleasant. Not that mine have been very pleasant, either, but he doesn't even have my super-roach thing going on. He is totally vulnerable in every way. As both Mr. Gabriel and the demoness (before our deal) made perfectly clear on a couple of memorable occasions.

His face is grim as he looks at me, not speaking. I wait, letting him have this tiny allotment of time in which to adjust. I hate seeing that expression on his face, though. He doesn't look scared, although I'm sure he must be, since he's not an idiot. He just looks really, really unhappy.

"I thought we were done with all this demon stuff," he says finally.

"Me, too." *Liar,* my brain whispers. But I'm not totally a liar. I did think we were done with encountering demons in our own world. And I thought Ryan was done completely. I never intended to involve him in the two future trips when they happened. If they happened. Which maybe they might not, still.

"Okay," he says, clearly attempting to rally. "The first thing we have to do is get you off that show. There's got to be some way we can arrange that." He brightens suddenly. "Maybe you can switch to *Scarlet Pimpernel* instead! Then we could all be on the same show together! I could talk to Steven, see if there's anything he can do . . ."

He lost me even before he got to the part about us "all" being together on *Pimpernel* — as though we are now some kind of trio, him and me and Jules. As soon as he mentioned getting me off Peter's show, I knew at once that I didn't want to do that.

"I'm not switching shows."

"Cyn, come on. You can't just stay there and work with him!"

"How is switching shows going to make me any safer? He's still going to be here. He's still connected to me —"

"He's *connected* to you? What does that mean?"

I sigh, exhausted at the idea of trying to explain what I don't really understand myself. "Something to do with how he hitched a ride with me. He called it a *tether*. I didn't really get all the details. I was too busy trying to not lose my mind. But the point is that I'm not going to be helping anything by switching shows. If anything, it makes more sense to stay where I can keep a closer eye on him."

"It's not your job to keep an eye on him."

"Of course it is. Who else is going to do it?"

"Why does anyone have to do it? He's not our problem! We're *done!*"

"Oh, yeah? Are you ready to ditch camp, then? And leave him here to do who-knows-what to your beloved summer paradise? Anyway, he has to stay within a certain distance of me until I can break this tether thing or whatever it is, and so running away isn't really an option."

Ryan stares at me. "How much distance?"

"One point six three miles."

There is more staring.

"I know. It's all very random and confusing and upsetting. But . . . well, what if he's telling the truth? It's worth at least trying to find that out. If he's really not evil . . . then maybe there's nothing we have to do at all."

Ryan puts a hand to his forehead in the same kind of you're-giving-me-a-headache way that Peter did. "Do you actually believe him?"

"I don't know. I don't know what to believe. But I do know that switching shows is not the answer. I need to find out what's really going on."

We sit there for a few minutes, not talking.

Then he says, quietly, "Why did you even bother to tell me?"

Now I'm the one staring. "What kind of question is that? No more secrets, remember?" I feel like the world's biggest hypocrite, but I press on. "I thought you'd want to know. And I needed to tell you. Jesus, Ryan, who else am I going to talk to about this? I hadn't decided anything, I just . . . I just wanted to come find you so we could figure it out together."

61

"But apparently there's nothing to figure out."

"Yet! I'm just saying we should try to get more information first. I mean, what would we even do? Try to catch him? Banish him back to the demon world?" I try a tiny smile. "Did you even pack a strobe light?"

"Ha." Still not an actual laughing sound but less like hidden screaming than before. I start to breathe a little easier.

"Okay," Ryan says after a minute. "I guess that makes sense for now, anyway. Let's . . . see what happens. If people start acting like zombies or, you know, dying, at least we'll know who to blame."

"Right. And then we can . . . figure out what to do. Together."

"Right."

We keep sitting there, not speaking. I do not think I would describe this as a comfortable silence. I think a more accurate description would be that it's a terrifying silence in which my boyfriend is possibly thinking secret thoughts about being mad at me and how maybe I am not quite worth all this demon baggage that I seem destined to drag around forever.

"We okay?" I ask, not looking at him.

He sighs, and for a second I stop breathing entirely. Then he reaches over to take my hand. "Yeah, we're okay. I'm sorry. I just . . . really hate demons, you know?"

"You and me both, mister."

We fall into silence again, but he's still holding my hand, and so that makes it much less ominous. I think this time we're just not ready to rejoin the regular world quite yet.

"How's the show?" Ryan asks.

"Oh, my God," I tell him. "It's amazing. I mean it's really amazing. Demon or not, he's really talented."

"Well, that's good, at least. I guess. I mean, I was hoping. You'll have to tell me what it's about and everything."

"Is *Scarlet Pimpernel* all that you dreamed it would be and more?"

He pinches me lightly on the arm. "Shut up. It's only the first day. But yes, so far, everyone seems really great."

"I heard the chorus singing as I came up here. They sounded pretty good already!"

He gets up and then turns and takes my hand again.

"Let's go to lunch. I want . . . to not think about demons for a little bit. Okay?"

"Okay."

He pulls me to my feet, and I grab him in a spontaneous hug. And then I have trouble letting go.

"Hey," he says, hugging me back. "It's okay. It'll be okay."

"Promise?"

"Yes. I promise. Whoever this guy is, he can't be worse than Mr. Gabriel, right?"

"Right." God, please let that be the truth.

I force my arms to disengage from their slightly too-tight embrace and hold his hand again instead. Then we start walking down the hill.

Jules has saved us both seats at lunch.

She looks at Ryan with poorly concealed concern/curiosity but doesn't ask any questions. We try to get caught up in the ongoing conversation about everyone's first rehearsal and who already has a crush on someone in their cast and which directors are new and who wishes they were in a different show already.

At least half the camp appears to have a crush on Peter.

"Is he as delicious up close as he is from a distance?" Ryan's friend Toby, who is rather delicious himself with his perfect ebony skin and perfect dancer's body, asks this while peering toward the other end of the dining hall, where Peter is sitting at an over-full table with some of his many admirers. Toby was cast as Snout in *A Midsummer Night's Dream*. He's sitting next to Maria, who is playing viola in the *Brigadoon* orchestra. I've been glad to discover that Ryan's group of friends at camp is not entirely made up of superstars like him and Jules. I mean, he is friends with several of the other kids who often get leads, but plenty of his friends are chorus-level or musicians or backstagers. They're all really nice. Like his friends back home. He's got good taste in friends, that Ryan.

I glance at Jules. My inevitable and immediate thoughts about her being the exception to this rule aren't really fair, since she's been nothing but nice to me. I just . . . can't like her. Or how close she and Ryan are. Or how much shared history they have. I think it's just not physically possible for me to like any of that.

Toby pokes me in the arm for taking too long to answer.

"He is a very attractive young man," I confirm. "That is my objective opinion."

"I'd like to give him my objective opinion," Maria says.

Toby pokes her now. "That doesn't even make sense, love."

Maria shrugs. "Everyone knows what I meant. The exact syntax was irrelevant."

Everyone is curious about Peter's show, and I oblige them with a description of the plot and assurance that the music is incredible. Ryan's friend Belinda, who is in the chorus of *Aftermass,* walks by just as we're talking about it and joins our conversation. "Did you tell them about the drama?"

"What drama?" everyone asks at once.

Ryan stares at me, clearly thinking about the demon-related drama, but I give him a tiny shake of my head. "I didn't see very much, but someone named Darleen may or may not have pushed another girl off the stage?" I look at Belinda for confirmation. Everyone else does, too.

She squeezes in to sit down next to Jules. "Oh, my God. Cyn, did someone tell you the backstory? Those two have been fighting for, like, ten years now. It's crazy that they ended up in the same show this year."

Toby rolls his eyes. "Belinda likes to exaggerate." It's her turn for a poke in the arm. "Ten years ago they were six years old, Drama Queen. It's more like five years of mutual hatred."

"Six," Belinda insists. "They were nine. I remember. I was here that year."

"But why?" I ask. "What happened?"

"Well," Belinda says, "what I heard is that Darleen got the lead in the Lower Campers' production of *Cinderella,* and Celia was the understudy, which made her crazy mad. And then she tried to arrange it so that Darleen had an 'accident' so that she could go on in her place."

"That's not what happened," Maria says. "They were nine! It wasn't anything so violent. Celia was just really mean to her, and she turned a bunch of the other girls against her."

"There was definitely some violence, though," Toby says. "I heard that Steven had to physically pull them apart after opening night because Darleen jumped Celia the second the curtain went down."

"However it started," Jules says to me, "they totally hate each other now, and something always happens before the end of the summer. This is early, though! Usually we get through at least a week or two before things blow up."

"That's our camp," Ryan says. "Drama onstage, drama everywhere else, too." He points back and forth between me and Belinda. "You guys will have to keep us informed."

Belinda waggles her eyebrows as she gets back up with her tray. "Of course!"

The conversation drifts on to other shows and other famous feuds between campers (although everyone agrees that there is nothing that comes even close to rivaling the Darleen-Celia thing) and then to what everyone has scheduled for the afternoon. Some days there's a second rehearsal period, but other days there are electives that we all chose ahead of time. Ryan tried to get me to sign up for improv with him, but I just couldn't imagine that being anything but terrifying. Yes, sure, I want to learn and grow as an individual, but not by making a fool of myself in front of others. I signed up for archery and painting instead.

I have brief second thoughts as I watch Ryan and Jules head off to improv together (of course), but I turn determinedly away and head for the archery field. Lisa R. bounds up beside me on the way. "You picked archery, too, right? I'm so glad. No one else I know signed up for it."

She barely knows me, but I refrain from pointing this out. "It sounded like fun," I say instead. "And a nice break from set construction."

"I hope I don't shoot someone's eye out!" she says cheerfully.

I laugh before I can help it. I like Lisa R. She reminds me a little of Leticia.

That gives me a twinge. I miss those girls already. I resolve to write them all long letters tonight after dinner. In which I will say nothing about demon campers. Especially not to Annie. I just want her to be happy and have delightful falling-in-love times with sweet, sweet William and not have to think about anything scary or upsetting in any way. Besides, it's not like there's any reason she needs to know. Even if Peter does turn out to be evil, he's stuck here, tethered to me, and so poses no danger to Annie whatsoever.

Unless he was lying about that part. Which, if evil, he totally could have been.

But I'm not going to go down that road. Watch and wait. That's the plan. I'm going to stick to the plan. It's a good plan. Easy.

The rest of the day passes with no more demon revelations or even any eyes getting shot out during archery. I am starting to get the hang of this camp thing, I think.

After dinner and evening activity (a performance by the extracurricular musical improv troupe, followed by solicitations to sign up and join them, which I decline), I walk with Ryan and some of his friends to the point where we have to go in different directions to go back to our bunks.

"Good night, sexy," I whisper, kissing him perhaps a teeny bit longer than is really tasteful for a public leave-taking, but screw it. I had a rough day.

He rewards me with one of the smiles that justifies me calling him that, which I hold carefully in my mind to gaze upon with my inward eye when I get into bed.

Everyone drifts off to their bunks, and I walk the final length of the path alone to number 6.

Just as I'm reaching the door, a shadow moves beside the path.

A big shadow.

I stop, looking back over my shoulder, but everyone else is out of sight already.

I debate running. Or screaming. But I really don't want to be the crazy girl who ran screaming around camp the third night. And maybe it was just a shadow. A harmless, totally non-demony—

"Hey." The shadow is closer. And it is talking to me.

"Uh, hello?" I whisper. I don't know why I'm whispering.

"Come here." The shadow moves around the side of the bunk.

Nope! I head for the door.

Something grabs me and pulls me off the path.

"Hey!" I shout. But I'm still sort of whispering. It's something about the dark and the trees and all the nature.

Stupid nature.

"Leave Peter alone," the shadow says menacingly.

"What?" I'm still trying to make out features of some kind. It could be a bear for all I can see.

The shadow leans closer, and I see a face in the darkness. Not one I recognize. Also, not a bear. He's a teenager. Human. Just . . . very large.

"Leave. Peter. Alone."

"Who *are* you?"

"Hector."

Ah. Peter had neglected to mention that his human helper was here at camp.

"I'm not doing anything to Peter."

"You'd better not. He worked really hard to get here."

"No, he didn't! He — well, you know how he got here."

"You don't know how hard it was for him. How long he's wanted to escape. What he had to endure! You don't know anything. And you don't have to. You just leave him alone, that's all."

Well. Peter certainly has a devoted friend in Hector here. That's nice for him.

"Sure, fine. Whatever you say. Now how about you leave *me* alone, okay? I'm going to bed."

"I'll be watching."

"What?"

The shadow hesitates, seeming to realize how that sounded. "I mean, not watching you go to bed," he amends. "I just mean . . . you know what I mean."

"Sure," I say again. "Have a good night, Hector."

I go inside.

"Hey Cyn," various voices say.

"There's a letter on your bed," Sasha adds.

I can see immediately that it's from Annie. No one else uses quite so many unicorn stickers on an envelope. She must have mailed it on the day I left for it to have gotten here so fast.

I'm smiling as I pull it gently open. This is what I need. No more demons or overprotective shadowy bear-shaped human helpers. Not for the rest of the night, at least.

I lie back, happy to see it's a long letter. Good old Annie.

Dear Cyn, it begins. *Are you already having the best summer ever????????*

I make a tiny chuckling sound that is also almost the sound of a quiet desperate sob.

Yup, I think back at her. *No question. Best summer ever.*

Sure.

Chapter | 05

Annie's letter is filled with adorable descriptions of things William has done and said in the very short time between when I last saw her and when she started writing. There are also several stick figures depicting Annie's ideas of what camp is like and what Ryan and I are doing whenever we get alone together. I make sure to find a good hiding place for the letter before I go to sleep. No need for the other girls to know my best friend is a horrible pervert.

Sleep is slow in coming, however. I lie there in the dark, listening to the shifting of Caroline on the bunk above me and someone (Hana?) snoring quietly from across the room. I've been doing my best to not freak out all day, but now that I'm out of immediate distractions, I feel the freaking out starting to happen.

Because, you know, demons.

Again.

Well, one demon, anyway. And way less terrifying than Mr. Gabriel. At least so far. But then, Mr. Gabriel was less terrifying in the beginning, too. I try to take comfort from the fact that Peter doesn't give off any trace of that same creepy vibe I felt right away from the librarian. I try to believe that he's telling the truth about not wanting to kill anyone. I keep trying to believe it as I lie there for what seems like hours until I fall asleep.

Sleep fails to be the escape I was hoping for. All night long I see red halos, flashing everywhere and then vanishing as I try to see who they belong to. I run down corridors after bear-shaped shadows that turn when cornered and reveal glowing red eyes and pointy needle teeth and tentacles where the arms should be. I run screaming for help, to find Ryan, to find anyone, but everyone I see has a red halo now, and no one can help me. I'm alone. And running out of places to hide.

Then suddenly all the faces merge and change into that of Mr. Gabriel. He looks at me, smiling his too-wide demony smile, wings and horns stretching outward as I watch in horror. I try to back away but his dark swirly black-hole eyes have caught me and something is wrong with my roachy resistance because I can't run, I can't break free, he's got me trapped. He steps closer, still smiling, and I see that he's covered in blood. He smiles even more when he sees me noticing this.

"They're all dead now," he says, jerking his head back to make me look behind him. I gasp at the pile of bodies. Ryan. Leticia and Diane. My parents, my teachers, as soon as I think of someone I see them lying there, dead eyes staring at nothing, mouth slack, limbs motionless. But not Annie. She's not there. I grab on to a sliver of hope.

"You didn't get her," I tell him. "You will *never* get her."

He laughs, and keeps laughing, and then Annie is there beside him, laughing, too. "You never saved me," she says. "He's had me all this time. He will always have me. I'm damned forever, damned for all time, and it's your fault. *All. Your. Fault.*" Her laughter turns to screaming. *"Why didn't you save me?"* She runs at me, shrieking, tentacle-claws waving.

I wrench myself awake, swallowing the scream that wants to rip from my lungs. *Just a dream,* I tell myself over and over. *Just a dream. Mr. Gabriel is dead. You killed him. You killed him, and Annie is fine. Annie is more than fine. Annie is safe at home, canoodling with sweet, sweet William and drawing pictures of me and Ryan doing naughty things on the backs of unicorns in the woods.*

I lie back down, willing my heart to slow to a normal kind of rhythm. I don't go back to sleep.

Later, I walk slowly to breakfast, trying to make small talk with Susan about orchestra rehearsal. There is a cute oboe player in her rehearsal group, apparently. She still doesn't seem to appreciate how awesome it is that she's in the pit orchestra for *West Side Story*. I feel I should try to educate her, but I have bigger things to worry about right now. Even shaking off the dreams for what they were — just dreams, dammit — I am still faced with the very real issue of Peter and what to do about him.

I always assumed that if demons ever reared their falsely attractive heads again somewhere in the human world around me, there would be an obvious threat, a clear enemy to pit myself against. Peter . . . does not fit the expected criteria. Is it possible that he's really telling the truth? That he's not evil? That would be nice to believe. I certainly don't want to fight demons if I don't have to. With Mr. Gabriel, there was no choice — he was brainwashing Annie and killing people and doing so many very bad things that required immediate action and eventual fighting to the death. But if all Peter wants to do is create amazing shows with outstanding music and production value . . . where's the bad there? Wouldn't the bad thing be depriving the world of his talent? What if he could go on to usher in the next golden age of musical theater? Do I really want to stand in the way of that?

Susan seems to sense that I am not focused on her descriptions of the oboe player. "Earth to Cyn," she says, nudging me. "Are you in there?"

I force myself to smile at her. "Yes, sorry. Just . . . thinking. But also listening. Have you talked to him yet?"

She looks at me, incredulous. "Of course not. What would I say?"

"How about, 'I like the way you play that oboe, mister'?"

She laughs. "You clearly have never had a crush on an oboe player."

"Are they so different from the rest of us?"

"Completely. Like aliens, really. I need to take things really slow."

"Well, let me know if I can help. I may not know about oboe players, but I know about crushes."

"But . . . isn't Ryan your boyfriend?"

"Yes. Now. But first he was a boy who made my brain evaporate every time he was in the room."

Susan considers me with renewed interest. "So how did you make that change?"

"Oh, he still makes my brain evaporate."

"But how did you start talking? How did you, you know . . . get closer? Make things happen?"

Oh, easy. I got him to follow me into the library where we caught the new librarian in demon form. Fighting evil together is a great way to form romantic bonds! "It . . . took a while. But it definitely got easier once I actually started talking to him." I hesitate, then add, "I accidentally tackled him in the hallway once, near the beginning. That turned out to be a good icebreaker."

"Hmm." Susan seems to be giving this a lot more thought than I intended. I had been kidding. Mostly. Luckily, we have now arrived at breakfast, and I head off to find Ryan.

Along the way, I notice Peter walking toward a table in the back. Toby is walking beside him. They are talking and laughing like best friends. At least four other campers lurk behind them, clearly intending to follow them to a table but trying to appear as though they are not doing that. Many other admiring eyes are watching Peter make his way across the dining hall.

Ryan's eyes are on Peter as well, but I would not describe them as admiring.

Maria follows his gaze. "Looks like Toby's making a play for the playwright."

"Are you still a playwright if you write musical theater?" Craig asks. "Or is that just if you write straight plays?"

Discussion ensues, but I can't pay attention. I sit and try to act normal, like I'm not at all worried about Toby getting too close to our new demon friend or about myself and how I'm supposed to talk set design with Peter now that I know what he is, but Ryan keeps giving me concerned glances over his waffles. Finally I have to kick him under the table and hiss, "Quit it!"

Jules (who is, of course, sitting right beside him) can't help but notice this exchange.

"What's up with you guys this morning? Lovers' quarrel?" She smiles to show that she's joking.

I want to punch her.

"Everything's fine, Jules," Ryan says unconvincingly.

I steal a bite of syrupy waffle from Ryan's plate *(that's right, Jules, because he's my boyfriend and I can eat off his plate anytime I want)* and chew slowly, giving myself time to think of something to say.

"Yeah," I say at last. "Ryan just hates when I get distracted with set stuff."

"Well, that's your whole *job*," Jules says. "It makes sense you get distracted with it sometimes. Don't mind him; Ryan just can't stand not being the center of everyone's universe at all times."

"Hey!" Ryan says. But he's kind of laughing.

I laugh, too. But I don't like having my boyfriend explained to me by other people.

Finally it is time to go to morning rehearsal. I walk with Sasha, who is gushing excitedly about the show. I make encouraging noises but can't really add meaningfully to the conversation. This is the longest walk ever. I don't know what to hope for or expect at the end of it.

As we approach the theater, Sasha skips on ahead. A giant bear-shadow-boy leans out from under a nearby tree and glares at me. In the daylight I can see that he has really unfortunate acne. I roll my eyes at him and walk inside.

Peter grabs my arm and whisks me toward the stage.

"Don't worry," he says, "I told Michael we'd be working backstage the whole time today. And probably from now on, really. He's more than happy not to have me out there watching. Also, you probably need to get the tech crew started on things to do while you're working on the design. Do you have any ideas yet?"

"I've been a little distracted," I say pointedly.

He stops when we get backstage and turns to face me. "Well, stop it. Whatever your personal issues are with me, you have a job to do. One that affects both of us. I know you want that Tony. Not that the camp award means anything in the big picture, obviously, but I know you want to be the best, and to be recognized for it. So do I. And I want this show to be amazing. In every way. Including the design. So if we need to talk about . . . things . . . let's get it out of the way right now so we can both get on with what we came here to do."

I notice that his halo is masked again. I don't know why he bothers, although I am secretly glad he does. Seeing it just makes everything worse. The color . . . brings back too many memories.

He waits while I stand there staring at him, trying to think.

Can I do this? Can I believe him? Can I work with him even if I'm not sure I can believe him? I told Ryan that staying on the show was the best course, and I meant it . . . but it's not like I can just pretend that everything is fine now. He's a demon! He doesn't belong here. He's screwing up my best summer ever!

But. So far, he hasn't done anything demonlike. And he does seem really, really devoted to his show. And the show is really, really good. And what are my other options? Stay here to keep an eye on him but not work on the show? That wouldn't be possible even if I wanted to do that — Michael would kick my ass to the curb, and they'd find someone else to design the set.

And . . . *I* want to design the set. I was so excited yesterday, before I found out about Peter.

He's still watching me, waiting for my decision. Which makes me wonder: what would happen if I refused? If I said I wouldn't work with him? Would he just be disappointed? Or is there some more important reason he needs to keep me close by? Maybe he's afraid I'd try to leave camp entirely, which would mean he'd have to come along, because of the tether.

Or that he'd have to find a way to stop me.

"Please, Cyn. I know we can do an amazing job on this show, working together. Don't let a little thing like nonhuman DNA get in the way." He's trying to be funny, I guess, but he mostly seems nervous. He keeps pushing his glasses up on his nose, reframing those big blue eyes. Which are currently giving off just the slightest hint of puppy-dog pleading. It's kind of adorable, really.

Don't forget what he is, Old Cyn whispers from the back of my brain.

I won't. I just wish I knew for sure whether demons could ever be trustworthy.

Probably not, Old Cyn says. *So don't trust him. Not all the way. Also, stop thinking about him being adorable. Only Ryan is adorable!*

"All right," I say finally, not really knowing what's going to come out of my mouth until I start talking. "I'm going to believe you. For now. I'm going to trust you that you're not evil, and you're just here to do theater. And we are going to work on this show and make it awesome. And also, you are going to tell me what needs to happen for this tether thing to be broken so that I can eventually be rid of you. Sound like a plan?"

He gives me a radiant smile so engaging and contagious that it almost has me smiling back before I catch myself.

Dammit. He really is as charming as he thinks he is.

"Yes. Thank you, Cyn. You won't regret this."

"We'll see. Oh! And call off your bear-boy."

"What?"

"I got a visit from Hector last night. You didn't mention that he was here at camp."

"Oh. Sorry. I'll tell him to back off. He can be a bit over-protective."

"Thanks." I pause, then can't help asking, "What's he doing here, anyway? Aren't you afraid someone is eventually going to notice him lurking in the shadows? He's not exactly inconspicuous."

"He only lurks occasionally. He's registered as a camper. It seemed the best way to keep him close by in case I need him. He's doing backstage stuff on *Brigadoon*."

"Couldn't you have arranged it so that he was on your show? I mean with your magical demon powers?"

"Sure, but . . . well, look, I love the guy, but honestly, there's such a thing as too much Hector-time, you know? Plus, you saw how he gets. He'd be hovering over my shoulder all the time. Or yours. Anyway, it's better if no one catches on that there's any connection between us. I told him to keep his distance as much as possible."

"Hmm." I'm trying to picture Hector painting flats with the other set kids and am having a very difficult time. I give it up; my poor brain doesn't need any extra challenges right now.

Peter touches the sleeve of my T-shirt lightly with one finger. "So . . . are we good? Focus on the show and not on our respective backstories or places of origin? Yes?"

"Yes." But then I give him my best steely glare. "Unless you give me a reason to doubt you. The slightest reason."

"Yeah, yeah. But don't worry. I won't. Really. I'm nothing like the other demons you know, I swear."

"Hmm."

"Okay!" he says, clapping his hands excitedly. "Let's talk backdrops." He whips out a copy of the score plastered with sticky notes and bookmarks, then plunks down to the floor and gestures for me to join him.

After a second I do. This is what I came here for in the first place; if I'm not going to ditch, then I might as well get started.

We talk backdrops. And risers. And lighting. Before long,

despite everything, I feel myself starting to get swept up in the excitement of envisioning the stage and how to bring this show to life.

What else am I supposed to do?

Before I know it, camp life begins to fall into a pattern. The sleeping part of this pattern is not very awesome, because I keep having those demony nightmares, but I guess that's not so surprising. Obviously, encountering another demon, even a (probably) non-evil one, is going to make my subconscious start coughing up all its dark and terrible memories of Mr. Gabriel. And anyway, that's only when I'm sleeping. The daytime parts of the pattern are much, much better.

The rest of the set crew actually have a few days of technical-skills classes before they need to start working on the set construction, which gives me a little time to figure out the plan. Peter and I spend morning rehearsals discussing the ideas that I've sketched out the night before. We've got several aspects of the set design in rough form already, and I have to say, I'm pretty pleased with how things are shaping up.

And Peter . . . is proving to be a lot of fun to work with. When I let myself not think about the whole demon thing. He knows every part of the show by heart, of course, and he's ridiculously entertaining when he acts out little snippets while we try to decide on design ideas. He's not a performer; his voice doesn't carry anything like the power and intensity of Ryan's, for example, but it's sweet and clear and relentlessly on key, and he does an adorable falsetto whenever he sings the girls' parts.

Stop thinking he's adorable!

Oh, relax, Old Cyn. I'm just saying.

Peter and I are in agreement that minimal is probably best for the overall design; it's a desolate postapocalyptic cityscape, so we're thinking dark shadows and angles and corners and very little color. There are lots of scene changes, so we need to build in easy transitions and make sure everything is portable and quick to move around. The story has many layers to it, and I want to reflect that in the set, incorporating different levels into the vertical construction and using rotating set pieces that reflect the different angles of events that take place within the musical. Peter is on board for all of this. He's super quick to get what I'm talking about, every time, immediately seeing what I'm going for and jumping in with ideas to help clarify or expand on what I'm thinking.

I don't want to admit it, but we actually make a pretty good team.

Hector doesn't make any more late-night appearances, but I do sometimes see him out of the corner of my eye, loitering passive-aggressively.

Speaking of the corner of my eye, I finally figured out that the tether is the thing I was catching glimpses of in the days leading up to camp. It only happens when Peter's at a certain distance and a certain angle . . . like our relative placement to each other occasionally makes the tether almost visible, and my almost-seeing it is what kept making me so jumpy. Because really, how often do things you almost-see out of the corner of your eye turn out to be happy surprises, like cake or bunnies?

Far more often they are spiders dangling from the ceiling. So jumpy is totally reasonable. But knowing what it is helps a lot.

I still don't like it.

"When are you going to tell me how to dismantle that thing?" I ask the next time I catch almost-sight of it.

"Once we're done with the set plan," Peter assures me. Again. "I need to do some research, and you know I'll have a lot more time once we're all done with the initial decision-making part and I can just set you loose to work your magic in physical form with all of your . . . what do you call them? Minions?"

"Yes. And quit it with the flattery." Although of course I don't really mind the flattery. "Just promise me you'll figure it out as soon as you can and set me loose for real."

"I promise." He pushes up his glasses and smiles at me.

"Hmm."

After dinner one night, Peter comes up to me at the canteen. I am sitting with Ryan and Jules and Craig and Maria and Sasha and Lisa R. and Susan, discussing everyone's most- and least-favorite types of chocolate. Maria has just shocked everyone with her revelation that she doesn't like chocolate at all. "Not even *Reese's*?" Sasha asks, unable to accept this confusing position. Sasha has an enormous stash of mini Reese's Peanut Butter Cups in the cubby beside her bed. Her mom sends her a fresh supply every week.

"Cyn!" Peter says excitedly, ignoring everyone else. "I just had the best thought about Act Two. Do you have a minute?"

"Sure." I squeeze Ryan's hand. "Back in a sec."

"Hi," Ryan says past me to Peter. He hasn't released my hand. "You must be Peter."

"Yup," says Peter pleasantly. Very pleasantly. He smiles at Ryan, and everyone gets a little quiet.

"I'm Ryan," Ryan says. "Cyn's boyfriend."

"I know who you are," Peter says. Then he turns to me expectantly.

I introduce him to the rest of the group as quickly as possible and then pull him away before things can get any more awkward.

"What the hell was that?" I whisper at him furiously once we're out of earshot.

"What?"

"You were . . . I don't know. Trying to provoke him. Or something. Cut it out."

"I don't know what you're talking about," he says. He glances back over his shoulder. "Who's the blond girl?"

"That's Jules."

I try to say it absolutely neutrally, but something must come through in my voice, because Peter's attention is instantly focused on my face. "Oh? And who is Jules? Old girlfriend?"

"No! They're just friends."

"Really. They look . . . pretty comfortable."

"Yeah. Like friends. Did you actually have an idea, or did you just come here to make trouble?"

He grins, and I have to look away. It's not a Ryan-level smile, obviously, but I still don't like the way it makes me feel.

Or that it makes me feel anything. I mean I'm not feeling *feelings,* nothing like that, just . . . somewhat fluttery in the stomach region. Or possibly a little lower. It's something about the glasses, I think. And the eyes. And the cheekbones. *He's a demon,* I remind myself.

And you have a boyfriend! Old Cyn shouts from the back of my brain.

I know. Shut up.

"So?"

"Right." He looks back once more, though. "They're both *very* attractive."

"*Peter,*" I growl.

"Okay, okay." He gets down to business. I forgive him when I realize it is a pretty good idea. We've just started set construction for real, but only really just started, so there's still time to make changes to the plan. I whip out my notebook, which I keep with me pretty much all the time for just this sort of reason, and we grab a seat on the bleachers to sketch out what he's talking about. I don't realize how much time has passed until Ryan comes over.

"Hey. It's almost last call. You guys almost done?"

I glance up, startled. "It is? Oh, wow. I had no idea. Sorry, sweetie. We just got caught up."

"I guess you did," Ryan says, looking at Peter.

"Sorry, sweetie," Peter says. "I didn't mean to steal your girl for this long. We can finish up tomorrow."

I give Peter a what-the-hell? kind of look and stand up. "Yeah. See you tomorrow," I tell him, pulling Ryan away.

"I don't like that guy," Ryan grumbles as we walk off.

"I don't know why he was acting like that," I say. "He's usually really nice."

"I'm sure he is," Ryan says. "To you."

I stop walking and turn to face him. "What's that supposed to mean?"

Ryan gives me an exasperated look. "He likes you."

"What?"

"It's obvious, Cyn."

"You're crazy. Also, he's a you-know-what."

"So? Have we not learned, to our great sorrow, that you-know-whats can develop inappropriate romantic attachments to humans? And vice versa?"

"And vice versa?" I repeat, staring at him. "Are you seriously suggesting what it sounds like you're suggesting?"

Ryan meets my gaze for a second, then drops his eyes.

"Sorry. No, of course not. I just . . . I just don't like that you have to spend so much time with him."

"Well, get over it, please. I have to spend time with him to work on the show."

"Fine, but you don't have to like it so much."

"Argh!" My expression of frustration is apparently a little too loud, and several heads turn to look at us. "Are you *jealous*?" I ask him. "Of Peter?"

"No!" Ryan says, also a little too loudly. "I just thought we were going to be spending more time together this summer, and instead, it seems like every time I turn around, you're working with him on the show."

My mouth literally drops open. "Seriously? You're going to complain that we're not spending enough time together when you have had Jules glued to your side since the second you got off the bus?"

"Jules has been my friend for practically my whole life!"

"Just your friend? The whole time?"

Now it's his turn to stare. "What? Where is that coming from?"

"Why does everyone I talk to express shock that you're my boyfriend and not hers?" I ask him. "Is there something you would like to tell me?"

"No," he says firmly. He takes a breath and looks me in the eye. "I don't want to fight about this. I don't want to fight about anything. I just . . . I just want you to be careful. I'm worried that you're forgetting what Peter is."

"Well, I'm not. But he's not like Mr. Gabriel. He's not a bad guy. And he's not the enemy."

"I know. I do. But I still don't like him. He's . . . smarmy."

I shake my head. "I can't believe you just said *smarmy*. Who even says that?"

"When the shoe fits . . ."

"Who says that either? What's gotten into you lately?"

"I don't know," he says. He puts an arm around me and pulls me in for a hug. "I'm sorry. I'm being an ass. I mean, aside from being legitimately concerned about demons and things, which you have to admit is not unreasonable. But I didn't mean to blow up at you. I'm just getting anxious about lines and stuff. We're supposed to be off book in a few days, and I'm nowhere near ready."

I make him wait several seconds before I hug him back. "Well . . . stop being an ass and I'll run lines with you."

"Deal."

"Good."

The next morning at rehearsal, I watch Peter as he inspects the revised sketches I worked on before bed. Ryan's crazy. Peter likes to flirt, but he likes to flirt with everyone. Boys, girls, counselors, even that asshole Michael. He just likes the attention, I think. He isn't really interested in anything other than his show and getting the tether broken as soon as he finishes figuring out how. I am a bit surprised that he's not more eager about that, but I guess there's really no rush. . . . It's not like he's going anywhere until after the show is over. And it doesn't seem to be affecting anything on my end. I can't feel it, and the range it lets him get from me is bigger than the boundaries of camp, or close enough.

I don't think I can feel it, anyway. I mean other than the corner-of-the-eye thing. Unless . . . unless maybe it's also the thing that's making me feel those uncomfortable fluttery feelings when he smiles at me.

Or is causing the nightmares.

Suddenly Peter and the tether have my full attention.

"Is the tether thing having any effect on me?" I ask.

He looks up. "What do you mean?"

I shrug. "I don't know. It connects you to me, right? So is it . . . doing anything to me?"

His mouth tilts up on one side. "Why? Do you feel like it's doing something to you? Making you want to spend more time around me, perhaps?"

"Is that going to happen?"

"Are you sure it's not happening already?"

"Peter. Quit it. I'm being serious."

He shakes his head. "You shouldn't be aware of it at all. It's not made of demonic energy — you'd be able to see it like you see halos otherwise. It's more like . . . well, you saw Aaron summon his demoness, right? Inside a containment diagram?"

"Yes, although he was a little light on the containment aspect."

Peter laughs. "Yeah, that's Aaron. Anyway, the tether is kind of like a big invisible containment diagram, with you as the focal point. So it moves around with you, and I have to stay within its boundaries wherever it goes."

"But there's a way to break it? You're sure?"

"Yes. I just . . . haven't quite figured it out yet. I arranged things in a bit of a hurry and hadn't really planned ahead for everything. But I will figure it out, I promise. Before camp is over, for sure."

"So at the end of the summer we can go our separate ways? Forever?"

He looks wounded. "Yes, although I don't know why you're quite so eager to be rid of me. We work really well together. We could . . . do it again, you know. I could come to your school, be a transferred senior or whatever . . ."

"No!"

"Why not?"

"We have already had our fill of demons at school, thank you very much."

"But I'm not like those other demons. I'm different. You like me."

I stare at him. "No I don't!"

"You don't like me?" He flashes me the wounded look again. It is a confusing mix of melodrama and apparent sincerity.

"I don't . . . I don't *dis*like you. I don't feel anything for you. I just don't want any more demons in my life. Surely you can understand that."

He looks at me silently for a moment. "But what if I want to be in your life?"

"Well, we can't always have what we want, can we? And besides, you don't like me. You just like messing with me. You like stirring up trouble. But you can find someone else to stir up trouble for. The world is a big place. Lots of options out there."

"True. But you . . . you're special, Cyn. I can't use my demonic powers on you. But I also don't have to hide what I am. With anyone else, I'd have to pretend to be human all the time."

"You'll get used to it. Are you done yet? Sketches approved? I would like to get back to work."

"It's great. I love everything," he says.

"Good," I say, reaching for my notebook. He doesn't let go.

"Let go," I say.

He smiles at me instead. "Make me."

"I don't have time for your nonsense, Peter. Let go."

He leans closer. "Or what?"

"Peter, come on." We're alone in the alcove behind the stage. "If you're trying to use your demony charms on me, it's pointless, remember? I have natural resistance."

"Only to my demon magic. Not to my magical personality." He takes a step closer.

I laugh before I can help it. "Trust me. I'm resistant to that, too."

His hand creeps forward until it's touching mine on the edge of the notebook. "Are you sure?"

I snatch my hand away, but not before I feel a tiny electric shock. "Yes! Ew! Cut it out."

He sighs and holds out the book. "Fine. Take your lovely sketches and go."

"*Thank* you."

I flee for the workroom, where the rest of my crew is. I can feel his eyes on my back, but I don't turn around.

That night, I dream about Peter. Not nightmares, which is a nice change, but . . . not very comfortable dreams, either. In the dreams I find him very attractive. I mean, he *is* attractive, that's not really debatable, but in the dreams I *feel* attracted to him. Very attracted. My brain replays the scene from earlier today, and this time when he touches my hand I don't pull away. I let him come closer.

He sets the notebook down and takes hold of my wrists, backing me gently against the wall and coming closer still. I look into his bright-blue eyes, and I don't want to look away.

"You do like me," he says.

"Yes," I whisper.

He puts his head next to mine, his breath tickling my neck. "What was that? I couldn't quite hear you."

"Yes." The word barely makes a sound. He takes one hand

and brushes the hair back from my face, and his fingers deliver tiny electric shocks where they touch my skin.

"Yes what?" he asks softly, holding my gaze.

"Yes, I like you."

"Do you like when I touch you?" He runs his fingers gently along the edge of my throat.

"Yes." Still just a whisper.

"Do you want me to kiss you?"

No, Old Cyn says in the back of my brain. *No no no! You want Ryan to kiss you. Not Peter! PETER IS NOT YOUR BOYFRIEND!*

I know, I tell her. *But . . . I want . . .*

No! she says again.

"Yes," I tell Peter.

He leans toward me, and I close my eyes, and it feels like a small eternity before his lips finally brush mine. The tingly electricity this time shoots all the way down to my toes.

I jerk awake, eyes flying open, half expecting to find Peter there in my bed with me.

That was . . . very realistic.

Also . . . just a dream. Like the nightmares. Also like the nightmares, it does not mean anything. I do not want to kiss Peter. Just like Mr. Gabriel is not really here, back from the dead, to torment me. I have a lot going on, and my subconscious is working through its problems in my sleep. It's probably all very healthy for my psyche. Nothing to be concerned about.

I close my eyes again, but it's a long while before I can relax enough to fall back to sleep.

Chapter | 06

At breakfast I act perfectly normal. Because it was just a dream, and it didn't mean anything.

After a while we become aware of some kind of quiet disturbance going on at the end of the dining hall. Steven walks over to where he makes the morning announcements, but something is clearly wrong. He's usually full of energy and looks like he can't wait to share whatever tonight's evening activity is or remind us about care-package rules and regulations, but this morning he just looks tired and a little grim. Conversation dies down as everyone turns to look at him.

"I have some disappointing news to tell you this morning, campers," he says, getting right to the point. "Jeremy, who as you all know was directing the Lower Camp production of *You're a Good Man, Charlie Brown,* was called away from camp suddenly last night and won't be able to return. I'm sure I speak for everyone when I say it won't be the same around here this summer without him. But assistant director Marlena will be taking over for him, and I know she'll do a great job."

Steven steps away without making any other announcements, and a buzz of reaction begins among the campers. Belinda rushes over and squeezes in beside me at the table.

"I heard that Jeremy didn't even tell Steven he was leaving," she says in the low, excited voice she uses for gossip sharing. "Just left a note. *Super* not cool. Steven was really pissed about it."

"I'll bet," Jules says. "That's so weird, though. I wonder what happened."

"Family emergency?" someone suggests.

Ryan and I lock eyes across the table. There's no reason to be suspicious, and yet . . . *family emergency* was how our high school excused the sudden disappearance of Signor De Luca after Mr. Gabriel killed him.

Jules notices our eye-locking. "Did you guys hear something else? Spill!"

"No," Ryan says. "I didn't know anything about it until just now."

"Me neither," I say. "I don't think I've even seen Jeremy since the show announcements. He was the tall, skinny guy with the receding hairline, right?"

"Yeah," Maria says. "That's him. He's been working here for years. I can't imagine he would have just abandoned the show unless something really awful happened."

It's very difficult, but I manage not to look at Ryan again at that. But I'm sure he is also feeling a deep sense of certainty that something awful did happen.

But I can't really believe it was Peter. I look around, but I don't see him anywhere.

As soon as we can get away without it seeming too weird, Ryan pulls me outside. "You know it was Peter," he says. "Had to be."

"I don't know any such thing," I tell him. "And neither do you."

He stares at me. "I can't believe you're defending him!"

"Let's . . . let's just go talk to him, okay? Maybe there is some perfectly reasonable explanation. Maybe there really was a family emergency! They do happen, you know. That's why everyone believed it about Signor De Luca."

Ryan makes a face, indicating how unlikely he thinks that is, but agrees to go with me.

We race up to Blake, which seems the most likely place to find him.

Peter's smile freezes when he sees that Ryan is with me. "What's he doing here?"

"We need to talk," I say without preamble. "Now."

The three of us head out a little ways into the woods. Peter looks back and forth between us. "What's this about?"

"I think you know what it's about," Ryan says.

"Stop it, both of you," I say. I turn to Peter. "What happened to Jeremy?"

Peter looks blank. "Who's Jeremy?"

I give him an impatient glare. "Don't play dumb. And don't

lie. Jeremy's the counselor who suddenly and mysteriously disappeared last night."

Peter looks . . . not exactly surprised. But not exactly like he knows all about it, either.

"Huh," he says. "I — huh."

"What does that mean?" Ryan asks.

A giant shape suddenly emerges from the surrounding trees.

"Peter? Are they bothering you?"

Ryan stares up at Hector. "Who the hell are you?"

I glare at Peter. "What's he doing here?"

Ryan whips his head around to stare at me. "You know this . . . guy?"

Oops. How did I not tell Ryan about Hector?

"Everything's fine, Hector," Peter says. "We're just talking."

"Hector is Peter's . . . companion," I tell Ryan apologetically. "I may have forgotten to mention him."

Ryan's expression is not very pleased. "Forgotten to mention him. I see. Anything else you've forgotten to mention lately?"

"Please," I say. "I really just forgot. He hasn't been an issue."

"He's a gigantic demon sympathizer who apparently lurks around and watches Peter and anyone who talks to him! How can he not be an issue?"

"Hector is not the problem!" I snap. Possibly more out of guilt than anger, because Ryan's *anything else* comment was a bit too on the mark. But I'm certainly not going to go into the demon-world stuff now. "He just stands around in the shadows most of the time. Well, and he's working backstage on *Brigadoon*. But we need to focus on Jeremy, remember?"

Ryan glares at me a moment longer, then gives me a reluctant angry nod. But it's clear that we will be continuing the Hector discussion at a later time. Yay.

We all turn to look at Peter.

He lets out a long, slow breath before he speaks. "Okay. So, first of all, no, I did not kill Jeremy. But . . ."

"But you know who did?" Ryan asks.

"Hush," I say. "Just let him talk."

Peter smiles at me gratefully, which doesn't help Ryan's mood. I don't smile back.

"I don't . . . exactly know who did, no. But I'm pretty sure someone did, that he didn't actually just go home. And the reason I know this is because I have not been entirely one hundred percent honest with you, Cyn."

I can feel Ryan's triumphant glare without even looking at him, but I refuse to acknowledge it.

"About . . . ?" I prompt Peter instead.

"The tether," he says. "I didn't lie, I just . . . didn't tell you the whole truth."

"That's still lying," Ryan says. My heart twinges guiltily.

"So tell me now," I say.

Peter looks around, in that way people do when they are trying to avoid getting to the point even when they know they can't really avoid it. His eyes finally settle back on mine. "Okay. So, what I said about the tether working like a containment diagram is true. Mostly. I mean totally true, for me."

"But you're the only one it affects. Aren't you?"

"Well . . . not exactly. The tether sort of has two parts. One part connects me to you. The other . . . connects me to the demon world. I can't get all the way free of you or the demon world until we break the tether. And while it's there . . . it's . . . *theoretically* possible that someone else could use it to get from the demon world to this one."

I stare at him, unpleasant crampy feelings starting to manifest inside my stomach. "Are you saying there's another demon tethered to me now?"

"Well, no. Because that part of the tether really does only affect me. But I think another demon traveled along the first part of the tether and is now, um, here. On the loose. I knew someone was fighting me on the far end, trying to keep the tether in place, but I thought that was just because they didn't want me to escape. I never thought . . ." He trails off and looks up at me earnestly. "I swear, I never thought there would be any danger to anyone but me."

"So basically what you're saying," Ryan says slowly, "is that you kind of left the door open, and someone else came through?"

"No! Well, okay. Yes. But it's not like I was careless. I just couldn't close the door all the way until the tether could be broken. And I can't break it, not even with Cyn's help, which is all I thought I'd need, because someone is holding it in place."

"Why didn't you tell me this before?" I ask.

He gives me a condescending look. "Oh, because *that* would have been a good idea. It only would have made you more nervous about me, and about what else might happen. I wanted to just take care of it and not have to mention it at all. It's not like there was anything you could have done. I thought that once I shook loose whoever was holding on to the other side, we could just, you know, proceed as planned. I was working on it. I just hadn't exactly figured it out yet."

"So who came through?"

"I don't know."

I take a step closer to him. "Find out," I say quietly. "Find out and figure out how we can make them go back."

"Or what?"

"Or I'll figure out how to make *you* go back."

"You can't," Peter says quickly. But something in his eyes makes me think maybe I can. He looked a little afraid there, just for a second. I store this knowledge away for later use, if needed.

"Don't you threaten Peter!" Hector rumbles, stepping closer.

"Back off!" Ryan tells him, stepping closer, too.

The woods are starting to feel very crowded.

"Stop fighting!" I yell at everyone. "We all have the same problem here. We need to get rid of that other demon before it hurts anyone else." I turn to Peter. "Is there anything else you know about what's going on that you haven't told us yet?"

Peter hesitates, and I grab his shirt. "That's a yes or no question," I say, ignoring Hector's shout of objection behind me. "You should not have to think that hard."

I let go before Hector is provoked to make me, but I don't move away.

"Okay, okay!" Peter says. "Sorry. I'm not used to full disclosure. It's . . . not generally how demons operate."

"Even the non-evil ones?" I ask sarcastically.

He ignores this and continues. "The demon who came through couldn't have done so in full physical form. Not via the tether. He's only here as energy, or spirit, or whatever you want to call it. But he must be able to either manifest physically for very short periods of time, or else take temporary possession of others' bodies—that's the only way he could have killed someone. And I'm sure that's what happened. I felt something last night, a surge of energy, but I didn't put it all together until you told me about Jeremy just now."

Ryan holds up a hand. "Wait. So you're saying this demon can possess people? Like, just take them over and make them do what he wants?"

"Well . . . yes. Pretty much."

"So anyone at camp could be the demon."

"Temporarily, yes."

"And Cyn wouldn't even be able to tell, assuming this new demon knows to mask the halo."

"Right."

"Is that, like, common knowledge down there now?" I ask Peter. "The halo thing?"

"Yeah," Peter says. "Pretty much. I told you, Aaron's a talker. And he knows a lot about you, Cyn."

Ryan sighs bitterly. "Well, this all sucks a whole lot."

"Agreed," Peter says.

Ryan glares at him. Again. Or maybe just more, as he's never really stopped glaring this whole time. "Don't agree with me! This is all your fault! You should never have come here in the first place!"

I put a hand on his arm. "Ryan . . ."

He shakes me off, whirling to face me. "Don't try to calm me down. This is your fault, too! If you'd never —" He breaks off abruptly.

Oh. I look at him sadly. "I thought we were past that argument. You know I had to go."

He takes a deep breath, visibly trying to regain control of himself. "Whatever. I guess it doesn't matter now, anyway. What's done is done. We just need to put a stop to this as soon as we can." He turns back to Peter. "You'd better figure out how. Really soon."

"Everyone is so bossy today," Peter mutters sullenly.

"I need to go. I'm late for rehearsal." Ryan doesn't quite look at me while he says this. Then he leaves.

I stand there, looking at Peter.

"Do you swear that's everything?"

"Yes," he says at once. He seems slightly more at ease now that Ryan is gone. "Someone else came through, and now he's here, and he must have killed Jeremy to gain strength. Now that I know he's here, I might be able to trace where he's gone."

"You keep saying *he*. Can you tell it's a male demon, or are you just being sexist?"

"It's just a feeling, mostly. But I can say *he or she* if you really insist."

I decide that would probably be more annoying than it's worth. "Whatever. Just please go and find out as much as you can as soon as you can."

"Yeah, yeah." Peter says. "Come on, Hector."

"Hey," I say, a question suddenly occurring to me. "What do you feed on?"

"Pardon?"

"You said you don't kill people. . . . If you don't feed on death or souls or whatever, what do you feed on? You must need something for strength, and I'm guessing it's not the dining hall food. What is it? Pain?"

"No," Peter says. "I don't know how many times I have to tell you. That's not my thing at all."

"So? What is?"

He smiles a little wearily. "Drama."

"Come again?"

"I feed on drama. Fictionalized drama to some degree, but the real power comes from real drama. Love triangles, best-friend breakups, cheating husbands, secret baby daddies, all that daytime-talk-show-type stuff."

I blink at him a few times, trying to decide if he's serious. I can't tell.

"Are you messing with me?"

"No!" he says. I wait for the *well, okay, yes,* but it doesn't come. "I don't know how it works exactly, whether being able to use drama as my source of strength grew out of my love of theater or if I was drawn to theater in the first place because of it or some combination of both. But for whatever reason, that's where I get my energy. Luckily, the people involved in theater are often partial to drama behind the scenes, as well. Like Darleen and Celia in our show. Man, those two alone can keep me going for days. Did you hear what happened yesterday? Darleen was just standing there minding her own business, and Celia comes striding up —"

"Great. I'm glad all the fighting is serving a higher purpose. I don't need to hear all about it."

Peter shrugs. "Suit yourself. You're missing out, though."

Something else occurs to me just then.

"Is that why you keep trying to provoke Ryan? For the drama?"

"Oh, no," Peter says. "I do that because it's fun. He's very entertaining."

"Stop it."

He grins at me. "Unlikely. Sorry, sweetie."

Before I can say anything else, he disappears into the trees, Hector trailing menacingly behind him.

I walk back to the theater and slip backstage, not that slipping is really required, since Michael doesn't pay much attention to me most of the time. The design is basically done, so it's all construction now, and my team has that pretty well in hand. I supervise and pitch in where needed. Peter does not reappear for the remainder of morning rehearsal period.

When it's time for lunch, I decide to stay behind in bunk 6 instead. I don't feel ready to see Ryan. I'm still trying to sort out my various emotions. I'm mad at him for being mad at me about the demon stuff, since there's no way I could have not gone after Annie to the demon world, and he knows it. He knows it even though he tried to stop me. And if I could forgive him for that, he should be able to forgive me for going. And I thought he *had* forgiven me — that's the part that is really making me mad. I thought we were past all that. But apparently he's still nursing that resentment, and it was just sitting there beneath the surface, waiting to come back up for air.

But right alongside the mad is the guilt, and I don't know what to do with that part, exactly. Obviously this afternoon was not the right time to tell him that, yes, I'd still been keeping a fairly big demon-related secret from him. But I need to tell him. Soon. But when I tell him, he'll be mad. And I don't want him to be mad. More mad. But if I don't tell him, and he finds out some other way, that will be even worse. He really might not forgive me if that happens.

But what if I tell him and he can't get past it? Isn't it better to maybe just hope that he never needs to find out at all?

There is a decided silence from the inner Cyn, including the voice of Old Cyn, who really thinks I should know better by now. And yes, of course, I should know better by now. I promised no more secrets. So I should tell him. But he's already so mad at me. Surely it can't be the wrong choice to wait until he's not so mad and then tell him. Right?

More silence. I hate when my inner monologue goes unacknowledged.

Stupid various inner aspects of me.

More letters have arrived: another from Annie, and a joint one from Leticia and Diane. L&D's letter lacks the artistic quality that Annie's has, but their handwritten back-and-forth dialogue more than makes up for it. I feel like I'm sitting in the cafeteria with them, like we're all still together and nothing bad is happening and everything is just good and nice and perfect like it was a couple of weeks ago.

Stop whining, I tell myself firmly. *It will be okay. This is nothing like what you went through last fall. Nothing.*

And that is true, and I know it, but it still sucks that there are demon things happening again.

Especially for Jeremy, Old Cyn points out. Suddenly I feel even more awful. What is wrong with me? How can I worry about Ryan being mad at me when some nice innocent counselor is dead? If I hadn't come here, Jeremy would still be alive. If I hadn't . . . If I'd never . . .

I force myself to stop. Dissolving into guilt and panic is not going to help anything. I take a deep breath, and then another. Focus. I can't help Jeremy now. All I can do is try as hard as I can to make sure no one else has to die.

I have painting that afternoon, where we have been experimenting with various techniques in preparation for choosing one to use for a final project. I like this class; most of the kids in here are not artists, and so there's a general sense of fun and messing around, because we don't feel like we're supposed to be perfect at this. (I may be handy with set-design sketches, but that doesn't mean I can make a good painting. Trust me.) Today I am obviously in no mood to paint, but I also feel like I have to keep going through the motions of camp life until we figure out what to do next. I stare at my canvas and consider attacking it with dark colors and heavy brushstrokes, or maybe just ripping it to shreds with a steak knife, but I remind myself that I am more likely to be functional and useful if I work on staying calm rather than whipping myself back into an emotional frenzy. So I try to channel my inner Annie. I paint delicate lines of bright, pretty colors and attempt to change my mood from the outside in.

Surprisingly, it kind of works. The happy colors and shapes and thinking about Annie have me feeling a lot better by the time class is over.

I go back to the bunk to rest and clean up a little before dinner. Lots of the girls, including me, tend to shower at this time of day instead of in the morning, to avoid having to get up extra early before breakfast. The hot water finishes the job of washing away my bad feelings, and by the time we leave for dinner, I'm ready to find Ryan and make things feel okay between us again.

I see him on the food line and gently bump him with my hip. "Hey."

"Hey," he says back, slipping an arm around my waist. This exactly perfect response is one more reason why I love him. Nothing says *we're okay* like an arm around the waist. I lean into him and feel my heart unclench inside me.

Dinner consists of meat- and veggie burgers with a heaping side order of more gossip. Belinda is buzzing from table to table gathering more rumors about Jeremy, and people are talking about whatever the latest argument was between Darleen and Celia. No one seems to notice that Ryan and I aren't really participating. I hope Peter is able to find out something fast. Maybe I should have offered to help. But this feels like a Peter-and-Hector kind of job, really. If I can't rely on my halo spotting, which I can't, then I'm not sure how much use I'd really be.

Evening activity tonight is a practice concert by several musicians, including Susan. I try to locate her cute oboe player, who she said would also be playing, but I can't quite make him out from where I am sitting. The concert is in the open-sided theater that Ryan's show rehearses in, and despite everything it's lovely to be sitting in the night air, listening to what turns out to be a really nice concert. The music is not from any one show in particular; this is a group that plays together during one of the elective sessions in addition to whatever show they're each assigned to. Ryan sits beside me, holding my hand, and for a while I let myself just listen to the music and focus on the very comforting feeling of his fingers wrapped around mine.

After, when everyone goes to the canteen, I hold Ryan back. "Let's stay here," I say. "Just for a while. I don't want to hang out with everyone else tonight. Just you."

"Okay." We find a spot in the corner against one of the outer columns. I lean my head on his shoulder. Our knees are gently touching. He takes my hand again and holds it.

"Tell me more about this *Scarlet Pimpernel*," I say after a few minutes of comfortable silence. "I don't think I really understand the plot."

"Well," Ryan says, stroking my hand while he talks, "it's set during the French Revolution, and all kinds of bad things are happening in France. Percy and Marguerite run off to England and get married. Citizen Chauvelin, aka yours truly, is devoted to the ideals of the Republic and wants to execute everyone who opposes it. Also, he used to be sort of together with Marguerite, which becomes important later."

Hmm. He hadn't mentioned that part before. But I don't want to interrupt.

"Right after they get married, Percy finds out that Marguerite gave information to the Republic that led to one of his friends being executed. He shuns her but doesn't explain why. Then he recruits a bunch of his friends to help him start rescuing French aristocrats before they can be executed. He becomes the Scarlet Pimpernel and spends all his time as Sir Percy acting like an idiot so no one will ever suspect that he's actually this daring mastermind. Chauvelin becomes obsessed with capturing him, and he blackmails Marguerite (after trying unsuccessfully to win her over by reminding her of their past relationship) by threatening to kill her brother unless she helps him find out the true identity of the Scarlet Pimpernel."

"Does Marguerite know it's her husband?"

"Not yet, no. She arranges to meet the Scarlet Pimpernel, and he hides in the shadows so she can't see his face. She tells him Chauvelin's plan, including about her brother, and says that Chauvelin blackmailed her before, too, for the information about Percy's friend who was executed, and Sir Percy is all happy and relieved that she's not willfully helping the enemy. Everyone ends up in France to try to save the brother, but Marguerite is captured by Chauvelin, and he sentences her to death by guillotine and sings a song about how he'll never have her back and she can go die on her own, et cetera."

"Charming."

"Hey, he's a man of strong principles. And she broke his heart and insists on staying true to a man everyone believes is a moron."

"Still, guillotine is pretty harsh."

"True," he concedes. "Anyway: eventually Chauvelin,

cunning devil that he is, lets Marguerite and her brother think they're escaping so he can follow them to the Scarlet Pimpernel. Marguerite finally learns it's her own husband, and then there's a big duel where Chauvelin fights valiantly but ultimately fails to capture his nemesis. Percy and Marguerite live happily ever after."

"But not poor Chauvelin."

"No. He lives on bitterly and in disgrace."

"Hmm. I think I'd like this story better if Chauvelin won." I refrain from saying "And Jules got executed." Barely. "And the love story doesn't sound very good if they spend the whole show not talking to each other."

"No, no," Ryan says. "The love story is great. They have this deep connection, and then they both think they must have made it all up, because how could it have gone so wrong between them if they had really known each other . . . because Percy doesn't realize then that Marguerite had been coerced into giving information about his friend, and Marguerite doesn't know why Percy turns away from her as soon as they get married. And so they're both still deeply in love but think they're alone, but they're not really, and eventually they come back together with an even stronger bond after everything they've been through."

We're both quiet for a minute.

"So even though there was this whole perceived breach of trust thing, they eventually forgive each other and come to a greater understanding?"

Ryan squeezes my hand in the darkness. "Yes."

This is it. This is the moment I should tell him about the

two other trips I have to take to the demon world. I open my mouth to begin, when suddenly there is a flash of light and we're both temporarily blinded.

"Hey, you two!" a voice says from nearby. "What's goin' on?"

After what seems like several minutes of violent blinking, I start to be able to see again. And then I wish I couldn't.

The figure before us takes on disturbingly familiar features. Mostly familiar, anyway. But completely disturbing. Ryan makes a sound beside me that indicates he might be trying not to throw up his burgers. I silently second the sentiment.

It's Aaron.

Chapter 07

"Aaron?" Ryan and I say together.

"Long time no see and all that, huh?"

Aaron looks, in some ways, just as I remember him. Forty-somethingish, short brown hair shiny with product, old-school concert T-shirt (this time it's the Violent Femmes). In other ways, he looks very different. For example, he now has a long, sinuous tail that curls around into the air behind him. It is black and white and scaly, and reminds me of one of those zebra moray eels they sell for tropical aquariums. He also has what appear to be fish fins coming out of the back of his shoulders. And possibly what are gills on the sides of his neck.

"What are you *doing* here?" Ryan asks in bewilderment.

I experience several emotions at once. The top three are: (1) anger at Aaron for appearing right then, right when I was about to fix the lying and come clean and tell Ryan before he found out some other way (like, say, by Aaron appearing and saying the demoness has summoned me back for one of those additional two trips I promised her); (2) sorrow at the prospect of what is about to happen between Ryan and me when Aaron answers his question; and (3) slowly rising terror at the idea of actually having to go back to the demon world, which I'd still been half-successfully managing to convince myself might not really ever need to happen.

Aaron does a quick look back and forth between us, and I see that he sees that Ryan really has no idea why Aaron is here. I send Aaron urgent telepathic begging to please please please please please not tell him.

Miraculously, Aaron seems to understand what is happening and (equally miraculously) takes pity on me.

"My beautiful mistress wishes a word with our Cynthia here," he says. "In person."

"I don't think *that's* going to happen," Ryan says. "We are done with all of that stuff."

"That's not what I hear," Aaron says, smirking. "I hear you've got a demon friend right here in Camp Whatever-It's-Called. Looks like you two can't help but get involved with our kind at every opportunity."

"*Our* kind?" I ask, both curious and eager to jump on any possible tangent topic of conversation. "So you're one of them now?"

"Well, not exactly," Aaron admits. "Not yet. But I will be! In time. Off to a nice start with the tail, huh?" He waves it slowly around, looking back at it admiringly over his shoulder.

"Lovely," I say. "Really suits you."

"How do you know about Peter?" Ryan asks. His eyes narrow suddenly. "Do you have something to do with what's happening?"

"Simmer down, tough guy," Aaron says. "I don't know what you're talking about. I just know that Peter is here, thanks to Cyn, to follow his dreams and stuff. How's all that going, by the way? Has he won over Broadway yet?"

"Not quite," I say, trying to think. I need to get Aaron alone somehow. The fine print of my deal with the demoness prevents her from snatching me away in front of people who don't know about demons, and that obviously doesn't include Ryan. But I can't let him find out this way. I just can't.

"Anyway, Cyn is definitely not going anywhere with you," Ryan says. "So you can go right back where you came from, and send her regrets."

"Ryan, wait," I say slowly. "Maybe this is actually a good thing. Maybe the demoness can help us figure out what happened with Peter's tether."

"No. No way, Cyn. I watched you get sucked down there once already. And you've told me how horrible it was. You are *not* going back to that awful place." He glances at Aaron. "No offense, man."

"None taken."

"But we need help," I persist. "And if she wants to talk to me, maybe I can make a deal—"

"What? No! No more deals! Cyn, are you *nuts*?"

"Okay, not a deal. Bad choice of words, sorry. But . . . a trade, something. Peter obviously doesn't know how to fix things on his own. And I don't know about you, but I am not filled with overwhelming confidence regarding Hector and any useful skills he may have."

"Cyn . . ."

I turn to Aaron. "Can you give us a minute? Please?"

"Sure. I'll just be over there somewhere." He points to the expanse of moonlit nature outside the theater and strides purposefully away.

Ryan is looking at me with an expression I don't like one bit.

"You've already made up your mind to go, haven't you?"

"Ryan . . ."

A thought seems to strike him. "Did you . . . was this your idea? Did you summon him here somehow?"

"No! Of course not!"

"Well, I don't know, Cyn. You certainly accepted the invitation mighty quickly. You didn't seem nearly as surprised as I was, either."

My stomach twists in an agony of guilt. I could still tell him, right now. The reason why I wasn't entirely surprised to see our old friend. But he's already mad, and clearly not in a very understanding or forgiving mood. Dammit, why couldn't Aaron have waited just a little longer to show up?

Ryan leans forward. "Cyn, this isn't Annie's life on the line this time. You have absolutely no responsibility to help Peter. None. He used you without your consent. His problems are not your problems. You can walk away. I know why you couldn't before, but this is not the same."

"No, it's not . . . but people are still dying, Ryan. At least one so far, anyway, and he won't be the last if we don't do something. And no one else here is equipped to deal with demons."

"Peter is! And his freakish sidekick, too!"

"I know, but . . ."

"No buts, Cyn. If you do this, you're doing it because you want to. Not because you have to. And I'm sorry, but I can't get on board with that." He stands up.

"Ryan, wait, come on."

He shakes his head. "You don't need me here. You're not going to listen to me anyway. You're going to do what you want, just like always. No matter what the consequences are."

He walks off into the darkness.

I didn't like that reference to consequences. I want to run after him to ask what he means, exactly. But I don't. Because I need him to go away so I can go with Aaron without further argument or explanation.

I will just have to make it right later. Somehow.

Aaron, whistling, ambles back over to where I am sitting.

"You didn't tell him, you bad girl."

"Shut up, Aaron."

His eyebrows shoot up. "Hey, is that any way to talk to me after I covered for you?"

I sigh wearily. "No. I'm sorry. Thank you for not telling him."

"I can't believe you didn't tell him by now."

"I was going to. I *am* going to. I just haven't gotten the chance yet."

"Mm-hmm." Aaron looks at me a second, then rubs his hands together briskly. "Well, anyway. Ready to go? Never a good idea to keep a demoness waiting."

Suddenly the terror feelings completely drown out the anger and the sorrow ones.

"What does she want? Do you know?"

"She wants you to fulfill your part of the deal. Trip number two, at a time of her choosing. Which is now." He reaches a hand down to help me up, and I take it, to be polite, even though I kind of don't want to touch him. His hands still look (and feel) like normal hands, but my eyes keep darting to those fish-fin-shoulder things, which are very much creeping me out. He must have cut little fin-holes in his shirt for them to stick through. I can't quite imagine the physical procedure of Aaron getting himself into his clothes with all the extra appendages. Not that I'm trying very hard. *Ew.*

A new thought occurs to me, which I guess I hadn't dared to wonder about before. "Is it going to hurt? The last time . . . it was pretty terrible."

"No," Aaron says. "That was different, that whole thing with the vortex and all the demons going down at once with their consorts. This . . . won't be like that." He hesitates, then adds, "But how long can you hold your breath?"

"What?"

He grabs my wrist. "Deep breath now and hold it, okay? Go!"

I barely have time to inhale before there's another flash and everything swirls away into a chaotic mess of color and sound. And then keeps swirling. I can't see because nothing will hold still—everything is motion and noise, and if it weren't for still being able to feel Aaron's hand tight around my wrist, I wouldn't even know he was still there beside me.

I brace for the pain despite Aaron's reassurance, but he wasn't lying about that. There are no feelings of knives slicing me open, which is definitely a plus over my last journey. But my chest is already starting to object to the not-breathing, and I have no idea how long this trip is going to take or what will happen if I do try to breathe.

The colors continue to swirl by, but they are getting darker, and the wind rushing around me starts to feel heavier somehow and Aaron's grip gets a little tighter, and just when I am starting to feel like I can't possibly hold my breath for one more second we . . . arrive. The colors settle into a slower-moving spectrum of black and gray and blue and violet, and Aaron lets go, and I take this as a sign that it's okay to breathe again, which is good because it's either breathe or pass out at this point.

"Home, sweet home!" Aaron says jovially.

It's . . . different, but the same. But different. The land-scape once again refuses to settle down completely, and things seem to shift from harsh metallic angles and edges to softer, rounded, bloated shapes to something like an underwater sea-scape, except without the wetness. But the giant arena is gone, or else we're just in a different location. That probably makes more sense. I'm sure the demon world is a big place, and I only saw one tiny fraction of it last time. Not that that wasn't more than enough, of course.

Aaron leads me down shifty alleyways and across streets/

rivers/big blobby things. I look around nervously, remembering how the demoness had told me last time that I would be "meat and prey" to everything else down here. It's hard to even tell if there are demons anywhere nearby, with all the shifting and shapes and my constant effort to stay close to Aaron, who is moving pretty fast. Which I try to hope is because he's eager to get back to his mistress and not because he's afraid of something catching and killing us.

Suddenly we turn a corner, and there's an enormous castle. Well, sometimes it's a castle. In between shifting into a mountain and something that resembles sea coral stretching up into infinity. In all aspects, it's dark and sharp and forbidding.

My first internal reaction to her dark, scary place of residence (since surely that's what this is) is to feel it's surprisingly wrong. I realize I had sort of fallen into thinking of the demoness as the good guy, since, you know, compared with Mr. Gabriel and Principal Kingston, she totally was, and some part of me was expecting her to live in a pink Disney-princess castle or something. *Dumb, Cyn. She's still a demon. And not one of the alleged few non-evil demons, either. Just a regular evil one willing to make alliances when it suits her interests.*

I have to remember that. The demoness is not my friend.

She is not the good guy.

We go inside.

I watch Aaron's tail as I follow him down dark corridors and up long and twisty stairs. It's so weird that he has a tail now. He's really on his way to becoming demonified, or whatever the appropriate term is. He seems super happy about it, but then, this is what he always thought he wanted. It's just that usually when people get what they always thought they wanted, they end up realizing they were wrong. Like Annie did.

I guess I'm another exception, though. I wanted Ryan, and I got him, and I still want him. I wasn't wrong. I just . . . wish it weren't so complicated.

It doesn't have to be, Old Cyn says from the back of my brain. *Just tell him the truth!*

It's too late for that now. Confessing after the fact gets you no points.

It's not entirely after the fact, she insists. *There's still the third trip.*

I don't even want to think about that. I ignore Old Cyn and her overly idealistic perspective until she goes away.

Eventually Aaron and I come to some kind of smallish throne room or audience chamber (I don't really know the terms for various castle parts), and there is the demoness, part fishy and part human.

"There you are," she says. "Finally."

"Why, I'm fine, thanks for asking," I say. "And yourself?"

She gives me a look. "I have no time for pleasantries. Maybe later. Give me your power."

"*Lend* me, you mean," I say. "Remember, you have to give it back."

She doesn't say anything, just looks at me, and I feel that horrid sensation of having my roachy goodness pulled away and stretched over to where the demoness can use it. She wears it like a coat, almost. Like a coat that settles in and becomes, temporarily, a part of her. And I am left coatless and cold and unable to protect myself from the elements. Or anything else. I sink down slowly into a chairlike thing nearby, trying to adjust. At least this time I can just hide out here in this room, instead of having to race around dodging demons and trying to rescue people while not getting eaten or otherwise becoming dead. Always good to look on the bright side, when possible.

"Ahh," the demoness sighs, stretching luxuriously. "I could get used to this."

"No, no," I correct her. "You could not, because you have to give it back. We have a deal."

"Yes, yes," she says. She glides airily (swimmily?) toward the door.

"What do you need it for this time, anyway?"

She pauses, apparently torn between wanting to go and wanting to stay and talk about her problems. Talking about problems wins by a snout.

"There are still those who are . . . resistant . . . to my style of ruling," she says, turning back to me. "No demon sits easy on the throne until she crushes all who might oppose her. Which is to say, no demon ever sits easy on the throne, because there are always enemies lurking somewhere, plotting to bring one down." She shrugs. "It's what we do. But some of my opposition have been proving especially troubling of late, and I want to put a stop to their annoying behavior before it gets out of hand. It shouldn't take long. Stay here with Aaron until I return."

She finishes her journey to the door and goes through it and away.

I expect Aaron to complain about being left behind, but

apparently he knew this would be the drill. He settles down into another of the chairlike things. "So when are you going to tell him?" he asks.

I'm too tired to have this conversation. I'd forgotten how weak I feel without my demon resistance. "Soon. I don't know." I give him an angry look. "I was actually just about to when you appeared, you jerk. I mean literally just about to. My mouth was open and everything. And now we're fighting again, and I'll have to wait until things calm down."

Aaron shakes his head. "Just tell him. Don't wait for the perfect time. The longer you wait, the worse it will be."

"Why are you giving me boyfriend advice?"

"It's not boyfriend advice. It's general common sense advice. You know you should tell him. You feel guilty about not telling him. He suspects there are still things you haven't told him. By telling him, you address all of these issues."

"And maybe drive him away forever," I mutter.

He rolls his eyes. "Humans are so melodramatic. You won't drive him away forever. He loves you. He wants to trust you. Just let him see that he can."

Aaron is making sense, which can't be right. I attribute this impossibility to the strange shifty context of the demon world in which we are temporarily kicking up our heels. "I will. Eventually."

He shakes his head again but says nothing.

"So," I say, wanting to change the subject. "How are you liking it down here?"

He grins widely at me. "It's so awesome. You have no idea."

"Really?" I cannot help being skeptical. "I mean, really?

This is really what you want? To be here, with them? To become one of them, at least as far as that is possible? Don't you miss being with other humans?"

"Yes, this is really what I want, and no, I do not miss other humans." He pauses. "Well, maybe Erica from the store. She was cool. But honestly, that's about it."

"Do the other demons even talk to you? I got the sense that they don't think much of humans."

"Well, they don't, in general. But it helps to be consort to the queen. And it helps to no longer be fully human. Plenty of them want to be in my good graces in hopes of getting into *her* good graces, which gets me all kinds of fun perks and stuff. Most of them are idiots, but still, the benefits are worth it. And there are others who are really brilliant and interesting. I mean, some of them have been alive for thousands and thousands of years, Cyn! It's fascinating, the stuff they know, the things they've seen. And others are really curious about humans, and so I have something to offer them because of having been one myself."

"So basically you're selling us out to them?"

He smiles frostily at me. "This is where I belong now, Cyn. My loyalties are here."

"So I can't really trust you."

He laughs. "Could you really trust me before?"

It's a good point. Aaron only does what is best for Aaron. We have known this pretty much since the beginning with him. I have to remember that, too.

And yet . . .

"Hey, so do you know anything about this tether situation with Peter and me?"

"I know the tether formed when he made himself a tiny stowaway on your return trip the last time you were here."

"Tiny?" This part is new.

Aaron laughs again. "Yeah, apparently that's how he got through without anyone noticing. He made himself tiny and hid inside your pocket or something. Crude but effective. But then of course he had to spend some time working back up to full size once he got up there."

A terrible thought suddenly occurs to me. "Wait — what effect does it have on the tether for me to be down here? Did we pull Peter down after us?" I'm still mad about his lying, but not enough to wish that on him.

Aaron waves a hand dismissively in the air. "Oh, no, don't worry about that. The tether between you and Peter only exists in the human world. Since you're not there right now, the center of the tether is the place from which you left the human world to come here. He can't go more than the allotted distance from that corner of the theater, but otherwise he's not going to be affected."

I sit back in my chairlike thing, relieved. I hate when I think of questions like that too late. I decide to keep thinking of more questions, since Aaron appears to be in a chatty, sharing kind of mood.

"Is it really true that Peter feeds on drama?"

Aaron shrugs. "As far as I know. Demons feed on what they desire most. Most demons, being demons, desire most to kill and hurt things, and to suck up their life forces and watch them weaken and wither and die. But Peter, for some reason, has been obsessed with humans and theater and theatrics of both the stage kind and the interpersonal kind for as long as he can remember. So, yeah, I think it's true. He picked a good focus for his tether, in that case. You can't seem to avoid the drama even when you try."

I decide to ignore that last part. "So, how do we break it? He seems to think someone down here is interfering somehow."

"Hmm." Aaron visibly goes into bookstore mode before my eyes. "There's probably a couple of options. . . . Hold on, let me consult my references."

He gets up and jogs through the door, presumably on his way to where he now keeps all his books and stuff. I wonder if he brought that computer and ancient printer with him, too.

While I'm waiting, I decide to explore the room. It hits me then that I'm no longer terrified. This is *much* different from last time. Last time there were demons everywhere, some of whom were actively trying to kill me, and there was so much at stake, and I had to find Annie before it was too late, and everything was horrible and scary and full of danger and pain. This time . . . I apparently just need to hang out here with Aaron until the demoness gets back. That doesn't seem so bad, all things considered.

It's pleasantly non-shifty in here, everything staying in the same form from second to second; I wonder if the demoness somehow made it that way for me on purpose. If so, that was unexpectedly nice of her. I push myself up out of the chair to take a better look around. It's like a mix of temple and tea-room. There's an actual throne/altar thing at one end on a dais, with elaborate sculptured forms in the wall behind and above it, where I suppose the demoness holds court or what-ever. Although the room is on the small side . . . maybe she just has a throne in every room so she can sit on one wherever she is. Everything is dark and angly like the outside was. There are pictures on one wall, actual framed images like a person might have hanging along the side of the stairway in their pleas-ant suburban home showing family and vacation shots, but when I get closer I begin to see bits of bodies and blood and quickly decide I don't want to know anything else about what they might depict. The area where Aaron and I were sitting is almost cozy, in an alien kind of way, with three of those chair-like things and a small black-velvet love seat arranged around a coffee table shaped like some sort of creature I can't quite identify.

There's a window on one wall, and I wander over to see what it looks out on. We're several floors up, and I can see a lot of the surrounding . . . countryside? Cityscape? Random demony environment? The shiftiness is still visible to me from here (my understanding is that it's not really shifting; that's just my human brain's attempt to reconcile the impossible physical dimensions of the demon world with images it can comprehend), and so it's not a very comfortable view. I turn away before it starts to make me queasy.

But just as I'm turning away, I see something out of the corner of my eye that makes me turn back.

Several large dark shapes are approaching the window.

This is alarming for many reasons.

For one thing, as previously stated, we are several floors up. Which means the fact that these shapes appear to have head-parts that are roughly on the same level as the window indicates that they are of a very gigantic stature.

For another thing, the shapes, as they come closer, which they are doing very rapidly, are made up of scary demon body pieces, like wings and tentacles and horns and claws and teeth. So many, many teeth. Large, pointy teeth, which I can see clearly even from here.

Also, it soon becomes evident that they are not just coming in the general direction of the window; they are coming at the window. Directly at it. And did I mention very rapidly?

See? Corner-of-the-eye things are never any good at all.

"Hey, Aaron?" I call, not moving my gaze from the approaching figures. "Could you, um, come back, please? Right now?"

"Just a sec!" His voice calls from somewhere down the hall.

"Now, please!" I say with a bit more urgency. "Some . . . things . . . are coming."

"What?" His voice doesn't sound any closer. I begin to feel angry impatience. But mostly horror and terror.

"Aaron! Get back here right now, dammit! Big scary monsters coming this way! Really fast!"

Before he has a chance to respond, one of the approaching demon-parts (a furry hand-shaped appendage dangling at the end of a long translucent tentacle-arm) slaps itself against the window. The sound makes me yelp and jump back, but the window holds. I start to relax, thinking that of course the demoness would have good strong demon-resistant windows in her uneasy-throne-containing castle home.

Then another of the shapes slams full force into the center of the window, and tiny cracks begin to form, spidering out from the point of impact.

"Aaron!" I am kind of screaming now, because it seems entirely appropriate at this time.

The window shatters, and I fly backward to slam against the wall. Several of the unpleasant pictures drop to the floor around me, their frames breaking in small-scale imitation of the window's destruction a moment before. As I slide to the ground beside them, the first of the creatures (not the one with the furry hands) begins to pull itself forward into the room. This one has long, red, crunchy-looking limbs, sort of like an Alaskan king crab. They taper to long, sharp, terrible hooked points. It swivels its enormous dog-bear sort of head until its bright, beady eyes land on mine.

Then it smiles, and I start screaming in earnest.

Chapter | 08

Dimly, I am aware of Aaron finally deciding to come see what all the fuss is about.

"What the hell?" his voice says from somewhere to my right.

"Aaron!" I scream again. The dog-bear-Alaskan-king-crab monster is still pulling itself into the room. It has a lot of those red arms. Armlike things, anyway. Maybe they are legs. Whatever they are, they puncture the walls and floor and ceiling as the demon flings them forward and then inches itself farther through the window, ignoring the jagged bits of glass that pierce and tear its skin.

It is still smiling. It looks very, very happy to see me.

Its crazy eyes start to go big and black and swirly, and I jerk my gaze away before I can be sucked into any kind of paralyzing mesmo-glare, which I'm probably entirely susceptible to at the moment. I am newly aware of how much it sucks to have given away my defensive power while stuck in the demon world.

Also, I take back everything I said about this visit being so awesome compared with last time.

Aaron is frozen in the doorway. I'm not sure exactly what I expected him to do, but I vaguely assumed the demoness had left him here to protect me from any sort of bad things that might happen.

"What did you do?" Aaron shouts at me.

"I didn't do anything! These . . . things came out of nowhere and broke through the window! Do something!"

"Like what?"

"Like some kind of demony magic or something! Or humany anti-demon magic! Or throw a fucking chair at it, I don't know! Don't just stand there!"

But he does just stand there, and I realize he might be considering whether to just run away.

Fucking Aaron.

I push myself back to my feet and try to lift one of the chairs myself, but it's too heavy. So I go for the coffee table instead. I can't lift that enough to throw it, but I can at least push it over onto its side and get behind it. Not that I imagine it will prove much of a defense against the dog-bear-crab, but at least it might slow the thing down a tiny bit before it reaches me.

Suddenly the monster flinches, and I see that Aaron is throwing things at it. Throwing . . . books. And small objets d'art. And whatever else he can get his hands on. The creature roars and blinks to avoid having its eyes poked out by flying tomes and vases. I am grateful and relieved until I notice another demon squeezing past the first one now that there is enough room for it to fit. This one is more snakelike in body and has a more humanlike head (a long and horribly stretched human head, though). It doesn't have any arms, but it opens its mouth to reveal a very long tongue that immediately shoots toward me.

I scream and duck behind my table. This is not good. This is so not good. I want to go home. Right now.

Also, I suspect Aaron will be out of things to throw very soon.

I wait until the new snake demon has just thrown its tongue against the table again and then I fling myself forward and make a run for the door. I nearly knock over Aaron in the doorway, but he barely seems to notice. He is two steps behind me as we race toward the stairs and down and down and down.

There are angry, screaming, crashing sounds above and behind us. Sounds that include, perhaps, the door frame breaking apart as a giant dog-bear-crab monster forces its enormous bulk through the doorway. We reach the bottom of the last flight and look up to see its furiously smiling face staring down at us. The snake demon's tongue flails wildly, apparently caught between the other demon and the banister.

"Crap," Aaron says. We start running again.

"Where are we going?" I ask between breaths.

"Away from them! After that . . . I have no idea. I thought we'd be safe inside the house."

I want to be amused that he calls this enormous castle structure *the house,* but there's really no time for that now.

We race toward the large front room just inside the entry-way. I can't imagine that going outside is really a smart move, but obviously staying inside is not such a smart move, either, given the sounds and screams still coming from behind us.

Aaron throws open the door and abruptly slams it shut again. I catch only a glimpse of a giant toothy mouth before he does.

"Um," I say helpfully. This is really, really not good at all.

"This way," he says, darting down a side passage. I follow at his heels.

We keep running, but it's no use. The demons continue to pursue us. Eventually we are going to run out of house.

It happens even sooner than I expect. I don't know if Aaron just panicked or had some plan that didn't work out, but we end up at the end of a long hall that has no exit other than a door to the courtyard. We go through it because that seems better than just standing still and waiting to die.

So we go outside, and then we stand still and wait to die.

The snake demon reaches the courtyard first, having apparently slipped past the dog-bear-crab monster at some point during the chase. But the latter is not far behind, and it bursts through the doorway a second later. A few smaller but still pretty frightening demons appear next and fan out behind the first two until we are effectively surrounded. Courtyard wall behind us, monsters everywhere else.

Aaron decides the time has come to try diplomacy.

"What do you want?" he asks in an impressively level voice. "You must know whose home this is that you've wrecked with your giant selves. She's going to be severely pissed. But if we can resolve this before she comes back and has to deal with it, you can spare yourselves a lot of pain."

I'm not completely certain the demons can understand him. They give no sign of comprehension, anyway. But then one of the smaller demons toward the back — it's the one with the furry hands from earlier — says in a scratchy rasp, "You know what we want. Hand over the roach girl."

I wait, but Aaron does not immediately respond with "Never, demon scum!" or any such comforting refusal.

A thought occurs to me. What happens if I die while I'm down here? Does the demoness somehow get to keep my gift? Or will it die with me? I want to believe it will die with me. That kind of makes more sense, really. Also, if it's the other option, then I have to suspect the demoness of setting all this up in order to keep my strength forever. But no; if she can do that, she would have done it the first time. She must need me alive in order for it to work.

So, if that's true . . . Aaron won't want to hand me over, since that would mean his beloved mistress would lose her current advantage, wherever she is and whatever she's doing. Which must be something pretty terrible and dangerous for her to have called me, despite her apparently blasé attitude earlier. If she thought she needed my extra protection enough to use up one of her two remaining borrowing chances, then she probably really did. Aaron is probably just stalling for time.

I tell myself this to counteract the uneasy feelings that are happening because of the very convincing way Aaron seems to be considering the demon's demand.

"Aaron, you can't," I tell him firmly through clenched teeth. Crap, I really hope he's thought things through like I have.

"What will you give me if I do?" he asks the demons finally.

Stalling, I remind myself somewhat desperately. *He's just stalling.* I know we've already established that I can't trust him, and I don't . . . but I do trust him to look out for his own interests, and I know that keeping the demoness happy is at the very top of that list.

It's the snake demon who answers, somehow speaking around that impossibly long tongue. "Let you live," he says gruffly.

Aaron rolls his eyes at this. "Even you are not stupid enough to kill me, Argzyrl." (The word he says is not exactly *Argzyrl;* it's one of those harsh demon words that hurt my ears. But it's close enough.)

I turn fully around to stare at Aaron. "You *know* him?"

Aaron shrugs. "We've met. His even more horrible friend is . . ." (He says another name here, but I can't even try to come close to a phonetic representation of this one, sorry.)

The even more horrible friend lifts an arm-leg-claw thing in what might be a friendly wave.

I keep operating under the assumption that there will eventually be a limit to the insanity and horror, that at some point we will reach the end and things will not get any more horrible or insane. I suppose that could still be a valid assumption; it's just that we don't seem to be anywhere close to that outer boundary yet. Things just keep getting more crazy and awful.

I really, really hate it here.

"Look," Aaron says, "if it were up to me, you could have her, and good riddance. But you know it's not up to me. So I think you should all go home before we all end up in really big trouble here, okay?"

He's talking to them like they are children. Or mentally deficient in some way. Or both. I guess maybe they could be; even in my somewhat limited experience, there are definitely some demons that seem more like animals than intelligent beings.

"We have our instructions," Argzyrl says.

"Instructions from whom?" Aaron says, sounding genuinely curious.

I'm curious, too. Obviously. The only demon who has a personal vendetta against me is dead. What new enemies do I have that I don't know about?

Even-More-Horrible-Friend knocks Argzyrl across the courtyard with one of its arm/legs, and I get the sense that perhaps the snake demon has said too much. We are all at a standstill, watching one another and waiting for someone to make the first move. I'm not really sure why the demons are waiting; now that we have no place left to run, they could kill us in seconds, easy. My only guess is that they don't really want to hurt Aaron, since that would incur the wrath of the demon queen, which cannot possibly be a good thing.

Slowly, the demons start toward us. Now I think they are drawing out the killing process just for the pure pleasure of it. Aaron and I back up until we are pressed against the courtyard wall, trying to watch all the approaching appendages at once, as if we have the slightest hope of dodging them long enough to stay alive.

"Why are you doing this?" I ask desperately.

They don't bother to answer. They just take a few steps closer.

Suddenly there is a displacement of air in the courtyard, and everyone freezes, confused. The colors of the ground and walls and sky swirl angrily around for a few seconds, and the demoness's voice calls out, "What is the meaning of this?"

I am overwhelmed with relief. She is still my favorite demon ever, evil or not.

When the colors resettle, I see that she is more than a little the worse for wear. She's clearly been in some kind of massive brawl. I guess it's a you-should-see-the-other-guy type of situation, since she's still here and alive, after all. It must have been some fight, though, if she was that badly damaged even with my roachy resistance.

"You will all leave my house. Now."

I breathe out slowly and wait for them to leave.

But they don't.

They had turned at the demoness's appearance, but now they turn back to me and Aaron.

"Last chance, Aaron," Argzyrl says. "Stand aside or die."

"Are you seriously threatening my consort and my guest

in my own house?" The demoness sounds utterly amazed. "You know you will not commit such an insult and live."

"Our lives are forfeit," one of the other demons says, and that sends a chill right through me. Evil creatures willing to die for an evil cause are very, very scary.

The world slides suddenly around me, and then Aaron and I are standing at the demoness's side, behind the demons who were facing us a second before. They whirl around to relocate us, but in the meantime the demoness has opened a giant hole in the air.

"Go," she says to me. "Right now."

"Wait," Aaron says. He pushes something into my pocket.

Then the demoness shoves me through. I feel my roach power return as she does so, and the feeling of being at full strength again is the most welcome thing I can possibly imagine right now.

I look back and see the opening begin to close behind me.

But not before one of the demons hurls itself forward and clutches at me with its long horrible spidery legs.

Then the portal winks closed and I'm alone in the swirly darkness. With the demon.

I fight it the whole way back. It may only be a matter of seconds, but it feels much longer when you are grappling blindly with a disgusting monster intent on trying to kill you. The feel of its limbs is indescribably awful. I want to scrape off every part of my skin that it manages to touch.

When the world opens again and we tumble forward

onto . . . concrete? . . . the demon's grip fails. I hear a collective gasp as I scuttle back along the ground as fast as I can, away from the creature, and try to get my bearings.

The demon hears it, too, and rears up on several hind legs, glaring around with its misshapen bull/bug-like head. It hisses like a scorpion or a really, really pissed-off cat and then bounds off into the darkness.

Finally, I start to take in where I am and what's around me.

I'm sitting backstage in the set-construction area of Blake Theater. Peter is there. So is Ryan. And Hector. And . . . Jules.

Everyone is staring in the direction the demon disappeared.

Then Hector suddenly takes off after it.

Then, slowly, the rest of them turn back to look at me.

"Hey, guys," I say when I can't stand the awkward silence one more second. "What's going on?"

Ryan looks like he wants to kill me.

Also — I blink to make sure I have this right — he appears to be holding hands with Jules.

"I can't believe you," he says in a quiet voice. "I'm glad you made it back alive, but . . . I just can't believe you, Cyn."

Jules looks at him in a concerned, sympathetic way that makes me want to scratch her eyes out.

"Ryan, please. Just . . . just let me explain."

He shakes his head. "No. I can't . . . I need some time, Cyn. I just can't deal with you right now."

Then he walks away.

With Jules.

They are still holding hands.

I sit there on the floor, still shaking from the whole demon-portal-struggle-almost-dying thing, looking after them.

"I . . . possibly owe you an apology," Peter says.

I turn my head to look back at him. "What?" I am feeling . . . very confused. And immensely unhappy.

Peter comes over to sit across from me on the floor.

I'm still thinking about Ryan. "He didn't even ask about the demon that came back with me," I say. "Did you all not see it? Giant spider-bull-bug thing? Hissed at us and ran off into the night?"

"We saw," Peter says gently. He reaches out and pats my leg in what I assume is supposed to be a comforting manner. "I think your lover boy was too preoccupied with his other concerns to really take that in, though."

"Other concerns?" I feel like my brain is broken. And also my heart.

"So, I didn't actually realize that you hadn't told him about your deal with the demoness."

I stare at him mournfully. "You told him? About the two more times?"

Peter looks uncomfortable. "Well, he came looking for you, asking if I knew where you were. He mentioned Aaron's visit, and . . . and I said I assumed the demoness must have summoned you back for one of those return visits. It became immediately clear that he had no idea what I was talking about, but he wouldn't let it go until I explained."

"And you couldn't have made something up?"

Peter blinks, offended. "Hey, it's not my fault you lied to

138

him all this time. Besides, it was too late for that. I'd already said enough that he wasn't going to settle for anything but the truth."

"How . . . why were you all here, right here, when I came back? How did you know?"

"I could feel it, the portal approaching. I sent Hector to get Ryan, figuring he'd want to know, and when he showed up, he had Jules with him. I guess he'd been spilling his heart to her about you or whatever when Hector went to find him."

Ow. I look hard at Peter. "Thanks for softening the blow."

He shrugs. "I don't think you two belong together, anyway. He's too . . . uptight for you. You are not a girl who always plays by the rules. Ryan . . . is like a walking rulebook."

"That's not true!"

"Sure it is. And I'm sure it's one of the many things you like about him. He's gorgeous, he's smart, he's a good guy. He does the right thing whenever possible. But I'm not sure that's really what you need."

I laugh without any humor whatsoever. "Oh, and I suppose you know what I do need? Is it a deceitful demon who takes advantage of everyone around him?"

He jerks back. "Hey, where did that come from? I only took advantage of your presence in the demon world. Well, and our theater connection, to follow you to camp. I did what I had to do to get what I want. Same as you. You were willing to do anything to save your friend. No matter the consequences."

I flinch at the repetition of Ryan's phrase from earlier.

"That's different. I was trying to save Annie. You're just trying to be famous."

He looks at me. "You know that's not true. That's not what it's about for me."

"Whatever."

"Cyn, please." He reaches forward and takes my hand. I feel the demon-spark and try to pull away, but he holds on, staring at me intently. "You're the only one who can really understand. I know you're hurt and angry right now. But don't shut me out. You need me, especially now. And I need you. To finish this show and make it awesome and help me start to prove myself. And I need you to understand, because no one else does. You know it's not the fame I'm after, although, sure, I'm planning to enjoy that part, too. But it's the actual work that I want. The doing. The creating and breathing life into stories and working with sets and actors and music and lyrics and everything that makes musical theater the magical thing that it is. I crossed a whole world to find this. It's what I'm meant for, what I want more than anything. And you know. You know what that's like."

He's right; I do know. And I do understand. It's still different from what I was doing, saving my best friend . . . but it's not superficial. It's real. It's what he needs to go after.

No matter the consequences.

"But, yeah," he goes on, "now that you mention it, I do think I know what you need. I think you need someone who understands what it's like to want something so much that you'll do anything to get it."

"Not anything," I say. "I have limits."

"Fine. Not anything. But anything that doesn't completely shatter the boundaries of your moral code. And your moral code is . . . pretty flexible, from what I've seen so far."

I don't say anything. I don't even know why we're having this conversation. I should be going after Ryan. Or going after that thing that came back from the demon world with me. Or punching Jules in the face. But I don't quite feel up to dealing with any of it right now.

Unfortunately, I don't think not-dealing is really an available option.

"We need to do something about that demon," I tell Peter.

"Hector's following it. He'll let me know if he finds out anything useful. But for now I suspect it will need somewhere to hole up and get settled before it can cause any real trouble. Traveling like that takes a lot out of a demon. Just being here in your world takes a lot out of us at first. It's going to be weak and want to regain some strength before doing anything, trust me."

"Well, so that's why we should go after it now! While it's weak!"

"And what? Kill it? How are we going to do that?"

I glare at him. "What kind of demon are you? I mean, seriously, don't you retain any demon knowledge? Don't you know how to kill another demon? Or at least send him back where he came from? Are you any goddamn use at all?"

"Well," Peter says after a moment. "That seemed uncalled for."

"I don't think so. I think it's entirely called for. You need to start pulling your weight around here. You're the resident demon expert. You swear that you're not evil. So prove it. Helps us find the demon that killed Jeremy, and help us send that new demon back where it came from."

"Who's *us* in this scenario, Cyn? I'm not so sure Ryan is really on your team anymore."

"Of course he is," I say. "He might be pissed at me, but he wouldn't just turn his back on everything."

Peter looks unconvinced, but he doesn't say so. "Let me think on it. I might have some ideas. But you should know . . . I can't just go after the other demons and smite them with my awesome demon power."

"Why the hell not?"

"Because I don't *have* that kind of awesome demon power, Cyn. I'm not physically strong in that way. Not on a demon scale. We're going to have to find some other way to bring them down."

Wonderful.

"Fine. In the meantime, I'm going to bed. What time is it, anyway?"

"Late. You should be careful not to get caught if you don't want to get in trouble for being out after hours."

I laugh for real this time. "It's hard to feel really concerned about that right now."

Peter smiles one of his charming smiles back at me. "Understandable."

"I asked Aaron about breaking the tether," I say, abruptly remembering. "He sounded like he was making progress, but then these horrible demons attacked . . ."

I suddenly remember him putting something in my pocket before I left. I look down and see a small pair of what look like kitchen shears sticking out of my pants. I pull them out.

"Hey," Peter says. "Did Aaron give you that?"

"Yes. He slipped it into my pants right before the demoness sent me back."

Peter bites back a laugh, and I roll my eyes. *Boys.* "Into my
pocket, moron. Do you know what it is?"

"Your pocket?" he asks, still grinning.

"This," I say, holding up the shears.

He gets serious again. "Yes, I think I do, actually." He
reaches out a hand. "May I?"

I hand him the shears.

"Huh. Yes . . . I think this is exactly what we need. He's
done something. . . . I should be able to use these to break the
tether on both sides, even if someone's still trying to stop me."
He looks back at me. "Why would he do this? Did you make a
deal with him?"

I think back, suddenly alarmed. Did I? "I'm pretty sure I
just asked him if he could help. I didn't promise anything in
return."

"Hmm. That's unlike him. But maybe he figured he'd be
able to call in the favor later on. Or maybe he meant to bargain
with you and then didn't get a chance. In any case . . . I'm going
to try these out."

"Right now?"

"No time like the present!"

He stands up and then squints down, looking at something I can't see. Then, very carefully, he opens the shears and
snaps them closed again a few inches from his abdomen. I feel
a strange sense of release.

"You did it," I say. "That was the tether breaking, wasn't it?"

"One side," he says. "Now for the other . . ."

He repeats the gesture on the other side of his body. I don't feel anything this time, but his face relaxes into an expression of pure relief. "It's done. I'm free. Forever." He smiles at me again, and this time the smile is so happy and genuine that it's impossible not to smile back.

"Well, whatever his reasons were, I'm glad Aaron was able to help," I say.

"Me, too," Peter agrees. "Thank you, Cyn. For asking him."

I shrug. "Well, it's not like I wanted to be stuck with you hanging around for the rest of my life."

His smile twists. "Of course not."

Then he drops to the ground in front of me. "Let me thank you properly, if you don't mind."

Before I can ask what he's talking about, he leans forward and kisses me.

This is not the slow, delicate, delicious first kiss I had with Ryan. This is . . . fast. And determined. And . . . overpowering. I know I should be pulling away — Old Cyn is beside herself with hysterical objections in the back of my brain — but the feelings from my dream have taken over and his mouth is warm and soft and hard and insistent and for at least a few very long seconds I just . . . kiss him back.

His hand reaches out to touch my face and I feel the tiny shocks of contact along my skin. I catch myself making a small sound of pleasure in response and Peter hears it, too, because suddenly he pulls me even tighter against him, and his hand is gripping my hair and his tongue is in my mouth and he's right, I do want to kiss him, I do like him, I don't want to stop, I . . .

"No," I say, pulling back. "No, no. We can't do this. I —
I can't."

He stops at once, letting me go, and sits back on the
ground. "Okay."

We're both shaking a little from the experience, though. It
was . . . intense. On both sides, apparently.

"Did you make me dream about you?" I ask him after a
minute.

He looks surprised, and I immediately curse myself.

"You dreamed about me?" he asks, smiling again. "What
did we do in this dream?"

"Never mind. Shut up."

He lets it go, but he's still smiling. I can feel my face flush-
ing uncontrollably.

"This . . . that . . ." I gesture back and forth between us.
"That can't happen again. Understand? Ryan may hate me
right now, but I'm still his girlfriend, and I'm going to fix
things between us, and we're going to be all right. And you are
not going to screw that up for me. Got it?"

He twists his mouth to one side, then nods. "Okay. Until
and unless you tell me otherwise."

"I won't."

"Fine. But I don't think you really need my help to screw
things up, Cyn. I'm pretty sure that's happening quite effectively all on its own."

"Did you not hear me say *shut up*?"

He starts to give me another charming smile, then stops
abruptly.

"Oh," he says. "That's not good."

"What?" I am instantly on alert.

"Huh," he says, looking down at the kitchen shears, which he had placed on the ground beside him sometime during the kissing.

"So . . . the tether is indeed broken," he says slowly. "But . . . remember that other demon who used the tether to get here and do bad things?"

"Yeah?"

"I . . . I wasn't thinking. He's still here. On this side. And now that the tether is broken, there's no immediate way to send him back."

Chapter | 09

"Wait, what?"

Peter looks at me, shamefaced.

"I'm sorry. I didn't even think. I should have waited until we forced him back through to the other side. I was so excited to break it . . ." He swallows anxiously. "I can't believe I did that."

"Okay," I say, although it's not, of course. "Okay, well . . . what do we do about it?"

"I don't know! I need . . . I need to think. And maybe to consult some friends."

This takes me by surprise. "You have friends? I mean besides Hector?"

"Yes, I have friends," he says a little defensively. "I mean, not the kind of friends I'm on the phone with every night or having sleepovers with and braiding one another's hair, but

I have certain people I can turn to in an emergency. Some of them may know what we can do."

"And what do I do in the meantime?"

"Get some sleep. You have a big day tomorrow, trying to fix your broken relationship, remember?"

I remember. As Peter starts to leave, I also remember that there's a huge spider-bull-bug demon running around out there in the night somewhere, and that it's kind of a long walk back to bunk 6.

"Hey, Peter, wait! Will you . . . will you walk me back? Big, scary demons out there tonight, you know?"

He hesitates, and at first I'm afraid he's going to say no. But then he doesn't.

"Sure," he says. "Come on."

We head out of the theater together and into the dark starlit night.

I know there's no reason to think being inside my bunk will keep me safe, but I tell myself that the demon will want to remain in hiding and not draw attention by killing me in the middle of a bunkful of girls. Demons, I amend silently. Plural. Why do they always seem to multiply like that?

There's a letter waiting for me on my bed, and I can tell it's from Annie even in the nearly total absence of light (glow-in-the-dark cat stickers), but I decide to save it for the morning. I'm in no mood to appreciate anything right now, not even an Annie letter.

Unsurprisingly, despite the lateness of the hour, I am not feeling at all sleepy. Exhausted, yes, physically and emotionally, but still too worked up on all levels to feel anywhere close to falling asleep. I should be thinking about the demons, and what to do about them. Instead, I think about Ryan. Ryan, who is really, really mad at me. Who is now aware of the full extent of the lying, and possibly hates me for it, and who has turned to lovely, concerned Jules to comfort him in his hour of need.

I can't get the image of them walking off, hand in hand, out of my mind.

Hypocrite, Old Cyn hisses at me silently.

Yeah. She's kind of got me there.

I kissed Peter. And lying here in the dark, alone with my thoughts, I cannot pretend that I didn't enjoy it. I did enjoy it. Until the guilt and enough presence of mind to make me stop kicked in, I enjoyed it a whole lot. I suspect this makes me a horrible person. I have a boyfriend, an amazing boyfriend that I love, who has been with me through some of the worst experiences of my entire life, and instead of running after him to apologize and beg his forgiveness for the lying (about which he is one hundred percent totally justified in feeling angry and betrayed), I stay behind and make out with the demon who started all this trouble in the first place.

Well . . . I suppose to be fair, Peter didn't really start all this trouble. Mr. Gabriel started all this trouble. Peter just took advantage of my being in the demon world. But if he hadn't hitchhiked back with me, the second demon would never have shown up. I guess I can't blame the third demon on him, though. I don't know who to blame for that one. I guess me, since I'm the one who made the deal with the demoness to go back again to the demon world two more times. But I had to do that to save Annie. Which I had to do because Mr. Gabriel stole her mind and heart and then her whole physical body.

I realize that the lyrics to "Your Fault" from *Into the Woods* are spiraling through my head now, and that is *never* going to help me get to sleep. And the witch makes a good point in "Last Midnight" (her song in response to the flurry of accusations) about whether figuring out who to blame is really what's most important in a crisis.

So, okay. Stop worrying about whose fault everything is and try to use your brainpower for something productive, Cyn. What can you do to fix things? To at least start fixing them, anyway.

I'm not sure there's anything I really can do on my own about the demons. I have to rely on Peter to gather information on that front. And if he can't . . . well, he's been in contact with Aaron. Maybe he'll know how we can summon Aaron back here and see whether he or the demoness would be willing to help us somehow.

Ryan will not be excited about that plan, though. Ryan is already very much not excited about all of this. Not that I can blame him. I would be very happy to listen to alternate ideas regarding our best course of action if he has any, but I doubt he will. I doubt he wants to think about any of this at all.

I *can* try to do something about him being mad at me. Ryan is a reasonable person when he's not in the throes of anger, and tomorrow I will talk to him and try to explain why I didn't tell him about the extra demon-world trips. I know my excuses are not good ones, but . . . acknowledging that and apologizing should still count for something, shouldn't it?

I don't know, Old Cyn says. *How badly can you screw up and still expect to be forgiven?*

I liked it better when she was just calling me names.

Maybe I can make him understand. How I was afraid to tell him because I knew he'd be angry, but it was already done, and I couldn't change it, and . . . I couldn't even really regret it, because it was what I had to do to save Annie.

Shouldn't that be a good thing, being someone who would do whatever needs to be done to save the people she cares about?

I think about what Peter said, about my flexible moral compass. Which I guess is what made me feel like I could lie to Ryan about the details of my deal with the demoness. And so, yes, fine, maybe it's not okay for whatever needs to be done to be entirely open-ended. It does seem very Machiavellian, which is probably not a good adjective to attribute to one's core personality.

But if two people I love require different and opposing things, why is it wrong to try to shield one while doing what I need to do to save the other?

But you weren't shielding Ryan. You were shielding yourself. From having to tell him the truth.

Because otherwise you might have lost him.

I don't know if that's Old Cyn or Current Cyn or someone in between. I want to argue, but I can't. Because, of course, that's entirely correct. I lied to Ryan because I was terrified of what he would do if he knew the truth. I held back, deliberately, even after I promised not to.

Admitting I was wrong is not going to be enough, I realize. Not to fix how he's feeling right now. I need to make him believe that I will never do it again.

But can I really be sure I will never do it again?

What about kissing Peter? Old Cyn asks. *Are you going to tell Ryan about that?*

That's different. That has nothing to do with anything.

Old Cyn is pointedly silent.

There would not be any point in telling Ryan that I kissed Peter. Or that Peter kissed me and I kissed him back, which is technically what really happened. None. It didn't mean anything. That's a whole different area. People are allowed to have some secrets. You can't really tell another person everything! I mean, for example, there are things that go through my head sometimes that I will never tell anyone. Thoughts that shock even me at times. Keeping those things safely locked inside my own brain is not the same as actively keeping secrets. So there must be other exceptions, too.

I stop there, holding tight to that conclusion. I will tell Ryan everything about the demon situation, and promise not to hide anything else like that from him ever again. But I will not tell him about kissing Peter, and I think that is perfectly okay, and I don't want to hear one word about it from any voices in my head who might still be listening in right now.

That decision must sit okay with my subconscious, because I am finally starting to feel like I can sleep. I close my eyes and try to visualize tomorrow being a much, much better day than today.

But I should have known that tonight wasn't done with me yet.

And apparently my subconscious is not done with me, either.

The early dreams are guilty, skin-tingly dreams in which I replay my kiss with Peter, and then let it continue past the point where in real life I pulled away. Dream-Cyn does not pull away. Dream-Cyn takes Peter's hand and leads him deeper backstage, where we can do more than just kiss each other. The feel of his real-life hands on my face was electric. The feel of his dream hands in other places is . . . indescribable. And everything feels so real. He lifts my shirt over my head and I can feel the rough texture of the floor against my back. I can feel the flexing muscles of his arms as he wraps them around me, the strong pulse of his demon heart beating within his human-shaped chest. His mouth feels real against my skin, his teeth as they bite my neck, and oh, his hands . . .

Part of me is not okay with this dream and struggles to wake up. But not all of me.

Eventually, though, either through my own efforts or the unknowable logic of dream progression, the scene changes, and I'm alone and fully dressed (but still a little breathless) and walking through the aisles of an empty theater. No — not entirely empty. Mr. Henry is there in his favorite seat, grading English essays. He looks up as I approach.

"Careful, Cyn," he says. "He's coming."

"Who? Who's coming?"

He hands me one of the essays. I look down at the paper. At first it appears blank, but then red liquid marks begin to seep through until they form the words *MISS ME?*

The red liquid begins to spread out, covering more of the paper, and I drop it before it can reach my fingers. I look back at Mr. Henry. "Who's coming?" I ask again.

"I'm so sorry, Cyn. You were one of my favorites, you know." He packs up his things and starts to walk away. I try to run after him, but suddenly the seats are full of people, and I can't get through. Faintly, I think I hear Mr. H. humming "Safety in Numbers" from *The Boy Friend*. Which is weird because I know he hates that show.

I start to push past the people in the seats around me, but no one will move, and after a second I realize that's because they're all dead. There is blood everywhere. I try to climb over them, I need to get out of this place — the blood, the smell, is terrible — but I can't seem to make any progress. Blood gets all over me, my clothes, my face, my hands. I can't get it off.

Someone laughs. It's a loud, horrible sound that hurts my ears. I stare around wildly and see that it is Mr. Gabriel as he appeared in the library that first time we saw him in not-quite-human form. His horns and wings are black and sharp and awful. Seeing him there, even after all this time, even knowing it's a dream — and I do know it's a dream, even while it's happening — seeing him makes me feel like all the air in the universe has been sucked away. I can't breathe, I can't move, I can't do anything. I can't stand seeing him looking whole and happy and alive.

He's on the stage, watching me.

"I love this show," he says. "I mean, it's no *Sweeney Todd,* and the acting is horrible, but the body count is much, much higher."

I force my lungs to work, force my blood to resume its course through my body. I will not be afraid of him. He's not real.

"What are you talking about?" I struggle not to let my voice shake. "Why are you even here? You're dead! The demoness killed you!"

"Did she? Are you sure about that?"

"Yes!" He's not going to scare me about this. I was there. "I *saw* you. I saw you die. I watched it happen."

He starts a slow, casual single time step on the stage. Somehow the fact that he is wearing tap shoes is not strange at all.

"Good thing you know everything there is to know about demons, I guess. Otherwise . . . you could be in for a nasty surprise."

I renew my climbing over the dead bodies and finally force my way back to the aisle. I march toward the stage. "Say what you mean, dammit! If it's really you in my dream, then stop messing with me and say what you came here to say and then get the hell out of my head!"

Suddenly he's directly in front of me, and I scream and jerk back before I can help it. He grabs my arms, locking me in place. I struggle, but he's so strong I can barely even shift in his grip.

He is no longer smiling.

"All right, dear Cynthia. Here is what I mean: I'm coming back to finish what I started. I'm already here, in fact. I'm going to kill you and all your little friends. Except for Annie, of course. Annie is coming with me, like she was always meant to."

"You're not real," I manage, still trying to break free of his grip. "You're dead. I know you are."

His eyes are cold and black. "You're not nearly as smart as you think you are, you little bitch. I can't wait until I get to kill you. It's going to hurt a lot. Jeremy had it easy, but you . . . you're going to suffer. It's going to be so . . . much . . ."

He pulls me closer until his face is only centimeters from my own. *"Fun,"* he finishes in a whisper. Then he darts forward and licks my face.

I scream in horror, trying to push him away, to wipe off the sticky trail of his saliva, but he only laughs. "Oh, come on, Cyn. You like to kiss demons. I know you do. Don't you want to feel what it's going to be like for Annie? All the delicious horrible things I'm going to do to her?"

"Stop it!" I'm crying now, still trying to pull away. "Let me go!"

He does, suddenly, and I fall backward to the floor. He stands above me, looking down.

"Get ready," he says. "I'll see you tomorrow."

Then he disappears, and I wake up.

All of the other girls in my bunk are standing around my bed.

"Cyn?" Sasha asks. "You okay?"

I sit up. "What happened?"

The girls look at one another. "You were screaming," Susan says. "That must have been some nightmare."

"Yeah," I say, a little shakily. "Sorry . . . didn't mean to wake everyone."

"It's okay," Lisa P. says. "Almost time to get up, anyway." It's true; the morning sunlight is streaming in through the windows.

Sasha squints at me and leans forward. "What's that on your face?"

I get up and go into the bathroom. Sasha and Susan follow me, I guess to make sure I'm okay. Or maybe they're just curious to see whatever it is on my face. I stand in front of the mirror.

There's an angry red rash in a long vertical stripe just to the left of my mouth.

Exactly where Mr. Gabriel licked me in the dream.

Chapter | 10

I hold it together long enough to get dressed and get out the door.

Washing my face did nothing. I mean, it got rid of the sweat and salt from my tears (I was apparently crying in my sleep as well as screaming), but the rash is still there. I don't know what it means. I'm afraid of what I think it means. I need to talk to . . . someone. Can I go to Ryan? Surely he'll put aside being mad at me to listen to this.

At least, I'm pretty sure.

I need to talk to Peter, too. Peter will probably have more immediately useful insight. But I don't *want* Peter. I want Ryan. I want Ryan to slip an arm around my waist and pull me into a really tight hug and tell me everything is going to be okay.

I run ahead of the other girls to the dining hall and look around. Ryan is miraculously alone at a table; everyone else we usually sit with must still be on line for food. I start in his direction.

Jules steps into my path and puts a hand out to stop me.

"Cyn, I don't think he wants to talk to you right now. I think you should give him some more time." Then she notices my rash. "What happened to your face?"

"Jules, you do not want to mess with me today. Get out of my way, please."

"I'm just trying to tell you—"

I can't handle this right now. I really just can't. "Back the hell off, or you will be sorry. Can I be any more clear than that?"

Her eyes widen in surprise, and then she starts to look mad. "Look, Cyn. You can't stop me from watching out for my friend. You really hurt him."

That's it. I push past her *very* ungently and make my way over to the table.

"Ryan," I say. "I know you're still mad, but I need to talk to you. Right now."

He looks up, the start of what is clearly going to be something like *go away* on his lips, then freezes when he sees my face. "What happened to your—"

"I'll explain everything. *Everything.*"

Jules comes up from behind me. "I *told* her you didn't want to talk to her," she says, half apologetically, half like a bratty little tattletale. "She told me to *back the hell off*!" She seems to think he's going to come to her defense.

I don't say anything. I'm not going to beg him. He must know I wouldn't be pushing if it weren't really important. More important than what's happening in our relationship right now, even though that is really important, too.

For a moment he just looks at me. Then he shakes his head. "No."

"Ryan, please —"

"No, Cyn. I'm sorry." His face is set and closed. Like a stranger. "I can't just roll over every time you ask me. Your stuff is not the only stuff that matters."

I blink. "*My* stuff? Ryan —"

He shakes his head again. "I don't want to hear it. Not right now. You screwed up, and now you have to deal with it. Jules is right. I don't want to talk to you." Then his expression goes even colder, and he adds, "But that shouldn't be too much of a problem, since we all know you prefer to work alone, anyway."

I just stand there, trying to think of something else to say.

Then I realize that Toby and Maria and several others have approached with their trays in time to hear this exchange, and they are all standing awkwardly behind me, unsure what to do.

And then Peter steps up beside me with his tray. "Hey, guys. What's going on?" He plants himself at the table diagonally from Ryan.

"This is none of your business," Jules says.

"It's none of yours, either," I tell her. "But that doesn't seem to be stopping you."

She turns to face me, folding her arms across her chest. "Ryan was my business long before he was yours, Cyn. And he's made it clear that he doesn't want you here right now. So maybe you should just leave."

Ryan looks down at his tray and says nothing.

Peter looks at Ryan, and then at Jules, and then back at me. His eyes are glinting with pleasure, and I realize that he is — literally — eating this up.

Suddenly I want to be anywhere else in the world than right there. I can't stand the cold look on Ryan's face or Jules's self-righteous arm-crossing or the way everyone in the dining hall seems to now be staring at us. Also, I am definitely about to cry, and I don't want any of them to see.

"Fine," I say quietly, which is about all I think I can manage. I turn and walk out, no idea where I'm going other than away from that spot. But I look back when I reach the doorway, unable to help it.

Jules is now sitting across from Ryan, her hand on his, talking softly to him. As I watch, he lifts his head to look at her, and I see his expression softening now that I'm not the one he's focused on.

I leave before I start to throw up.

Everyone's at breakfast by now, so the paths are clear and quiet. The tears have begun by this point, but I try to ignore them. Crying isn't going to help. Crying is stupid. I head off into the fluffy green nature, swiping angrily at my mutinous leaky eyes, until I can't see the dining hall anymore. And then I find a bench and then I sit down and then I stare at nothing and try to think. Not about Ryan; about the other stuff. The demon stuff.

My stuff, apparently.

Okay, then.

First order of business: Could Mr. Gabriel really still be alive? Before today, I would have said absolutely not. Because: *I saw him die.* I did.

But . . . what he said in the dream is true. I don't know everything about demons. Maybe he *could* have survived somehow. I would think the demoness would have told me, or Aaron . . . but maybe not. Maybe they don't even know. Or maybe it's the kind of information they'd hold on to until they could use it to their advantage somehow. Because: demons. I have to keep reminding myself what that means. Not the good guys. At least not most of them.

And then there's the rash on my face. I reach up and flinch as my fingers brush the tender skin.

Something did that to me. I can't quite believe it's just some kind of dream-induced psychosomatic manifestation of inner stress.

Suddenly I hear footsteps approaching. My stupid heart immediately leaps up in hope that it's Ryan, ready to talk, but of course it's not. One of the counselors — I think his name is Luis — walks over and sits beside me on the bench.

"Hi!" he says.

"Uh, hi." I'm not sure how to politely express that I don't want company right now. "Luis, right?"

"Oh, I'm not Luis," Luis says. "Not right at this moment, anyway." He looks at me, and I know.

I fling myself from the bench and turn to face him from several paces away.

"It's you," I whisper. "Oh, God. It's really you."

Not-Luis smiles brightly. "Hello, dear Cynthia. I told you I'd be seeing you today. And here I am." He squints at me for a second. "You should really do something about that rash."

I stare, barely able to breathe.

"How — how can you *be* here?" I ask. *"I saw you die."*

"Yeah, you said that last night. It's going to be very tedious if we have to have the same exact conversation again. Do you mind if we skip it?"

I want to run. But I'm not sure I can make my legs work. I can't believe this is happening.

But it is.

There is no doubt in my mind who is looking out at me from behind those borrowed eyes.

"Fine," I say. "What's next, then? Is this the part where you kill me? What are you waiting for?" I'm not sure what I'm trying to accomplish. I think I just feel better talking than standing there silently and quaking in fear. "I mean, seriously, you've come all this way, why not just do it now? Come on over and kill me."

He gives me a mocking, fake-sympathetic look. "It won't be nearly that quick for you, I'm afraid. And besides, I'm not ready. I've only got this body for a few more minutes. I need to wait until I have something a little more . . . long-term. So I can take my time."

He smiles again, and I only barely manage to remain standing. *That is not going to happen,* I tell myself. *He's not going to win. We're going to stop him. He's not going to torture and kill me.*

But there was a whole lot of awful and malevolent promise in that smile.

And as Peter pointed out last night, there is some question as to who *we* actually includes right now. Which makes me feel very horrible and alone.

"Well!" Mr. Gabriel/Luis says, standing up. "I should get going. I just wanted to say hello. In person. I'll see you again very soon."

And then something happens, and it's just Luis standing there, looking very confused.

"Cynthia?" he says. "How did I . . . I don't remember coming out here."

"Huh. That's weird," I say, pretty much on autopilot because my brain is still busy trying to keep me upright and not screaming or sobbing or vomiting. "Here, let me walk you back to the dining hall."

I escort the still-confused counselor back to the doorway, but I don't go inside. I can't. I can't go running back to Ryan in front of everyone, even though I want to do that very, very much. And I can't go running to Peter, either, since that would also necessitate going back in there and possibly over to that same table.

Instead, I will walk calmly and slowly over to Blake and wait for Peter to arrive for morning rehearsal.

Peter will help me figure out what to do. He's a demon. He'll know. And he'll help me.

Because Ryan was wrong about one thing. I definitely don't want to be working alone.

Not on this.

When Peter arrives, he's clearly prepared for me to be mad at him for enjoying my personal drama this morning, but there's no time for that. Instead, I fill him in on my dream (only the part about Mr. Gabriel, obvs) and then on my real-life encounter with Mr. Gabriel in Luis's body.

"Well *that's* not good," he says when I am finished. We are sitting on the floor near the loading dock, where we can talk privately. Behind me, the doors are open to the beautiful summer day that I can't in the least appreciate at the moment.

"So he's the one who climbed up your tether to get here," I say. "He must be, right?"

"It appears so," Peter says. "You're sure it was really him?"

"Totally. Except for the part where it's *impossible*, obviously."

"Okay," Peter says, mostly to himself. "Okay. So, this is even worse than I imagined. But . . . okay. What really matters now is what we do next."

I look at him expectantly.

"I didn't mean that I *know* what we should do next," he clarifies. "I just mean . . . that's what matters."

"Great," I say. "Very helpful."

"Can we expect any assistance from Ryan?" Peter asks me. I give him a dark look, and he holds up his hands defensively.

"Hey, I need to know what our assets are before I can help you devise this brilliant plan we're going to come up with."

My dark look dissolves, no match for my resurging sadness. "I don't think so. At least . . . not right now." I look up at him half hopefully. "Did anything else happen after I left?"

He shakes his head. "Not really. Jules told Ryan he's doing the right thing. Ryan didn't say very much. Everyone else tried to pretend nothing weird had happened. Oh! But Belinda said there was some new escalation in the Darleen and Celia situation, so I'm hoping for something to happen during today's rehearsal."

I feel a sudden suspicion. "Did you arrange it so that they'd both be in your show?"

He grins. "Luckily, they were both right for different parts. Much easier to make use of existing drama than to try to stir up new drama. I figured the two of them together would be enough for basic sustenance, and then anything extra would just be a nice bonus. Like this morning!"

My dark look is back with a vengeance.

"Hey," he says, "still better than killing people, right?"

I can't really argue with that. But: "Speaking of killing people . . . we need to stay on topic here. I don't want anyone else to die. And Mr. Gabriel is going to have to kill someone to get stronger, right?"

"Oh, definitely."

"Did you contact any of your . . . friends?" I ask.

"I sent some messages," Peter says. "And I had Hector do the same, through other channels. But these things can take time."

"What about Aaron?" I ask. "Could you contact him? Maybe he could help us."

Peter looks very skeptical.

"He helped us with breaking the tether," I point out. "And he didn't leave me to be killed by the demons when I was down in the demon world."

"He probably didn't leave you because he knew the queen would be pissed," Peter says. "And I'm not entirely sure the tether breaking was meant to be helpful. I mean, that's what led to us breaking the tether with Mr. Gabriel stuck on the wrong side."

"But Aaron couldn't have known you'd use the shears right away. And . . ." I think back, trying to remember the exact course of my conversation with Aaron. "I'm actually not sure I mentioned the other demon to him. I told him you thought someone was interfering, making it hard for you to break it . . . and then he went to look stuff up and then horrible demons started coming through the window and there wasn't a lot of productive talking after that."

"Oh," Peter says. "If he didn't know, then . . . hmm." He thinks that over for a minute, then sighs. "Well, regardless, this probably isn't the most helpful line of reasoning. We can sit here guessing all day, but I don't think it's going to get us any closer to a solution."

"Okay," I say. "Let's go back to how Mr. Gabriel is still alive. Because, *what the actual fuck,* Peter?" The crazy terrible impossibleness of Mr. Gabriel being here is still trying to sink in, but I think my brain is, understandably, resisting. "He was *dead.* I swear he was dead. Very, very dead. Lying on the ground with his limbs spread all around and the demoness stabbing him and stabbing him with her stinger things long after he stopped moving."

"I do have a theory about that," Peter says, pushing up his glasses. "It's possible, if someone was prepared and waiting, that his spirit could have been captured and preserved at the moment that it left his body."

"That's going to take some more explaining."

"If Mr. Gabriel had some ally waiting, just in case he didn't win, that ally could have trapped his spirit before it dissipated. So his body would have died, but his spirit would have remained behind."

"Mr. Gabriel was sure he would win," I say. "I can't imagine him preparing a plan B."

Peter shrugged. "Well, maybe someone did it without his knowledge. They wouldn't need his active cooperation in order for it to work. All they would need was an appropriate container and to be present at the time of death within a reasonably close distance. Any of the demons watching the battle would have had the opportunity to get close enough. Then they could have captured his departing spirit in the container, stopping him from truly dying a complete death."

"Okay . . ." I say. "First of all, *why didn't someone tell me that could happen?*" Because that seems like really, really important information that everyone left out. That killing a demon doesn't always mean they are one hundred percent dead. "Does this kind of thing go on all the time?"

"Oh, no," Peter says. "It's pretty rare. But it does happen.

Every once in a while a demon ends up near death with enough time to make the arrangements. If he can find someone he can trust, willing to help. Which is what makes it so rare, since there's not a lot of trusting and helping among demons, generally."

My brain hurts.

"Okay, let's say that your theory is correct. He still has no actual body, though, right?"

"Right. He has to borrow other bodies, like you observed today, until he either finds someone willing to give up their body permanently or builds up enough strength to create his own. But re-creating his own physical form from nothing would take a tremendous amount of energy."

"But didn't you —"

Peter shakes his head. "I came up physically; I just had to build myself back up to full size. And maintain my human appearance, obviously. But Mr. Gabriel is nothing but spirit right now. He would have to actually create a new physical body. Huge difference, and much, much harder. No, I'm guessing he'll go for taking someone else's permanently. He'll still need to build up strength for that, but not nearly as much."

"And now we're back to the part where he tortures and kills people."

"Yup. I think —"

Suddenly Peter's eyes go very wide. He appears to be looking at something behind me.

It's really just never, ever a good thing when someone does that. It's even worse than the corner-of-the-eye thing.

I turn slowly around.

The spider-bull-bug demon is looming in the loading-dock doorway.

I didn't really get to take in the full picture of it last night, what with all the fighting and portaling and distracting hand-holding of people who should not be holding hands. It's *enormous*. And disgusting. And . . . right there. I should probably move away to some much greater distance. But its repulsive presence is sort of hypnotic, and I'm finding it hard to gather myself together and send the appropriate messages from my brain to my muscles. My eyes keep trying (hopelessly) to make sense of the way its body is put together, like where the spider legs become the furry bull portion of its chest and parts of its head, including thick, dirty, yellowing horns, and then somehow there's this beetle-ish face with antennae and the front pincers of what might be a stag beetle. I'm not sure about the stag beetle part; I don't really know my insect types so well. Honestly, it could be anything. If I'm going to keep encountering demons in their confusing mishmash animal-part forms, I might want to start studying up, maybe.

Peter tugs gently on my arm. "Get up, Cyn," he says quietly. "Right now, please."

My legs, fortunately, seem to be open to suggestions from others, and I find myself obediently getting up. Peter pulls me backward with him several slow and careful steps. Running seems like a better idea, but that idea is immediately followed by the very terrible and compelling mental image of the demon bounding after us, legs and pincers outstretched, provoked by the sight of fleeing prey. So I content myself with the slow and careful backing away.

For a moment the demon just stands there glaring at us. Then its insectoid mouth opens.

"Stay away from my brother," it says in a horrible gravelly voice that sounds like broken machinery trying to claw its way through a block of concrete.

I turn to stare at Peter. "This thing is your brother?!" I ask.

"No!" Peter exclaims, visibly horrified at the idea. "I swear, I've never seen it before last night!"

We turn back to look at the monster. I'm not sure, but I think it might be rolling its eyes at us.

"Not him," it says with disgust. "The other. The one you call Gabriel. We are brothers."

There are several seconds during which Peter and I are both absolutely speechless.

I find my voice first. "*Mr. Gabriel* is your *brother*?"

The thing nods.

"Really?" I go on. "Because he never mentioned you."

"I never knew he had a brother," Peter says. He gives the demon a fairly obvious once-over. "Kind of kept you out of sight, I guess, huh?"

"You would have been Annie's brother-in-law," I add, helplessly fascinated by this horrible notion.

The demon is not interested in our commentary.

"Stay away, or I will crush you."

"Okay, first of all," I say, getting a little annoyed now, "he's the one who followed us here and took over poor Luis's body to threaten me this morning. We had nothing to do with it. Second of all, we are going to find a way to kill him for good this time, so you can take your warnings and threats and shove them up your spidery ass."

I'm not actually sure that spiders have asses. I guess they must, right? I mean all creatures need to excrete bodily waste and stuff, don't they? I realize this is not a helpful tangent, but now I can't stop trying to picture the ass of a spider. I may be slightly hysterical. Or perhaps my brain has finally broken once and for all.

"You," the thing says, taking a step closer to me. *Now* I can stop thinking about spider asses. Now I'm back to being terrified, which is very good for clearing one's mind of all extraneous thoughts.

"You are the one who ruined everything," it says. "I should kill you right now."

Peter steps in front of me, which is both sweet and slightly irritating.

"You know what I am, don't you?" I ask it. "You can't use your demon magic on me."

"I can use legs and teeth," it says, which, unfortunately, is true.

It lunges forward, much more quickly than I would have guessed possible, and Peter rushes to meet it, seeming to grow larger as he does so. I kind of forgot that as a demon, he has the ability to adjust his size and appearance. I am no longer irritated in the least by the way he stepped in front of me a few seconds ago. He blocks the monster's advance, gripping two of its spidery legs in his hands, but I can tell immediately that it's not easy for him.

"You know that's a bad idea," Peter says to the monster while holding it back, at least temporarily. His voice is amazingly calm. "You know your brother wants to kill Cyn himself. If you kill her now, if you even touch her, how do you think your brother is going to feel about that? I think he'd be pretty pissed off. I think you'd be in deep, deep trouble if you did that."

The demon backs off, looking, if I'm reading his bug features correctly, a little frightened.

"True," it concedes. "I must not be hasty. Brother said to wait."

"If Mr. Gabriel were *my* brother, I'd be damn sure not to make him angry at me," Peter goes on. "He doesn't really seem the type to forgive and forget."

"He . . . is not," the demon says. It seems to shrink into itself, thinking about this. Then it straightens up again. "It does not matter. He will share my body and we will kill her together. I will still get to taste her blood. And then we will kill the rest of you. And then we will go after the other."

"What other?" I ask warily.

The demon smiles a horrible insect smile. "Aaaannnnnnnie," it breathes. "We will have her together. Brother has promised me."

With that, he lashes out at Peter with one long spidery leg, knocking him to the floor, then bounds out through the loading-dock doorway.

173

I run over to Peter, who is back to his normal shape and size and appears a little breathless and in pain but not actually bleeding or broken.

I look down at him. "How has no one else noticed that enormous disgusting thing running around camp?"

"Come on, you remember how these things work," he says, rubbing his hip where the thing jabbed him. "Most people don't see what they can't believe is real. And the demons use their magic to encourage that."

"Right," I say. Because I do remember, of course. But not being suspicious of a demon who maybe acts a little shifty but looks human and has a job seems different from completely not noticing a giant spider-bull-bug monster frolicking around in broad daylight.

I help Peter back up to his feet.

"So, point of information," he says once he's upright again. "That thing is very, very strong. I would never be able to take it in a fight. Not one lasting more than about two seconds, anyway."

"Good to know," I say. Although it's not good to know, of course. It actually kind of sucks to know. But I guess it's still *useful* to know. Despite the suckiness. And Peter did already indicate that he's not the fighting type. "But, somehow, we still need to kill it. Kill both Mr. Gabriel *and* his delightful little brother. I mean, I don't think asking them nicely to stop what they're doing and go home is really going to work."

Peter takes his glasses off and cleans them on his shirt. "Well, technically, you can't kill Mr. Gabriel. Not here."

"What do you mean?"

"He's not entirely here in this world. Part of him, the core part, his essence, is still back in the demon world in whatever container someone trapped it in. I'm guessing it might have been Mr. Spider-Cow there, or one of his no doubt equally charming friends. But in any case, you can't truly destroy Mr. Gabriel until you destroy both parts—the spirit part that's up here now, and the core part still hidden away down below. Including whatever is holding it. If you kill him here, you'll really just be sending him back to the demon world. Which is still good—much, much better than having him running around up here, causing all kinds of harm. But, you know . . . just so you know. To kill him for good, you'd have to go back down there to do it."

I look at him. "You are full of good news today, Peter," I say.

"Sorry," he says. "Just telling it like it is."

"I am not a big fan of how it is," I say.

Slowly, by unspoken mutual consent, we start walking back to where set construction is happening and other campers are going about their normal routines, oblivious of the danger in their midst. The whole loading-dock area seems tainted now, pulsing with some spidery demonic residue or something.

"Ugh," Peter says, looking down at his hands. "I kind of want to take a bath in bleach now. I can still feel it on my skin."

"Thanks for talking it down," I say. "I . . . really don't want to be killed by that thing. Or, you know, at all. But especially not by that thing."

"Hey, what are friends for?"

I glance at him sideways as he continues to examine his outstretched hands with an expression of extreme distaste. *Are* we friends? Maybe we are, at this point. I seem to have fully accepted his claims about not being evil, and he did just save my life. He's not exactly a prince as far as ethical behavior goes, and, yeah, the drama fixation is kind of annoying, especially when he clearly derives so much pleasure from my personal issues involving Ryan, but no one's perfect. And anyway, I'm rather short on demon-fighting allies at the moment. At least ones who are talking to me. I can't afford to be overly picky.

"So, now what?" I ask him.

"Now we spend the rest of rehearsal doing what we're supposed to be doing. We still have a show to work on, and until I hear back from one of my contacts, I'm not sure what else we can do."

I start to object—we can't just wait around and act like everything's normal!—but then Peter staggers suddenly, careening into me. I grab him before he can fall over.

"Peter?"

"Correction," he says in a strained voice. "*You* spend the rest of rehearsal doing what you're supposed to be doing. I need . . . I need to sit down."

I help him over to a nearby metal folding chair.

"What's wrong?"

He leans over and rests his forearms on his thighs. "That thing . . . even stronger than I thought. I really am still feeling it on my skin. It's still . . . draining me . . . something . . ." He shakes his head. "I need to . . ." He turns his hands over, palms up, and I see a flare of red demon energy.

Then he slides out of the chair and onto the floor.

"Peter!"

I kneel beside him. At first I think he's unconscious, but then his eyes flutter open. "Got it," he says. "Done. That was a nasty trick. Evil bastard."

"Are you going to be okay? What happened?"

"I'll be okay. It left behind a sort of delayed-activation poison. Something in those wiry fibers on its legs."

I shudder, remembering all too well what those legs felt like when I was fighting them off in the portal.

Oh.

"Will it . . . I touched it, too, last night . . ."

He shakes his head again. "No. Just a demon thing. You're fine. And I'll be fine. I just have to remember not to touch it again without protecting against that."

He seems to be regaining some of his strength, but he still needs my help to get back up into the chair.

"What can I do?" I ask.

He smiles up at me weakly. "Find some excuse to get Celia and Darleen back here. Tell them it's something about one of their songs. That should get them going."

"Seriously?"

"Seriously. I wasn't kidding about the drama thing. I'll need it to recover from this." His smile disappears suddenly and he looks at me like he's just thought of something. "It doesn't . . . it doesn't hurt them. If you were thinking that. I mean, I'm not taking anything from them in the way Mr. Gabriel was sucking out students' life energy. I only take what they already put out into the world around them. I just encourage them to put out a little more sometimes."

"I didn't —"

He reaches for my hand, and I let him take it. "I swear, Cyn. I'm not like that. I'm not doing anything to hurt them. I want you to understand."

I give his hand a tiny squeeze. "I understand. It's okay. I'll send them back here."

He releases me and nods in relief. "Thanks."

I go out into the theater proper. Fortunately, Michael's running a scene that neither Darleen nor Celia is in, and they're both sitting in the audience, several rows apart, studying their scores. I talk quietly to one and then the other, and they both head backstage. As they get closer to the stairs, I can see them speeding up, both trying to be first.

After a moment, I head backstage myself toward where my summer minions are working on set construction. I want to be doing something about Mr. Gabriel and his deranged spider-brother, but it seems clear that we're going to need some outside help to deal with them, and Peter's in no shape to do anything right now, anyway. But as soon as he's better, I'll ask him about contacting Aaron to see whether the demoness might be willing to help us. I don't want to wait for his other friends to get back in touch, and I realize the only reason I've been reluctant to bring in Aaron is because I know Ryan would hate it. But Ryan has removed himself from the situation and has therefore lost his vote. So I am not going to care about what kind of plan he would or would not like. At all.

Nope.

I feel a sad sigh coming on and fight it back down instead. The only cure for grief is action, as one of my few nonmusical favorite inspirational quotes goes. (George Henry Lewes, nineteenth-century English dramatist, novelist, actor, philosopher, scientist, etc. Seems like a smart guy.) So I'm going to take action. As soon as Peter is strong enough to help me.

In the meantime, I might as well see how the platforms for Act 2 are coming along. That counts as action, too.

By the end of rehearsal, Peter is looking much better. Darleen and Celia had a brief blowup and had to be separated by Michael, again, but everyone's come to expect that from them by now, and so the disruption didn't last very long. Peter is going to check in with Hector to see if any brilliant ideas have come in from any of his sources, and we will reconvene after lunch. Ordinarily I would suggest skipping lunch under these circumstances, but Peter says he still needs a bit more rest, and I'm actually kind of starving, since I didn't end up eating anything at breakfast.

I stop back at bunk 6 on the way to lunch, hoping maybe Susan will be there so I can walk with her to the dining hall instead of all alone, and I notice Annie's letter still sitting unopened on the milk crate that serves as my night table. With everything else going on, I'd forgotten all about it. I sit down on the bed and carefully tear open the envelope without beheading or de-footing or otherwise maiming any of the glow-in-the-dark cats. This is exactly what I need. I am going to just take a little break from today's fresh new dose of horrors and lose myself temporarily in some entertaining stories about sweet, sweet William and all the other happy and demon-free news from back home. Just for a few minutes.

But the first line after her bouncily penned "Dear Cyn" nearly makes me drop the letter in shock.

Guess what???? We are all coming up to see your show!!!!!!

No. No no no no no.

Annie can't come here. Not now. Not when Mr. Gabriel is here. Him and his horrible brother. This — she can't — I won't —

I close my eyes and take a deep breath, trying to calm down. My heart is pounding faster than a Gilbert and Sullivan patter song being sung by a real show-off, and my legs feel shaky and weak even though I'm already sitting down.

This can't happen again. He cannot get at her.

He cannot.

HE CANNOT.

I just wish I knew what we could possibly do to stop him.

Chapter | 11

Once again my first impulse is to run to Ryan, but there is no way I'm going to let myself do that.

Anyway, this is not really an emergency. The show is still more than a week away. Maybe we'll have fixed everything by then and it will all be fine.

Old Cyn snorts derisively in the back of my brain.

It could happen! I retort angrily. *I don't think the time issue is the greatest part of this challenge. If we're going to figure out some way to stop Mr. Gabriel and his horrible brother, it could happen tomorrow as easily as next week. So stop with the attitude, please. If you don't have anything useful to contribute, you can just be quiet.*

Silence. Which is too bad, because I was kind of hoping maybe she would have something useful to contribute.

Because I've got nothing.

I could write back to Annie and tell her not to come . . . but she would immediately be suspicious and insist on knowing why. And I can't tell her why. It's been so hard for her to even begin to feel safe. I can't let her know that Mr. Gabriel is still alive, and here, and still wants her.

I could try to come up with some alternative believable reason (*a lie, you mean,* Old Cyn says in my head, sounding suspiciously like Ryan, but I ignore her) . . . that the show was canceled, or something . . . but . . . I guess I don't have to decide that just yet. There's still some time.

Right now . . . I don't know what to do right now. I've completely lost my appetite for lunch, so there's no reason to make myself face the dining hall. I could go to find Peter, but if he admitted needing rest, he probably really does.

I decide to do the one thing that almost always makes me feel better when things are crap. I dig out my headphones and my music and go outside.

Nature is there, bright and beautiful, all green and brown with sunlight dancing on the leaves, and there are no giant spider monsters immediately visible anywhere. I head off on one of the paths into the trees, scrolling through my albums. As much as I love Sondheim and his dark and complicated masterpieces, today I think I need something a little . . . happier. I stop on *Guys and Dolls* and press play. Good, old-fashioned, smart music and snappy lyrics and a sweet, wonderful ending where everything turns out okay for everyone. That's what I need right now.

I walk, and listen, and try not to think too much about anything. When the lunch period is over, I'll go find Peter, because that will just have to have been enough resting, and then I will ask him to contact Aaron and then I will do whatever I have to do to get the demoness to help us again. Until then, I am just going to try to regain my equilibrium.

And for a little while, that actually seems to be happening.

It's not until I'm up to "If I Were a Bell" that I even see another person. It's a man, approaching my path from one of the connecting paths up ahead. After a second I realize it's Michael, asshole-director extraordinaire.

I am resolved that not even Michael will disrupt my carefully achieved and probably extremely temporary mental stability. I'm about to turn around and find some other direction to walk when I notice how strangely blank his face is. He hasn't seen me; he's looking straight in front of him and is far enough ahead of where I am that he wouldn't be able to see me unless he turned his head. But he doesn't turn his head. He walks steadily forward, not looking around, not seeming to be looking at anything at all, really.

Something feels wrong about this.

For a moment I'm tempted to ignore the sense of wrongness and stick with my original plan of turning around and walking away. But . . . I don't. Instead, I pause the music and take off my headphones and tuck everything into my pocket. And then I follow him.

He walks on, leading me deeper into the camp trails than I've yet explored on my own. He's not going in the direction of any of the theaters or activity buildings or offices.

The sense of wrongness gets stronger and stronger.

This can't be good, Old Cyn mutters in the back of my brain.

I could not agree more.

I hesitate, torn over what to do. Then I take a breath and jog forward.

"Hey, Michael?"

No response.

I reach out to take his arm and try to pull him to a stop, but he shakes me off without even glancing at me and continues walking. His expression doesn't change.

Crap. This *definitely* can't be good.

I try pulling his arm harder. I try standing in front of him and physically blocking his way. Finally, I try slapping him across the face.

At first nothing happens. His face remains blank, and he keeps trying to walk forward.

Then he stops and turns toward me, and his eyes become alive again.

I can instantly tell it's not him on the other side.

"I wondered why it was taking him so long," Mr. Gabriel says through Michael's mouth. "That's what I get for leaving him on autopilot, I guess."

"What are you doing to him?"

He smiles one of his terrible smiles, which looks extra hideous on Michael's hijacked face. "What do you think?"

I swallow, my throat suddenly very dry. "You're not going to kill him."

"Oh, no. No, of course not."

I don't relax, because obviously this is not the end of the story.

There's a rustling in the trees, and then Little Brother creeps out onto the path.

"*He's* going to kill him," Mr. Gabriel goes on.

Of course.

Crap.

"But . . ." stalling, not that I expect my brain will come up with any brilliant ideas for what to do in the next few seconds. "But what will happen to you if Michael dies while you're inside him?"

"Michael? Oh, good. You know him! That's even better." His smile gets wider. It's very disconcerting to see Michael's face wearing such a pleased expression. He never looks that way at rehearsal. "I won't still be inside, of course. I'm just helping him get to where he's going. Then my brother will kill him, and I will feed on the terror and pain and death."

"Couldn't you . . . couldn't you just drain off some of his life force like you did with the kids at school? Do you have to kill him?"

Mr. Gabriel throws his/Michael's head back and laughs. I can't really blame him. But again: stalling.

"I'd forgotten how amusing you could be, dear Cynthia." He shakes his head, still chuckling. "I don't *have* to do anything. I could just siphon off some of his energy and leave him alive. I could take it all, killing him, but in such a quick and painless manner that he wouldn't suffer before he died. But I *want* him to suffer before he dies. I want to watch him realize what's happening, and scream, and try to run but not be able to get away. I want to watch my brother drag him, screaming, closer and closer until he can feel the nice man's fists flailing against his head, and the limbs frantically struggling to break free. I want to watch as my brother slowly reaches forward with his sharp, shiny pincers and rips off the nice man's screaming face and eats it." He leans forward and adds in a low voice, "Do you want to watch, too?"

"First of all," I say, trying to keep my voice from shaking. That was a very horrible vivid picture he just painted in my mind. "Michael is not a nice man. So if that's what you're expecting, you're going to be sorely disappointed. He's a total asshole. Second of all . . ."

Mr. Gabriel waits patiently, eyebrows raised in expectant invitation.

"Second of all, you know I can't just stand here and let you kill him. Asshole or not."

"And how exactly are you going to stop me?"

Such a good question.

"I'll use my super-roach powers," I say spontaneously. "I'll share them with Michael to protect him."

Mr. Gabriel laughs again. "*First* of all," he says, mockingly, "your powers don't work that way. And second of all, your *powers* can't even protect *you*. Not from my brother. Not physically. Not if he really wants to kill you. And especially not from the two of us together."

"Can we kill her now?" the brother asks eagerly. "She is irritating and would be better dead. I want to taste her blood."

Mr. Gabriel's smile disappears as he whips his head around to face his brother. "What did I say?"

The monster shrinks back abruptly, seeming to become smaller. "She . . . this one dies last."

Mr. Gabriel walks Michael forward several steps. "And what will happen if you disobey me?"

The monster shrinks down even more. "Punished," he says in a barely audible voice.

Mr. Gabriel waits a moment, as if to be sure the reminder has sunk in properly, then turns back to face me.

"So, really, your choices are to watch or not watch. Up to you."

He turns back to face his brother, and then Michael's eyes go blank again. And then he blinks, and looks around in confusion.

And then he focuses on the spider monster.

"What—wh—" He loses the rest of the word as Little Brother takes a step toward him, front legs rising slowly into the air.

Then he starts shrieking.

Before I can think too much about it, I hurl myself forward and deliver a full-body slam, knocking Michael (and myself) into the bushes at the edge of the path.

Little Brother screams in anger and whirls toward us.

"Go! Go go go!" I scream at Michael. I push him stumbling to his feet.

He goes, still not really seeming fully coherent. But that's fine, as long as he gets out of here. Better than fine, probably. He runs, head down, legs pumping, back toward civilization.

Leaving me there in the bushes, alone.

With the demons.

I know Mr. Gabriel is there somewhere, although of course I can't see him. I wonder if I would be able to see him if he weren't hiding his halo, floating around like a poisonous red cloud or something. Then I decide that is not the thing I should really be focusing on right now.

Because Mr. Gabriel's little brother is *pissed*.

"I told you stay away!" he screams.

"Well you are not the *boss of me!*" I shout back. It's not my best line, I'll admit. But I'm under a significant amount of pressure here.

Little Brother does not like being shouted at, apparently. He surges forward, and I'm pretty sure he's forgotten all about Mr. Gabriel's recent speech regarding how he's not supposed to kill me yet. I scramble backward on my elbows deeper into the bushes, but the demon is coming at me like the runaway cart from *Les Misérables,* and, sadly, there is no Jean Valjean handily nearby to show up and save me.

And then suddenly something comes out of the trees and throws itself at the demon.

I have one crazy lunatic moment of thinking Jean Valjean has actually materialized in response to my desperate last thought before I realize that it's Hector.

I have no idea what he's doing here, but, man, am I glad to see that giant bear-shaped acne-faced boy.

Except . . . he's just a giant bear-shaped acne-faced boy.

He's going to get himself killed.

"Hector!" I scream. What *is* he doing here?

Mr. Gabriel's brother recovers all too quickly. He wraps his many disgusting legs around Hector and draws back his bullbug head to strike.

"No!" I scream. But obviously no one is listening to me.

Hector screams in agony as the monster drives his pincers into his neck and chest. He struggles and fights, tearing at the demon's face and legs, and apparently manages to connect with something, because Little Brother hisses in pain and pulls one of his legs swiftly out of reach.

Hector punches the demon in his furry bovine chest and shiny spider abdomen, fists flying, but it's clearly no contest. The demon regroups and attacks again, and again, and soon it's all over. Hector lies motionless at the demon's too-many feet.

Little Brother's head whips up as though he's listening to something, then he cringes in fear and perhaps pain. Awkwardly he crawls off, dragging his damaged leg behind him.

I get to my feet and rush over to Hector.

But it's too late. I can tell as soon as I reach him that he's not breathing. He's also bleeding from several puncture wounds in his face and neck and body. I grab him and shake him, trying to get some response, anything . . . but there's nothing. He's like a giant homely broken doll. There is a smudge of blue paint on one of his cheeks. His eyes are still open, and they stare glassily up at nothing.

He's dead.

I sit beside him for a few minutes, even though I know I should be getting out of there. It just seems wrong to leave him. Yeah,

I know we weren't best friends or anything, and I found his creepy loitering a little, well, creepy . . . but he was devoted to Peter, and apparently he just sacrificed himself to save me. He was one of the good guys.

I wish I were strong enough to carry him back to camp proper, but I guess that would raise a lot of questions that might be better going unaddressed. A dead camper would surely mean that they'd close down the camp and send everyone home, wouldn't it? I mean, at least this kind of dead camper, one murdered in the woods by an unknown assailant and sporting unidentifiable-weapon wounds. And getting sent home would only delay the inevitable, not to mention separate the team.

What team? Old Cyn whispers.

Shut up, I tell her. Anyway, it's not like Mr. Gabriel would give up just because we go back home. He'd follow us. And then he'd probably kill our friends and families like he threatened to do in the fall, and he'd still get Annie.

No, it's better that we take care of things here and now.

Whatever *taking care of things* might mean, given that we are clearly outmatched in every possible way.

I need to find Peter. Right now. And tell him what's happened.

I reach over and close Hector's eyes. Then I lean over and kiss him on his paint-smudged cheek.

"Thank you," I whisper. I hope he can hear me somehow.

Then I head slowly back toward the main campus.

Poor Peter. He's going to be really, really sad.

✳ ✳ ✳

I'm crossing the main intersection near the dining hall when Ryan and Jules step out right in front of me.

Ryan sees me, starts to look away, then looks back. His face looks alarmed. He comes toward me, Jules following just behind him.

"Cyn? What happened?"

I look down. My jeans are covered in dirt and leaves, and there are smears of blood across my T-shirt.

"It's not my blood," I say dully, attempting to push past him.

He grabs my arm. "What *happened*?"

I don't have any sad left inside me for Ryan things right now. I just feel empty and annoyed. "The usual," I tell him. "Demons, people dying, you know, *my* stuff. Don't worry about it."

"Who — who died?"

"Hector. It was almost Michael. I should have just let Michael die. If I'd known Hector would die in his place . . ." I have to stop and close my eyes for a second. "I have to find Peter and tell him." I try again to push past Ryan. He hasn't let go of my arm.

"Cyn . . ."

I sigh in exasperation. "Look, Ryan. I don't have time for this right now. I know you're still mad at me, and you probably have a right to be. But there are bigger things going on here. If you want to be pissed at me, fine. I still think you should help, though, because *people are dying,* and you are one of the very few who understand the situation and can help to do something about it. But I'm certainly not going to beg you. If you want to stand by and watch, that's your choice. But if you want to maybe put our personal issues aside and help to save some people, you can come with me. But we're not going to stand here and talk it out. Come or don't come. Up to you."

This time when I try to pull away, he lets me. I resume my travels. After a second, I become aware of Ryan falling into step behind me. And Jules, too.

There is hurried whispering, and then Ryan comes up next to me. "Are you okay?" he asks. His voice is soft and gentle, the kind of voice you'd use to soothe a wild animal.

I am in no mood for that.

"Nope." I don't stop walking. I don't even look at him. "Not okay. Mr. Gabriel isn't dead. He's the mystery demon that used Peter's tether to get here in spirit form. That horrible spider monster is his brother. They're going to kill us and take Annie. Oh, who is conveniently coming up for our shows, according to her latest letter."

Ryan grabs me again and spins me toward him. "Wait, what? Stop. Go back. What?"

I give him the quickest possible summary of the day's events. Jules has, of course, stopped with us, and is staring at me like she doesn't understand any of the words coming out of my mouth. I am in no mood for her, either.

"Why is she here?" I ask Ryan when I'm done. "I don't remember inviting her."

"I'm here because Ryan promised to finish telling me what the hell is going on," she says.

"It's none of your business what's going on," I say.

"If Ryan's in trouble, it's absolutely my business!" she says.

"Stop it, you guys," Ryan says. "Cyn, Jules is involved now, like it or not."

"Why? Why is she involved now?"

"Because she was there yesterday, remember? And I told her a lot of it already."

"Not enough, though," Jules says. "I still don't really believe any of it."

Now it's my turn to stare at her. "Did you have something in your *eye* last night when I fell out of a hole in the air with a giant spider-bull monster attacking me? What do you think that thing was? Someone's really good stage makeup?

"Cyn," Ryan growls. "Sarcasm is not going to help."

"Sarcasm almost always helps," I mutter.

Ryan takes a deep breath. "Okay. First, Jules, all that stuff I told you about demons is true. Peter is . . . a good demon. Mostly. He's on our side. Or at least we think he is. Or . . . Cyn thinks he is."

"I know he is."

"Fine. Whatever. There are two other demons here at camp with us. One of them is mostly here in spirit form, and he's the one who killed Jeremy."

Jules looks confused. "I thought Jeremy left because of a family emergency."

"That was a cover story."

"Made up by who? Who's trying to cover this up? Does Steven know?"

"No," Ryan tells her. "Made up by the demons. They

can . . . influence people. Make them believe things that aren't true, or not see things that are right in front of them, or lots of other things. But since we were already suspicious from our past experiences with demons, we pretty much knew right away that something bad had happened to Jeremy."

"Your previous experiences . . . last year at school. With the librarian demon who wanted to marry Cyn's friend."

"He wanted to do a lot more than marry her," I say.

"Right," Ryan says. "I'm not as easily fooled by them anymore, because I know about them. And Cyn . . . has a special resistance. I'm still vulnerable to their powers when they direct them at me. Cyn is immune."

"Why is Cyn immune?"

"I'm just special," I say, not really wanting Ryan to tell her what the demons call my special resistant nature. "Born that way."

"But they can still hurt her physically. Especially when they're in their real demon forms. Which brings us to the third demon, the one who came back through the portal with Cyn last night."

Jules holds up a hand. "You guys keep talking about this portal like I should know what that means. Portal from where?"

"The demon world," I tell her. "It's a long story."

Ryan gives me an exasperated look. "Cyn made a deal with a demoness when we were trying to stop Mr. Gabriel. The demoness helped us in exchange for getting to borrow Cyn's special resistance three times. The first time happened last year, in the battle with Mr. Gabriel and the other demons, and led to the demoness becoming queen of the demons. The second time happened last night."

Okay, so it's not that long a story. I still don't see why she needs to know all the details.

"Demon world," Jules says, looking back and forth between us. "Like . . . hell? You went to hell?"

"Basically," I say, not really wanting to talk about it. "It's certainly not heaven, anyway."

"So," Ryan goes on, "somehow this other demon got into the portal with Cyn, and is now here. At camp. In demon form. As you saw, he is very big and scary."

"And strong," I add. "Very strong, according to Peter. Too strong for Peter to fight him physically."

Ryan looks at me. "Crap. That's not good."

"No kidding."

"But . . . but what do they want?" Jules asks, seeming to be struggling (understandably) to keep up. "Why did they come here?"

"So . . . the second demon, the one without a real body . . . he's apparently the same demon we fought last year," Ryan explains.

"The librarian."

"Correct."

"Who you said was dead."

"Yeah. We really thought he was."

"So he's still trying to kill you guys? And steal away Cyn's friend?"

"Yes."

Jules stands there, taking all of this in.

"This is a lot to take in," she says after a moment.

"Feel free to leave at any time," I tell her. "You do not need to be a part of this."

"Cyn," Ryan says, "maybe she can help. You have to admit we could use all the help we can get right now."

Oh, so now it's *we* again? I know I should be happy about that, but I'm having trouble feeling it. I hate that it ever stopped being *we* in the first place.

"How can she help? Is *she* going to fight Mr. Gabriel's brother?"

"I don't know! But if she wants to help, then we're going to let her. If I can get along with Peter, you can get along with Jules."

"Hey!" Jules says, offended. "You're putting me in the same category as a disguised demon that you're only *kind of* sure is not a bad guy?"

Personally I think the comparison is insulting to Peter, but I manage not to say this out loud. Ryan is right, I suppose. We do need all the help we can get. Although I can't imagine how Jules can possibly help. Unless we can use her as bait or something.

That idea cheers me up just a little.

"Okay, fine. But *does* she want to help? Have you explained that she might, you know, *die* if she tries to help?"

"Hey," she says. "Standing right here."

I turn to face her. "Okay. Are you sure you really want to get involved with this? People died last time when they got involved. I know you and Ryan have been summer besties since the dawn of time, but this really isn't your fight. If you stay out of it, you'll probably be fine."

"Like Jeremy was fine?"

She has a point there, I have to admit.

"Ryan," she says, turning away from me, "I can't just sit by while someone — something — tries to kill you. I mean, could you? If it were the other way around?"

"No," he says. "Of course not. But I would never forgive myself if something happened to you because I got you involved in this crazy mess."

This is getting way more touchy-feely than I am comfortable with.

"Okay, fine," I say. "Jules is in. Great. Welcome to the team. Now we just have to figure out what to do. Which is why we're going to meet up with Peter and ask him to summon Aaron, so we can ask the demoness for help again." I turn at Ryan's sharp intake of breath. "I do not want to hear it," I say, pointing right at his lovely, angry face. "We don't have any other options."

"But —"

"I know you hate that idea. I get it. But as much as I want you to help me, as much as I want desperately not to have to face this without you, I am not going to reject our best chance just to try to make you happy. This isn't me ignoring your advice. This is me just knowing what the right course is."

I wait while he decides how he's going to respond. Finally he just closes his mouth and nods once, resignedly.

We go to the loading-dock area of Blake, which is where Peter and I had agreed to meet up. Then we wait in silence, everyone thinking their own separate thoughts. I hope Ryan is thinking about how he should have been with me today, but I'm afraid he's thinking about Jules instead and how bad he feels for dragging her into this.

I don't know or care what Jules is thinking.

I'm thinking about how I'm going to tell Peter about Hector. But as soon as he arrives, it's clear he already knows.

"How did it happen?" he asks, standing in the doorway.

"I am so sorry, Peter," I say, getting up and going over to him. "Hector attacked Mr. Gabriel's brother when he came at me after I stopped him from killing Michael. I don't even know what Hector was doing there."

"I sent him," Peter says. "To watch over you, in case either of the demons tried anything. He wasn't supposed to try to take them on by himself, though. He never was very smart about making good judgment calls in the moment."

"He probably saved my life."

Peter half smiles. "See what I mean?" Then the smile fades. "Poor Hector. He was just starting to like working backstage, too."

I think about the paint smudge on his face and I want to cry.

"I'm so sorry," I say again. "I . . . I left him there. I wasn't sure what else to do."

Peter nods. "I'll take care of it. Tonight." He suddenly seems to realize what I said earlier. "Mr. Gabriel's brother tried to kill Michael?"

"Just a coincidence, I think. Mr. Gabriel arranged it — he

was there, too — but he didn't seem to know I had any connection to Michael until I referred to him by name." I feel my fists clenching. "I should have let them have him. He wasn't worth Hector."

"Don't go there. You couldn't have just let him die. And you didn't know Hector was watching." He looks toward the stage area. "Is Michael here? I should find him and make sure he doesn't remember what happened. I'm guessing he's already managed to not-remember on his own, but just in case . . ."

He seems to notice Ryan and Jules for the first time. "Huh. Everyone all friendly again?"

"Not really," I say before either of them can respond. "But they're going to help us if they can."

"Okay. Let's . . . let's go over to my bunk. Bunk three. Everyone will be at rehearsal or afternoon activities, so we should have the place to ourselves. I'll meet you there."

"I'll wait for you," I say quickly. I don't really want any more alone time with Ryan and Jules right now.

Ryan takes the hint. "Fine. We'll see you there." He and Jules head out through the loading-dock doors. I sit back down to wait, not watching them go.

Peter comes back in just a few minutes.

"All okay?" I ask.

"Yeah. He repressed that memory so fast I doubt it will even show up in his dreams. But I gave him a substitute memory to make sure. He thinks he just took a nice walk this afternoon and ran into a camper who talked his ear off about what a great director he is, but he can't quite remember who it was." He jerks his head toward the door. "Ready to go?

I nod and we head out.

"Are you going to be okay?" I ask him.

He sighs. "Yeah. I'll miss the big lug, though." His face hardens. "And bug-boy is sure as hell going to pay for what he did."

"How did you get hooked up with Hector in the first place? He doesn't . . . didn't really seem the musical-theater type."

Peter surprises me by laughing. "No, he certainly was not. He learned about demons from someone he met in the comics world. That was his thing — comics, graphic novels, superhero memorabilia. He summoned me the first time because he wanted some rare first edition."

"Really? That hardly seems worth making a deal with a demon."

He glances at me. "Hey, everyone has their passions, theater nerd. Don't judge."

"Sorry."

"Anyway, something about him kind of endeared him to me. I offered him an ongoing arrangement, keeping him in Comic Con passes and whatever else he wanted in exchange for him becoming my musical-theater source. It actually took some convincing; his only real experience with musical theater was *Spider-Man: Turn Off the Dark.*"

"Ouch."

"Yeah. But I explained that there's a lot of good musical theater out there, too, and anyway, he didn't have to like it, he just had to be my supplier. He came around, although he never truly got into enjoying it for himself. But we had a really good thing going there for a while."

We walk in silence for a few minutes. Then Peter asks, "So Ryan's still mad at you but helping us anyway?"

I don't really want to talk about it, but maybe Peter wants to be distracted from thinking about Hector.

"Yeah. He saw me coming back from my encounter with the evil demon brothers and came over to ask what happened. I suggested that maybe our personal issues were less important than people getting killed and stuff. He saw my point, apparently."

"What about Jules?"

"They seem to be a package deal at the moment," I say darkly. "Ryan pointed out that she was there when Little Brother came through the portal, and so he had to tell her what was happening, and he made the pretty valid argument that we could probably use all the help we can get. It's not like there was any chance of getting her unglued from his side, anyway."

"True," Peter says. He looks at me for a moment. "You're hoping we get the chance to use her as bait, aren't you?"

I stare at him. "Can you read my mind? Is that a thing? That had better not be a thing, Peter. If you could read my mind all this time and didn't tell me . . ."

He laughs. "No. I swear. I can't read your mind. But it's pretty obvious how you feel about her."

I shrug angrily. "They have this whole history I know nothing about. And she loves to point out how much longer she's known him than I have. And since the fight, she's gotten ridiculously protective, like it's her job to make sure I never hurt him again. But *I'm* his girlfriend. Or I think I still am, anyway. And so in theory, at least, I'm the closest one to him now, and she must hate that a lot."

"And you hate that he's got a close female friend who is beautiful and talented and has known him a lot longer than you."

"Yeah."

He nudges me with his elbow. "Want to try to make him jealous?"

"What?"

"Come on. We can totally do it. It would be fun." He steps in front of me and looks into my eyes. "Don't you remember how nice it was to kiss me?"

"No!"

"No?" He leans closer. "Do you want me to remind you?"

I push him away. "No! Will you *stop* that?"

He grins. "Probably not," he says. "I may not be evil, but that doesn't mean I'm a saint." He looks at me a moment more, his smile changing into something slightly less impish. "Did you really have a dream about me?"

"Never mind," I say firmly.

"Ah. I'll take that as a yes. I hope it was a good dream. I bet it was."

"*Shut up,*" I hiss at him. "You are never ever to mention that again. Ever."

"Or what?"

"Or I will find a way to make you sorry. I swear it."

"Okay, okay. Sorry. It's just so hard to resist. Plus, I like thinking about it. And I like the way your face looks when I make you think about it."

"My face doesn't look like anything. And I'm not thinking about it. And speaking of my face, is this rash ever going to go away?"

"Hmm," he says. He reaches toward me but I jerk back out of range. "Oh, relax. I'm just trying to look at it. Hold still."

I do. I feel another of those tiny delicious shocks when he touches me, but I try very hard to pretend that I don't.

"I . . . think so. I think it will fade over time. It must be a physical reaction, since his essence shouldn't be able to affect you. But then, he did get into your dream. . . ."

I stop walking. "That didn't even occur to me. What does that mean? Could . . . could my resistance be wearing off?"

"No," Peter says. I'm immensely comforted by how sure he sounds. "If you're a super-roach, you're one for life. But . . . hmm."

"*Hmm*? What hmm?"

"I'm not sure. Just trying to sort out what your ability protects you from and what it doesn't."

I think about this. "He was able to use his powers on me when I let him," I say slowly, never really having reasoned this out before. "The halo thing, for example, when he did whatever he did to my eyes that makes me able to see them. I mean I didn't exactly *let* him, Principal Kingston was holding my arms, but . . . I had agreed to help him collect the other demons, and that was part of it. . . ."

"That makes sense," Peter says. "You'd opened yourself up in that specific case, so that allowed him access."

"But I didn't let him do this!" I protest, pointing to my rash. "And I certainly didn't invite him into my dreams."

"No . . ." Peter says, pushing up his glasses. "But dreams are . . . tricky. Maybe, on some level, your subconscious mind was open to him. If you were already dreaming about demons, for example, which would be understandable, maybe he could have used that as an entryway somehow."

He is making my brain hurt again. "Well, crap," I say. "How do I get my subconscious to keep him out?"

"I don't know," he says apologetically. "I think . . . I need to think about it some more."

"Well, share whatever you figure out, please. I need to know that kind of stuff."

"Yes, ma'am." He gives me a little salute.

We finally reach his bunk and head inside. Ryan and Jules are sitting beside each other on one of the beds. Just sitting.

"Okay," I start right in, wanting to get down to business. "I think we're all up to speed on recent events, yes? So the question has been what to do next. Unless anyone has a better idea, I think we should try to contact the demoness to ask for help with our evil-demon-brothers situation. I guess the first thing is to make sure we can even do that — contact her, I mean. But you said you've been in contact with Aaron before, right, Peter?"

"Yes. I can summon Aaron. I can't summon her, though. It would take a lot more power than I'm capable of to call up the demon queen in a containment circle."

"That should be enough," I say. "If we can get to Aaron, we

can ask him to ask her. Or, if necessary, to take me down there again to ask her in person."

Ryan makes an unhappy noise at this. I am tempted to make some unhappy noises myself.

"Sounds like a plan," Peter says. "Should I go ahead and do it right now?"

I look at Peter, surprised. "Can you? You don't need to . . . prepare or something? Aaron said . . ."

Peter rolls his eyes. "*Aaron.* Aaron likes to make a big production. Also he probably wanted to fix his hair or something first."

Ryan and I both burst out laughing. Because, of course, he did.

Our eyes meet, and just for a second, in our shared moment of memory and amusement, I forget that anything is wrong. I love the way his eyes crinkle when he laughs. It feels like ages since I saw him do that.

Then Jules opens her mouth, ruining it. "What's so funny?" she asks, looking back and forth between us. Ryan makes what is clearly a never-mind-you-kind-of-had-to-be-there gesture. She looks annoyed, which I am pleased about.

"Classic Aaron," Peter goes on, smirking. "No, none of that stuff is really necessary. I mean, to be safe, sure, you do want to make a containment circle, but you can do that with anything, really."

With no further preamble, he gets up and traces a large circle on the ground with his finger. A glowing ring of red energy follows the arc traced by his hand.

"Don't you need chalk or something?" Ryan asks.

"He's using his own demon energy," I tell him. "I can see it."

Peter nods and keeps working on his task. When the circle is done, he sits down and closes his eyes for a minute. We all wait, silently.

Suddenly Aaron appears in the middle of the circle.

"*There* you are!" he says, sounding relieved. "Thank God. We've been trying to contact you, but the queen's enemies are interfering. You guys are in serious trouble up here."

Chapter | 12

We all take a minute to recover.

"Uh, yeah," I say, finally. "No kidding."

Aaron pauses. "What do you already know?"

"We know that Mr. Gabriel is back. Oh, and that the demon that followed me up here is his horrible brother."

"Okay." Aaron nods. "So that's the first part."

"There's *more*?" Ryan asks.

Aaron suddenly notices Jules, who I notice has moved closer to Ryan since Aaron appeared. "Who's this?" He looks back and forth between me and Ryan. "Did you guys break up?"

"That's Jules," Peter explains, irritatingly, before I can hear how Ryan might have chosen to answer Aaron's question. I bet he did that on purpose. "She's . . . an old friend of Ryan's."

"Ah," Aaron says. He shares a knowing look with Peter that I don't like one bit.

"Anyway!" I break in. "You were saying?"

"Right," Aaron says. "So, everything that's been happening downside — the trouble that made my mistress call upon you in the first place, the demons that chased us, the chaos that's going on down there now — all of that was orchestrated by your Mr. Gabriel. Well, and his brother, but if you've met him, then you're probably pretty clear on who the brains of the operation must be."

"Yeah," Peter and I say together.

"Gabriel has apparently been stirring up trouble and gaining followers with the help of his brother for the past few months," Aaron continues. "He found out about Peter's little stowaway maneuver and realized he could use the tether to follow Peter to you, Cyn. And meanwhile, his supporters kept their forces moving against the queen, and Gabriel knew she'd call you when things got bad enough. And he made sure his brother would be ready to come back with you when she did."

"But . . ." I am trying to catch up with all of this very-far-in-advance planning. "Why didn't he just wait until he could get another body or whatever? And come back for real? Right now he's only sort of here and can't take over anyone for more than a few minutes at a time."

"He's a little impatient to get his revenge," Aaron says. "And I can only assume that since Peter provided such a convenient opportunity, he wanted to take advantage of it while he had the chance, and then worry about the other part later."

Peter has the grace to look chagrined. "Sorry," he mouths at me.

"Anyway, we're pretty sure he's just going to take his

brother's body and then work on adapting that into whatever he wants it to be, over time."

"But . . . then what happens to his brother?" I ask.

"Either he stays trapped in there underneath, or he gets pushed out and won't have a body anymore."

"And he's okay with this?"

Aaron laughs. "I doubt it. But from what I understand, Gabriel always was kind of an asshole big brother."

"Then why is his little brother *helping* him?" Jules asks. "This doesn't make any sense."

"You obviously don't have anyone maniacally evil in your life," Aaron tells her. "You don't really say no to someone like that. Not when he's about a zillion times stronger than you are."

"Cyn did," Jules says, which is such an unexpectedly complimentary thing for her to say that I don't even know what to do with it.

"Well, Cyn is blinded by love and loyalty," Aaron says, as if I'm not standing right there. "Also, she's got that roach thing."

Jules looks at me. "*Roach* thing?"

Thanks, Aaron. To Jules I explain, "That's what the demons call my resistance. I'm a super-roach. As compared to all you regular roaches, I will just point out." I sigh and add, "They think it's hilarious."

"*Anyway,*" Aaron says. "We have a plan, if you want to hear it."

"Why are you helping us?" Ryan asks suspiciously.

"Look," Aaron says. He sits down in the middle of the (to my eyes) glowing circle. "We all have the same goal here. To stop Mr. Gabriel. If he succeeds in regaining physical form and returns to our world with a body and a human consort, he can try to kill the queen and take the rule from her."

"Why is that even allowed?" I ask. "I mean, he lost, fair and square! He shouldn't get another chance."

"It's the *demon world*," Aaron says. "They aren't very big on fair and square. Certain things are frowned upon, but generally if you can get away with something, then that's that."

"I will never understand why you want to live there."

"*Anyway,*" Ryan says. "The plan?"

"Right. Basically, if you guys can force him back down here, we can set a trap and be ready for him."

"And how are we supposed to do that?" Jules asks.

"First, you have to reestablish the tether."

"What?" Peter and I ask together.

"If you re-create the tether," Aaron goes on, "you can force Mr. Gabriel back through it. It's not really gone, you see. It's just . . . in a few pieces. You only need to stitch them back together."

"But I don't want to stitch them back together," Peter says. "I want to be free!"

"Yeah, yeah," Aaron says. "And you will be. You can cut it again afterward, and my mistress will grant you an official ticket out so you won't have to worry about being dragged back ever again. Satisfactory?"

"Oh," Peter says, sitting back. "That's — yes. Definitely yes."

"Thought so," Aaron says, a little smugly.

"But . . . but . . . how do we force him back?" I ask. "And what do we do about his brother in the meantime?"

"Okay, so it's kind of a multipart plan," Aaron says. "First, you have to re-form the tether, like I said. Then you kind of have to wait for Gabriel to take over his brother's body and attack you. Then, you need to kill or hurt the body enough that Gabriel is forced to flee or risk being killed along with it. Then, at the moment that he flees the body, you will use a—I know you love these, Cyn—special magic item that my mistress will give you to force him back into the tether and into the demon world. And then we'll take it from there."

We all sit there staring at him.

"What?" he says finally.

"That's the plan?" Ryan says. "That's not a plan, it's a suicide mission."

"How are we supposed to hurt the brother's body once Mr. Gabriel takes it over?" I ask. "You have *seen* that thing, right?"

Aaron turns to look at Peter.

The rest of us turn to look at Peter, too.

Peter looks back at us like we're nuts. "Um, Cyn, do you remember how I had trouble just holding him back for a few seconds last night? In fact, I believe I distinctly said that I could *not* take him in a fight. I have not grown miraculously stronger since then."

"Cyn will have to lend you her power," Aaron says. "That will protect you from demon energy attacks."

"But what about his giant legs and those pincer things?" Peter asks. "I'm honestly more concerned about those."

"My mistress is willing to send you a gift of strength," Aaron says.

"She's going to lend me her strength?" Peter says, obviously impressed.

"No. Not hers. The strength of some . . . volunteers. It should be more than enough."

I study Aaron for a moment. "She really wants this taken care of, huh?" I ask.

"Yes."

"Enough to release me from my third visit?"

I see Ryan perk up with interest at this idea.

"No." Aaron looks at me seriously. "Do not try to weasel out of a previously made deal, Cyn. That is seriously bad form. I'm not even going to tell her you said that, because she would be very annoyed about it."

"I'm not trying to weasel out of anything! This would be a new deal!"

"No. It's not remotely an option. She is granting you a lot of help, without, I must point out, asking anything in return other than your cooperation with the plan. You're lucky that your goals align with hers right now, or you could be granting her another ten trips in return for her assistance."

Bah. Well, it was worth a try.

"*Anyway*," Peter says, trying to rescue the conversation from this latest tangent. "When is she going to give us these magical items and gifts of strength? Because I don't know how much time we'll have before Mr. Gabriel and his brother decide to make their move."

"Three days," Aaron says.

"That's too long," I say at once.

Peter nods emphatically. "A lot of bad things can happen in three days."

"Three days," Aaron says again, unruffled. "She has to finish getting everything ready. And in the meantime you need to reestablish the tether anyway."

"Which we do by . . . ?" I ask.

"I'll show Peter how," Aaron says. "It's not really very complicated. But Mr. Gabriel will know when I do it."

"Which means he will know we are up to something," Peter says.

"Which might provoke him to attack," I say. "So we shouldn't do it until we have the gifts from the demoness."

Jules has been following all this mostly silently. Now she raises her hand. "What happens if Peter can't hurt the brother enough to make Mr. Gabriel jump ship?"

Aaron cocks his head. "Then you'll all die, most likely. Gabriel will kill you all, maybe everyone else at camp, too, then go after Cyn's friend Annie, and then head home to take on the demoness."

"What's stopping him from going after Annie now?" I ask. "I mean, what's keeping him here at camp with us?"

"He can't travel very fast or far without a body," Aaron says. "In theory, he could jump from body to body until he got there, but he'd have to keep killing people to gather enough strength to keep going, and eventually the trail of bodies would add up and draw way too much attention. And then when he got to your friend, he probably wouldn't be strong enough to subdue her, anyway. She'll fight him this time, knowing what he is, and he'll be weak. No, he's got to take care of you first, secure his brother's body as his own, then go after Annie."

"Why doesn't he just take his brother's body right now, then?" Ryan asks. "What's he waiting for?"

"He needs a little more strength for that, too," Aaron says. "His brother will probably fight him once he realizes Mr. Gabriel doesn't intend to share."

"Which means he's going to keep killing people," I say. "Because that's how he gets stronger?"

"Yup," Aaron says. "You'll probably hear about some more family emergencies and things. Maybe a water-ski accident, someone busted for drugs and sent home . . ."

"We can't just wait around while he does that!" I feel Aaron should not really need this pointed out. "Tell the demoness to give us those gifts now so we can get this over with. We can't let more people die, and we certainly don't want to let him get any stronger, anyway!"

"*Three days*," he says again. Then he stands up. "Now if you'll excuse me, we're still dealing with your evil librarian's loyal faction down there. I need to get back."

"Will you be able to get up here again to bring us the magic stuff?" Ryan asks. "You seemed to be having trouble finding us before."

Aaron smacks himself on the forehead. "Right! Almost forgot." He turns to Peter. "Summon me again on the night of the third day."

With that he vanishes, and the glowing circle winks out.

"So . . . now what?" Jules asks.

214

"Now we wait," I say glumly. "I hate the waiting part."

"I hate the part where I have to fight the giant demon," Peter says. "Waiting seems kind of okay compared to that."

It's just about time for the next afternoon session, so we all head to where we're supposed to be. It would be bad to get kicked out of camp for not participating or whatever right about now.

At dinner, Belinda rushes over with new gossip to share. "Did you hear about Jessica? The counselor for bunk eight? She got busted for drugs and sent home!"

Ryan and Jules and I all look at one another, then stop before we look suspicious. Belinda darts off to the next table.

Another dead innocent bystander.

I hope the demoness hurries the hell up down there.

After dinner, Ryan asks me to take a walk with him. He must have prearranged this with Jules, since she doesn't try to tag along. We leave the dining hall and head out alone together along the path. By mutual unspoken agreement, we stay within the well-lit areas of the main campus.

I'm feeling way too many feelings to possibly sort them all out. I do know that I'm scared of what Ryan is going to say. And that I'm hurt by how he completely turned his back on me when I needed him. But there's also a lot of guilt and some anger and some jealousy all mixed up confusingly with love and longing and affection and pain. I desperately want things to be all right between us again, but given the events of the past couple of days, I'm having trouble picturing what "all right" would even look like.

215

"I'm sorry you had to go through everything today on your own," he says once the noise from the dining hall starts to fade behind us. We're walking side by side, inches apart. Miles. Not even close to touching. "I really am. I'm sorry I wasn't there with you when you found out about Mr. Gabriel. That's . . . a lot to deal with. Especially by yourself."

This sounds like just the introduction to what he really wants to say, so I remain silent and wait to hear the rest.

"I think you can understand why I was so upset with you, though, right?" He shakes his head, stops, turns to face me. "How could you not tell me?"

Ah, the million-dollar question.

"I . . . I don't know," I say slowly. "At first, I couldn't tell you because you were already so unsettled about the demoness and didn't want me to go after Annie, and I just didn't want to add any more problems to the ones we already had. And then . . . and then things were so good, after. Everything was so good and nice and I didn't want to screw it up. And I kept thinking, maybe it wouldn't ever need to happen, anyway. Maybe she'd forget that humans have short lives, or maybe at least it wouldn't happen until I was old or something. I never thought it would happen again so soon. And . . . I know you probably won't believe this, but I was actually just about to tell you when Aaron showed up. I hated keeping it from you, and when I realized demon stuff was starting to happen again, I decided I *had* to tell you, even if it made you really mad at me. And then right after you told me the story of *The Scarlet Pimpernel,* I literally thought in my head, okay, this is the moment, this is when I should tell him.

And then stupid Aaron appeared and ruined everything. And then Peter told you the rest while I was gone, and I lost my chance."

He's quiet again, and I make myself wait and not just keep talking in hope that I'll stumble upon the right thing to say to make him forgive me.

"I can understand some of that," he says. "But . . ." He stops, then starts again. "The last several months, I've felt so close to you. Closer than I've ever felt to anyone. And then to find out, after everything we went through together, after everything we shared, that you were keeping something that huge from me . . ." He shakes his head again. "Would you have told me if Aaron had shown up sometime during the spring semester? Or would you have gone off to the demon world without even letting me know what was going on?"

"I'm sure I would have told you," I say. I can hear Old Cyn raising her eyebrows in my brain, and I can't say this is unjustified. I'm not at all sure, not really.

"Are you?" Ryan asks. Maybe he can hear Old Cyn's eyebrows, too. "God, Cyn. What if you went without telling me, and something happened and you never came back? Just disappeared forever, without a word?"

"But that didn't happen. You can't be mad at me for something that didn't even happen. I screwed up, yes, I should have told you, but you can't start going down roads of imaginary scenarios and then add them to the reasons that you're mad. That's not fair."

"I'm not sure you get to tell me what's fair," he says. "I'm telling you how I feel, and part of that is based on all of those imaginary scenarios. Because they could have happened if things had gone differently. And apparently you never even gave that any thought."

"I was trying not to think about it at all!" I know this isn't the time for counterarguments; I should just be sorry and acknowledge how much I hurt him. But I can't seem to stop myself. "Going down there was *terrifying*. I will never be able to explain to you how terrified I was. And to know that I had to go back . . . You're right, I didn't sit around thinking about all the ways it could go wrong. I just tried *not* to think about it, because it was terrifying and awful and I didn't want it to be true. And, yes, maybe that was irresponsible. But I didn't do it intentionally to hurt you, and I think you should give me that much credit."

He sighs. "I know. I know you weren't intentionally trying to hurt me. But . . . I also know you have a tendency to decide what's best for other people as though you have some right to do that. And I don't like feeling like you might do that to me again. I need to have all the information and be able to make my own decisions."

"What are you talking about?"

He gives me a look. "You decided it was best for me not to know about your deal with the demoness. You decided it was best to go to see Aaron that second time without me and not even tell me you were going. You decided to make a deal with *the very evil librarian* without telling me about that, either. Which, may I remind you, almost got me killed."

That's quite a list. I didn't realize he'd been keeping score.

He stops and studies my face. "And I'm guessing you've

already decided not to tell Annie about Mr. Gabriel still being alive. Am I right about that?"

In other circumstances I would be thrilled to realize he knows me so well. But not now. I look away, unable to keep meeting his eyes.

He sighs again, unhappily. "You can't keep doing this, Cyn. How do you know it's best not to tell her? Who are you to make that call? Maybe you should trust your friends to decide these things for themselves."

I reflect silently on this for a minute.

"Okay," I say finally. "I know you're right about not telling you about the demoness. And I swear, I *swear*, I will not keep anything like that from you ever again. But I'm right about not telling Annie about Mr. Gabriel. You didn't see her down there when I went to rescue her, Ryan. Once the blinders came off and she really understood what was happening . . . she was out of her mind with fear. She's still scared, at least a little, all the time. It's taken her so long to relax enough to let William get close to her, so long to stop jumping at every shadow . . . I can't put her through that again. Not if there's a chance I don't have to."

"There might not be a chance," Ryan says.

"But there *might*. If we start to think there's really no chance at all, then I'll tell her. I promise. But not before. I'm not wrong about that. I'm not."

He falls silent again.

"Listen," I tell him. "This, this conversation right now, this isn't about Annie. This is about us. And I promise I will trust you to have all the information from now on." *Except for the kissing of Peter. Which does not apply.* I take a breath. "Is that going to be good enough or not?"

He takes a very long time to answer me. My heart passes the time by folding itself into tiny, jagged origami shapes inside my chest. I feel it stretching paper-thin, twisting and folding again and again into smaller and more awful contortions as I wait and wait and wait. I try to stand very still and not jostle it. Too much danger of ripping it apart entirely.

"I think so," he says at last. I continue my practice of stillness and non-jostling as he continues. "I want to say yes, but I'm trying to be completely honest. It . . . it might take some time for me to feel like I can trust you again. You kept me in the dark for a really long time. I can't just let that go with a snap of my fingers."

He stops. It's my turn to talk now. I force myself to let my lungs and throat muscles move enough to do so.

"I understand." And I do. But it still sucks. I suddenly find it impossible to look at him. I look down and study some of the very interesting rocks at the edge of the path instead.

"Cyn, I really wish I could say that we're okay again —"

"But we're not. I get it." I keep my eyes on the ground.

"Hey." He reaches over and lifts my chin up until I raise my eyes. "Not *yet*. No giving up, remember? I just need some more time."

"Okay." And then I make myself ask the next question, although I can only get it to come out as a whisper. "Am I still your girlfriend?"

"Yes," he says at once, and my heart unfolds, just a little. "Of course you are. And no more of this stupid avoiding each other or anything else. For one thing, we have to work together on this demon business. And for another . . . I missed you today. I hate feeling like things are screwed up between us."

"But we can't just pretend everything's back to normal when it's not."

He smiles. "When has anything ever been normal since we first met?"

I manage a weak half smile in response. "Good point."

"I think," he says, "we should go back to spending as much time as we can together and try to get past this. Okay?"

"Okay." *Try* to get past this. Because he still hasn't really forgiven me, and so there is still a thing to get past. Which I really do understand, and yet . . . I hate it. Because there's nothing I can do about it. All I can do is wait for him to feel he can trust me again.

You can not lie to him anymore, Old Cyn says. *That would be a start.*

True. And I won't.

Except about Peter.

Right.

I hear her eyebrows go up again, but I ignore them. Instead, I take Ryan's hand to see if he'll let me.

He does.

My heart unfolds a little bit more.

While we are waiting for Aaron's three days to go by, there are two more counselors with "family emergencies," and one camper who had some kind of nervous breakdown and had to leave.

That last one might be real and not a demon cover-up; some kids take theater camp very seriously.

Mr. Gabriel continues to visit me in my dreams, and every once in a while, someone I don't know winks or smiles at me as I walk by, making me sure it's Mr. Gabriel temporarily using someone's body to do some bad thing or other. It kills me to just stand by and let him, but there's nothing I can do until we're ready.

Peter continues to make appearances in my dreams as well. But I just do my best to pretend that's not happening.

And in the meantime, it's the start of performance week. They don't have regular tech week here; there's one tech rehearsal, one dress rehearsal, and then three performances. The shows are staggered so that everyone is able to see all the other shows in their camp section (Lower, Middle, and Upper). I have written back to the girls, telling them how excited I am that they're coming, and suggesting they wait for the final performance, since we'll probably have ironed out all the kinks by then. I am still resolved to not tell Annie what's going on. She sounds so happy in her letters and e-mails. There has been kissing with William, and he is officially her boyfriend, and Leticia and Diane are teasing her just enough to let her know they care but not so much that she's actually uncomfortable about it. (They have admirable finesse in this area from years and years of practice.)

I have kept my communiqués to Annie light and full of stuff about the shows and Ryan (only good things) and Jules (only bad things). I mention Peter only as smart and talented and not as attractive or liking me or having successfully seduced my subconscious mind or being a demon.

And although I know there are bigger and more important things going on right now . . . I can't help but notice that the shows are shaping up to be really good. Well, I don't know much about the plays or *How to Succeed* . . . or *Brigadoon,* but Susan says *West Side Story* is "incredible" (this from the girl whose initial reaction to getting into the *West Side Story* pit was a shrug), and I've seen firsthand how the actors are doing Peter's show every kind of justice. I try not to think too much about how all of these talented people might become dead very soon if we don't manage to make Aaron's plan work like it's supposed to. Or how any one of them could become dead before then if they are in the wrong place at the wrong time and Mr. Gabriel kills them.

I especially try not to think about the few who are already dead.

I peek in once or twice at *Scarlet Pimpernel* rehearsals, and that one will probably be the best show of all, at least in terms of performances. As much as it pains me to say it, Jules is excellent as Marguerite. I hate watching her onstage with Ryan, but I take comfort in the fact that he's not actually her love interest in the show, and she ends up with Percy (her husband), and Chauvelin ends up alone, so I can have him back when the show is over.

Well, probably.

Ryan is, as should go without saying by now, beyond amazing. I could watch and listen to him sing "Falcon in the Dive" all day long.

Except I can't, since I need to help backstage at my own

show. I'm not running the actual crew this time; there's a separate show-crew group in charge of that. My job is just the design and construction of the set, and I'll help backstage but won't have nearly as much responsibility as I did for *Sweeney*. That's okay, though. The set design was the part I was really excited about, and I think it turned out really, really well. Now that construction is finished except for a few last tweaks and paint jobs, I've spent a couple of rehearsals watching from the audience, and I can't even describe the awesomeness of watching the actors doing their thing in the environment I created for them.

When the evening of the third day finally arrives, I am both relieved and newly terrified. Although Peter has the most terrifying job of all, really. I only have to deal with Mr. Gabriel in spirit form, which I anticipate being a lot less horrible and scary than dealing with both brothers in that spider-monster body.

We all meet out in the woods that night for Peter's late-night summoning of Aaron. (He can't do it in his bunk at this time of night, since the rest of his bunkmates are in there, of course.)

Aaron doesn't waste any time; things are apparently still hot and heavy back at home. He quickly explains to Peter how to re-create the tether, then gives him what looks for all the world like lemon-lime Gatorade in a fancy bottle, telling him to drink it just before he's ready to fight Team Gabriel. Then he turns to me.

"This is what you must use to force Mr. Gabriel back into the tether." He hands me a folding Japanese fan like the kind they use in *The Mikado*.

I look at it sadly. I'm not sure why I expected anything more impressive. "It's not going to turn into anything else when the time comes, is it?"

"Nope. That's it. But trust me, it will work."

"So I just . . . *fan* him with it?"

"Yes. But, you know, vigorously. And don't stop once you've started, until Peter tells you that Gabriel's fled back down to the demon world. Peter's the only one who will be able to tell."

"Is Cyn the only one who can use the fan?" Jules asks. "I mean, in case something happens to her. Could Ryan or I take over?"

"Thanks for the vote of confidence, Jules."

"Hey, I'm just trying to be prepared!"

"That's a good question," Aaron says. "I didn't think to ask. I kind of just thought of it as Cyn's job, since she's the one he's after most of all." He thinks for a moment. "I would say, if Cyn dies or something, go ahead and give the fan a try. Can't hurt!"

This is not very comforting to anyone, but it seems to be all Aaron has time for.

"Good luck, you guys! Hopefully I'll be seeing you all again at some point, and everyone will still have all their limbs and organs and heads and things."

He vanishes, and we all go back to our bunks.

Shockingly, I have extra trouble trying to fall asleep.

Peter is reestablishing the tether right now. He may already have done it. Which means Mr. Gabriel will be able to feel it. Which means I will surely get another visit from him tonight in my dreams. A not-especially-happy visit, I imagine. He likes it when we are cowering in fear and uncertain what to do. He is less excited about evidence of organized action against him.

I consider staying awake all night, but if the fighting is going to happen tomorrow at some point, I should probably try not to be exhausted. I try counting sheep and reciting song lyrics backward in my head. Then I just curl up on my side and pretend Ryan is there with his arms around me, telling me everything will be okay.

That's what finally does the trick.

But I was right about Mr. Gabriel.

He's there right away, no preamble, no fancy set pieces. Just his angry handsome face, hanging in the air before me.

"I know what you're doing," he says. "It's not going to work."

"Okay," I say. "Thanks for letting me know."

"Don't be fresh with me," he says, and now he's got arms in addition to a head, because he's grabbing me and holding me in place. The rash has finally started to fade; I really hope he's not going to lick me again.

"Why can't you just leave us alone?" I ask.

"You know why," he whispers. His face is close to mine, like Peter's was in my first dream about him, his breath tickling my neck, but there's nothing erotic about this. He's hurting me with his grip and he smells like death and his skin is rough and scalding. "You took something that belonged to me."

"Annie did not belong to you!" I struggle hard enough to

push him away, which seems to startle him. "Why does it have to be her, anyway? Go find yourself someone else! Find yourself someone who *wants* to be a demon's consort. Like Aaron! He can't be the only insane person with a demon fetish out there."

"It has to be Annie. We were in love until you ruined it. I still love her. I want her. I don't want anyone else."

"You don't *love* her, you psychopath. You're just obsessed with her because you can't have her. It's really a very big difference. Maybe you should find yourself a therapist. Do they have those in the demon world?"

He growls and lunges at me, but I manage to move out of his way.

"You seem a little off your game tonight," I tell him. "Everything okay?"

"Mock me while you can," he says. I notice he doesn't try to lunge at me again. "Tomorrow you will regret every last word."

"Well, I guess we'll have to see, won't we?" I sound a lot braver than I feel. But really, what's the risk? If he wins, he's going to torture and kill me no matter what. I doubt I can do anything to make it worse at this point.

He vanishes, and I spend an uncomfortably long, lucid time waiting for him to return before the dream fades into something else and I'm back in normal sleep and dreaming mode again.

I get up early and shower before breakfast, just in case I don't have time later. I don't want to be dirty when everything goes down. I know that doesn't make any sense, but I always feel more ready to face things when I'm clean and have washed my hair. I even wear my special power-red underwear that I usually save for opening nights.

Look, sometimes that kind of thing really makes a difference in your confidence level. Don't judge me.

No one seems to have much of an appetite at breakfast, but everyone eats anyway. And then we all go off to rehearsal. It's the last day before tech starts, and we can't just sit around waiting for Mr. Gabriel and his brother to attack. And we're all pretty sure it won't happen until tonight. It's just hard to imagine fighting an enormous raging spider-bull-bug possessed by the spirit of his evil librarian big brother in the middle of the bright and sunny afternoon.

I'm so lost in my own worried thoughts on the way to Blake that it takes me a while to realize someone is calling my name.

Several someones.

No time for origami this time. My heart shrivels instantly into a tiny little ball of panic inside me.

I know those voices.

I turn around.

Annie and Leticia and Diane. And William. They are running up the hill behind me.

"Surprise!" Annie shouts, literally skipping with excitement. "We're early!!"

Chapter | 13

"What . . . what are you *doing* here?"

Annie reaches me and throws her arms around me, nearly knocking me to the ground. "We wanted to surprise you! We're staying at a place in town and figured we'll see a little of the area while we're waiting for opening night. But we wanted to come see you right away, obviously."

She finally notices that I am not returning her happy embrace. "What's wrong, Cyn? Are you okay?"

I don't know what to do. I don't want to tell her. But I don't want to lie to her. But I am not at all prepared for this moment and everyone is staring at me and I have to say something.

"Cyn?" Diane says, coming closer. "What's going on?" Leticia is right beside her. William hangs back, clearly confused by the unanticipated awkwardness of this reunion.

"Okay," I tell them. "First, you are all awesome and lovely, and under different circumstances I would be ecstatic that you came up early to surprise me. Really. But . . . there are some not-so-good things happening here right now." I look around, then take Annie's hand. "Come with me. I'll explain . . . what I can, but not here."

Annie's face has gone very pale. She's the only one who has some idea what kind of not-so-good things I might be referring to.

I lead them all to bunk 6; no one else should be there right now, since everyone is supposed to be at their morning activities. I wonder if all the sneaking around and skipping things that we've been doing has been successful because the demons have made everyone not notice a lot of things or if camp counselors are always this inattentive. I'll have to ask Ryan. Someday. If we survive long enough.

Annie, Diane, and Leticia sit on my bed. William and I sit on the floor facing them. William looks very uncomfortable. I reach over and pat his arm.

"Hey, William. It's good to see you. I apologize for all of the crazy that I am about to share."

"Um. Okay." He looks at Annie, then back at me. "Thanks?"

Annie is still sitting silently, eyes fixed on me with a heartbreaking mix of hope and fear. Leticia and Diane look nearly as confused as William. I can't believe I'm about to tell them what I'm about to tell them, but I don't see any other choice. Now that they're here . . . keeping them in the dark would be unfair. More than unfair. Possibly fatal. Of course, telling them won't necessarily save them from dying, but at least they'll know what's going on. Maybe it will reduce the amount of time they spend in paralyzed disbelief later, when things start happening. That could be important.

I take a breath and begin, looking at L&D. "So, remember all that stuff with Mr. Gabriel last fall?"

"Cyn," Annie says. "Are you sure?"

"I think we have to tell them," I say. "I don't think we have a choice anymore."

"Tell us what?" Leticia says, looking back and forth between us. "You guys are seriously starting to freak me out."

Annie gets up abruptly and comes to sit on the floor on the other side of William, taking his hand and holding it in her lap. He gives her a reassuring smile, and I am filled with gratitude for him. Annie deserves someone like that.

"This is all going to sound crazy. I'll just say that up front. But here goes. Okay. So, Mr. Gabriel was not just a creepy librarian trying to have an inappropriate relationship with our Annie." I look at her apologetically. She surely hasn't told William any of this. "I mean, he was that, too, but not just that. He —"

Suddenly there is a . . . feeling, in the room. Before I can pinpoint where it's coming from, William shifts beside me, and when he speaks, his voice is not his own.

"Now, Cynthia," he purrs, "you know it's not very nice to talk about people behind their backs."

Annie's head whips toward him. She knows the cadence of that voice as well as I do.

"No . . ." she whispers. She starts trying to pull her hand away from him. "Cyn, you said he wasn't, you promised . . ."

"It's not William!" I tell her urgently. "It's not him, Annie, do you hear me? It's . . ." Oh, God, this isn't going to be any better, but I can tell she already knows. "It's . . ."

"She knows who it is," Mr. Gabriel/William says, reaching out to touch her face with his free hand. "Don't you, my love?"

Annie screams and jerks away, trying desperately to get free. He grabs her by the hair and pulls her back. "Aren't you happy to see me?" There's an edge of anger in his voice now. "I've been working very hard to get back to you. The least you could do is show me that you've missed me." He gives her head a violent shake and pulls her closer to him. She's still screaming, pushing at him, trying to scramble back along the floor, her eyes as wide and white as I have ever seen them.

Leticia and Diane seem frozen in shock. I am, too, momentarily, but not for long. The sight of Annie back in that place of helpless terror . . . I can't bear it. I can't. I throw myself at Mr. Gabriel/William, knocking him away from her and back onto the floor. Annie screams again as his hand rips out some of her hair when I force it free.

"*Get out!*" I scream into his face, climbing on top of him to pin him to the ground. "Get out and don't you dare touch her again, you bastard! I will kill you, do you hear me?" He struggles to rise but I am filled with furious strength and I slam him back against the floor. "*I'm going to rip your fucking heart out and you will never ever touch her ever again!*"

And when I slam him down again this time, something flows out of me, some energy from deep in my soul, and it knocks him back again in a wave of invisible power. And suddenly he's gone. And it's only William there beneath me, looking confused and terrified and in pain.

I roll off him and sit back on the floor, feeling spent and a little like I might throw up. Annie is sobbing. William sits up and stares at me, then down at his hand, which is still holding a chunk of Annie's brown curls.

"What . . ." He swallows and tries again. "What just happened?"

Leticia is finally able to move and slides down next to Annie, wrapping her arms around her. "It's okay, honey. It's okay. Shh. It's okay."

Diane, still sitting up on my bed, clears her throat. "Cyn? You were, um, saying?"

I hold up a hand. "Wait."

"But—"

"Please, just . . . I need a second." I need a lot more than a second, but I know I don't have that luxury right now. I want to figure out what just happened. I pushed Mr. Gabriel out of William somehow; that much is clear. Is it possible my roachiness can be used as a weapon? Although I'm not sure I actually hurt him. I just . . . pushed him out. I'm pretty certain my resistance means he can't possess me. And surely what I felt flowing out of me and into William just now was some aspect of that resistance. What else could it have been? Mr. Gabriel said I couldn't share my power with Michael to protect him . . . but Mr. Gabriel is sometimes a very big fat liar.

Maybe . . . maybe I *can* share it, in the way I let the demoness borrow it. Only more voluntarily. Giving it, rather than just letting it be taken.

If I can do that, I should do that now. For all of them.

"Okay. I swear I am going to explain everything. But first, everyone needs to get in a circle and hold hands."

"What?" Leticia asks, still holding Annie. "Why?"

"Please. Just do it. I think I can protect us from what just happened happening again. And then I will tell you everything."

They do as I ask. Annie's sobs have reduced themselves to sniffles. I notice that she manages not to be next to William for the hand-holding.

I am going to need to fix that.

I hold William's and Diane's hands. Annie holds Diane's other hand and Leticia's, Leticia holds Annie's and William's. William has dropped the piece of Annie's hair, which is probably for the best. I ask everyone to be very quiet and to close their eyes. I close mine, too, trying not to think about the fact that I don't really know what I'm doing.

Instead, I try to think about how it felt to share my resistance with the demoness, and how it felt just now, forcing it into William. I want to find something in between . . . nothing quite so violent as what I did to push out Mr. Gabriel, but since Annie and the others don't have the demoness's ability to actively take hold of my protection and pull it over them . . .

I concentrate inward, grateful for everyone's patience when I know they must be terrified and confused and bursting with questions. I try to visualize my roachiness as a glowing energy force inside me. The demoness made my resistance feel like a thin-but-strong piece of fabric that settled onto and around her. But what I did to William felt more like something from inside me pushing out. I try to re-create that sensation, a little more gently, and then to send the energy out through my hands and into the rest of the circle.

After a moment, I feel it working.

William and Diane both tense on either side of me, and I hear Leticia and Annie breathe in sharply as it reaches them as well. I give it another few seconds, and then I try to will it to stop moving. To stay where I put it, in my friends. To protect them the way it protects me.

"Okay. You can let go."

They do, and we all open our eyes. I have no way to tell if it really worked . . . but I think it did. I feel a tiny bit weaker, which seems like a good sign. I mean, I wish I could share it without feeling weaker, but if I have less, that must mean that some of it is elsewhere, right?

"What did you just do?" Annie asks, sounding almost back in control of herself.

"You know how I told you I have that resistance? The roach thing?"

She nods.

"I think . . . I hope . . . I just shared it with you. With all of you. So that Mr. Gabriel won't be able to do that again."

"Do *what* again?" Leticia says impatiently. "Cyn, what the hell is going on? What . . . what *happened* to William before?"

"Yes," William says quietly. "I would really like to know that, too."

I look around the circle. "Mr. Gabriel was . . . is . . . not a human person. He's a demon. Principal Kingston was also a demon. And Ms. Královna, that sub we had for Italian after

Signor De Luca left. Only he didn't leave, he was murdered. By Mr. Gabriel. Because he tried to help us." I look at Leticia and Diane, who are staring at me with uncertain expressions. "Which is why I never told you guys what was going on. Because I was afraid he would kill you, too."

I keep talking, not wanting to give anyone a chance to interrupt before I get the basic story out there. "Mr. Gabriel wanted to steal Annie away to be his bride in the demon world. Having a human consort was one of the requirements for joining the battle for the demon throne, which he was trying to win. He messed with her brain a little, which is why she was acting so weird. Ryan knew what was happening, too, and he helped me try to stop Mr. Gabriel. And eventually I made a deal with Ms. Královna, and she helped me get what I needed to save Annie and defeat Mr. Gabriel and then we killed him and Ms. Královna became the demon queen and the rest of us came home and we *thought* that was the end of it.

"But apparently Mr. Gabriel didn't die all the way." I look at Annie, wishing so much I could make this not be true. "Someone did something at the moment of his death to save his spirit, or something — I still don't entirely understand this part — and now he's back, but only in spirit form. For now. But he can possess people for short periods of time, take over their bodies, which is what he did to William. There's another demon here, in physical form, who kind of looks like a giant spider-bull with some extra insect parts, and he's Mr. Gabriel's brother, and Mr. Gabriel is planning to use his body to kill me and Ryan and, oh, Peter, who is also a demon but not an evil

236

one, and . . . and as you just observed, Mr. Gabriel is still pretty obsessed with Annie and wants to get her back, too."

She whimpers a little at that, and I make my voice and my expression very firm. "That is not going to happen. I swear, Annie. I won't let him. We have a plan, and Peter is helping, and so is Ms. Královna again, because he's trying to kill her, too, and also that guy Aaron, whom you may or may not remember — from the bookstore? He's her human consort, and he lives down there now, only he wants to be there, because he's crazy and also he's not quite fully human anymore."

I stop, trying to think if I've left anything out.

"Oh, and there's also that girl Jules, Ryan's friend, she's involved now, too, unfortunately."

Everyone is quiet. I give them a minute to just kind of sit with all of this. I'm sure they need it. Their expressions are various forms of confused and alarmed and scared, but no one seems to be thinking that I'm messing with them or otherwise not telling the truth. I guess that's one upside to Mr. Gabriel's unscheduled appearance. Everyone saw William change into someone else. Well, except William himself, obviously, but he experienced it, which is probably even more convincing.

"I didn't tell you what was happening"—I am speaking just to Annie now—"because I was really, really hoping we could take care of it before you got here. So you wouldn't need to know that he was still kind of alive. I just . . . I didn't want you to have to go through that again. Please . . . please don't be mad. I had no idea you would come up early."

Annie lets out a long, slow breath. "I'm not . . . I'm not mad, Cyn. I understand why you thought that was the right thing. But . . ." She looks me in the eye, and I'm surprised by the steel in that gaze. "You can't do that. You can't hide things from me like that. Not these kinds of things. Promise me you won't ever do that again."

"But—"

"Promise me. I'm not a child, Cyn. You have to trust me to be able to deal with things. And this . . ." She gestures around, indicating the recent events of this room. "This was way worse than it would have been if you'd told me before now."

Ryan was right, dammit. I do keep deciding what's best for everyone else. Why does that always seem like such a good idea at the time?

"I promise. I'm sorry."

"Did I . . ." William looks at me and then at Annie. "Did I hurt you? It was like . . . I wasn't really there for a minute. But I almost . . . I almost remember . . ." He looks down at his hand again, now empty.

"It wasn't you," Annie says. "It wasn't your fault." I can see that it's hard for her to keep her eyes on his face as she says this. But she manages. She even gives him a tiny smile, which makes him smile back with visible and immense relief.

I'm such an ass.

She's a lot stronger than I give her credit for.

Diane turns to look at Leticia. "I *told* you something else was going on last semester. You owe me a dollar."

Leticia just nods, apparently not having anything to say. Which I don't think has ever really happened before ever.

"Well," I say, "you might as well come meet Peter."

We head over to Blake Theater. Peter runs out as we approach. "*There* you are! I thought . . . I don't know, that something might have . . . happened. Who, uh . . ." He stares at the new arrivals, and of course he knows exactly who they are, but tries to act as though he has no idea.

I make the introductions for my friends' sake — no need to really spell out for them how Peter was creepily and invisibly lurking around for a while at the beginning — as we head toward the backstage door.

Once backstage, everyone spreads out, just a little, to look around. Leticia peeks at the stage from the wings.

"Cyn, is this your design? It's incredible! I love all the different heights and the color scheme and all the pointy bits!"

I can't help smiling, despite everything. "Hey, no peeking! You should wait to see it from the front, during the show, as it is intended to be seen." Because we will totally still be alive then, and so that will be possible. "Also, keep your voice down. Trust me, you do *not* want the director to come back here and yell at us."

Peter backs me up on this. "Yeah, he's a total dick. We prefer to keep him out of our domain as much as possible."

I bring Peter up to speed on what has happened since breakfast, and I fill in the gaps in the story for everyone else — Peter's hitchhiking, Mr. Gabriel's tether-hijacking, my second trip the demon world, and how Mr. G's brother came back to camp with me. I also tell them about the plan for later.

"You should probably go back to your hotel until it's all over," I say.

They all look at one another, and I feel an argument coming on.

"I would rather stay," Annie says. "I don't want to be hiding under a bed somewhere in the dark, waiting to find out what happens."

"I'm with Annie," Diane says. Leticia and William nod to indicate their solidarity with this position.

"Guys," I say, "I don't think that's a good idea. I don't know how things are going to go later. I don't want you in harm's way."

"Cyn," Diane says, "you can't keep trying to protect people by pushing them away. And besides"— she grins at me —"who do you think you are? Our mother? You can't tell us what to do. We want to stay. We're going to stay. Stop arguing."

I look at Peter, but he puts his hands up as if in surrender. "Don't look at me. They're your friends. And honestly, I don't mind saying that increasing our numbers feels like a good thing. Even if they're only here for moral support."

I look back at the others, who are now standing with arms crossed, the embodiment of stubbornness.

"Fine," I say, since it doesn't look like they're going to give me much choice. "But you better not do anything brave or stupid."

I intercept Ryan and Jules on their way to lunch and steer them to bunk 6 instead, where Peter and the others are waiting. Ryan hugs Annie and Leticia and Diane hello, and acknowledges William with a friendly "Hey, man." He introduces Jules, and although the other girls are textbook polite in their responses, it warms my heart to see the frosty glances they give her on my behalf. I want to hug them all again myself.

"So, what do we do now?" Peter asks. "Just wait to be attacked?"

"I've been thinking about that," Ryan says. "It seems to me that we can choose our battlefield if we want to. I mean, they're going to have to come to us wherever we are, right?"

"That's true," Peter says, perking up at this realization. "Did you have someplace in mind?"

"It so happens that I do," Ryan says.

And that is how we all end up in the middle of the soccer field that evening after dinner. (We were pretty sure the demons wouldn't come for us in the middle of the dining hall, and it seemed like a good idea to ingest some protein and carbs before heading into battle.)

There's a full moon tonight, which is both appropriate and very handy, since the overhead lights of the soccer field are of course turned off in the absence of a game happening, and turning them on ourselves would draw unwanted attention. I've got my magic fan, and Peter has his vial of demon-strength juice or whatever it is. He's going to wait until the last possible second to drink it, which seems wise, since Aaron never said how long it would last. Ryan has the kitchen shears so we can cut the tether again after Mr. Gabriel has been sent back to hell where he belongs. Also, I think he just feels better carrying a weapon.

We sit in a circle in the very center of the field, facing out. Waiting. The soccer field was a brilliant idea; we'll be able to see the demons coming, and there's plenty of room to spread out if we need to. I have to admit it's useful to have four extra pairs of eyes in Annie, William, Leticia, and Diane, but I still hate that my friends are all here, right where all the bad things are going to happen. And Jules is here, too, obviously, with her pair of eyes as well, but I was already resigned to her having to be here. And also less worried about her well-being.

Suddenly I hear a sharp intake of breath from behind me, and Leticia's voice whispering, "Holy *crap*."

We all jump to our feet and turn to look.

Little Brother has appeared at the far side of the field.

"Do you think Mr. Gabriel is already inside him?" I ask Peter.

"No," he says. "I doubt it. I think he'll wait until the last possible second, like I will with the vial. He's not going to want to waste one bit of his strength."

The demons (I can only assume Mr. Gabriel is floating evilly and invisibly somewhere beside his brother) approach slowly. Probably to draw out the horrible anticipation, since our fear will only make them stronger. I want to believe that the leg Hector damaged the other day is slowing them down, but I don't see any sign of an injury. It's probably healed by now.

"Oh, my God, it's *literally* a monster," Diane says. She sounds fascinated despite herself. "And so big. And also *very* disgusting."

"No *wonder* Mr. Gabriel never mentioned him," Annie adds.

"Guys," I say, "I think this is a good time for you to not be standing right here."

"Okay," Leticia says at once. She grabs Diane's hand and

Annie's hand and jerks her head at William to include him, too. "Let's go. We'll just sit somewhere over there." They head for the bleachers, not running, but not exactly strolling, either.

Jules and Ryan should be going with them, but Ryan has already made it clear that he won't be leaving, and so of course that means Jules won't be leaving, too.

Peter takes out the vial and looks at me.

"Wow. I am really, really scared right now," he says. "I sure hope this works."

"Me, too," I say back. "On both counts."

Although . . . while it's true that I am scared (I mean, obviously), I realize I'm not nearly as scared as I was when I was facing my first demon battle. That time I was alone. This time . . . I think about Mr. Henry humming "Safety in Numbers" in my dream. Okay, *safety* would be a stretch, but it's definitely fortifying to have friends around at a time like this. Especially one who is about to transform into something huge and powerful and (hopefully) very deadly.

"What do you look like in your true form?" I ask Peter. We're still watching Little Brother approach. He is kind of taking forever about it. "Are you gross?"

"No, I'm not *gross*," Peter says, glaring at me. "What a thing to say."

"Sorry." I guess that wasn't very tactful.

"Hey, guys," Ryan says, coming over to stand beside me. "I think now might be a good time to get all the way ready, yeah?"

"Yeah," Peter says. "Watch out, everybody."

He opens the vial and downs the contents in one swallow.

"Ugh," he says, tossing the empty vial to the grass. "Tastes

243

like cherry NyQuil." Then his human outline starts to . . . dissolve. And he starts to get bigger. Fast.

The rest of us back away, staring. I notice that Mr. Gabriel's brother has paused in his approach to watch as well.

Peter throws his head back and his limbs seem to shoot outward, growing translucent. I hope he's not going to have tentacles. I hate those. I also suddenly wonder if it hurts him to make this transformation. I never thought to ask.

It certainly doesn't look very comfortable.

He continues to grow, and his outline re-forms in a new, much larger shape. His head begins to resemble that of an enormous horse, although the resemblance gets a little shaky once the huge, shiny, pointy antlers begin reaching up and out from between his ears. His arms have become graceful equine legs, but the hooves have long curved spikes arcing up and forward from their edges. The rest of him looks sort of like a dragon, with strong, powerful hind legs covered in green-black scales, rear feet sporting razorlike talons, and a long tail that splits into three thick yet oddly delicate-looking strands, each tapering to a deathly sharp point.

He was telling the truth. He's definitely not gross. He's by far the most attractive demon-in-demon-form I've ever seen. Luminous and glorious and just . . . just . . .

"Wow," Jules says admiringly, staring up at him. "He's *way* better than a spider-bull."

"Totally," I can't help breathing in response. He's like a beautiful antlery dragon-pony made of magic.

He's stopped masking his aura, and it shines strongly out,

representing, I hope, a vast reservoir of strength and power that he will very shortly use to smite our horrible enemies.

Mr. Gabriel's brother has resumed his creeping progress and is finally getting close. I still don't think Mr. Gabriel has taken possession. I wonder suddenly if maybe it's not too late to stop that from happening.

"You know he's not going to give you your body back once he's in there," I call out to the approaching monster. "He's just using you. He's going to steal your body and cast you aside."

"Liar," Little Brother says, turning his inhuman eyes to me. "We will fight as one. And win as one. And drink your blood as one and have your friend as one and return home to rule our land as one. You tell lies, like all roaches do."

"Look who's talking, bug-boy," Ryan mutters beside me.

The demon shudders suddenly and stops his advance. "Yes," he whispers to some unheard question, and he straightens just as a burst of red demon energy seems to settle into him. And then he seems to become confused, shaking his head back and forth and stumbling slightly. There is a struggle going on, and it's not the one he anticipated. His eyes roll in what I want to interpret as fear, although it's really hard to tell with those insect features. I almost feel sorry for him.

Almost.

Then he stops, and straightens again, and even with the inhuman face, I can tell that Mr. Gabriel has taken over.

"Trying to turn my own brother against me," he says to me, and I hear Annie gasp from the bleachers. There's no mistaking the change now. "I should have expected nothing less from you."

"Is he still in there?" I ask. "Are you pushing him down somewhere deep inside himself, or have you just pushed him out entirely?"

"He's still here," Mr. Gabriel says, almost fondly. "He was telling the truth about everything we will do as one. He won't be in control, of course, but I'll probably still let him come up and sample all the upcoming delights. Including killing all of you. Except for Annie, of course. Annie we get for dessert. Forever."

"I told you, you will never touch her again," I say in a low, barely controlled voice, meaning every word with all my heart.

"Okay!" Peter says. "Enough talking. Get out of the way, please. I need to kill this guy."

Chapter | 14

We get out of the way, running back over to the bleachers, where the others are watching in horrified silence. As we run, I feel Peter take hold of my strength, and I realize suddenly in panic that I never took back the protection I lent to Annie and the others. I'm not even truly sure I know *how* to take it back, but I yank blindly at it, no time to be gentle, sorry, guys, and use the momentum that comes with it to push it toward Peter instead.

And then I sit down heavily. I'll never get used to that feeling of having it all borrowed at once that way. God, I hate this. I feel so weak and exposed.

"You okay?" Ryan whispers, instantly at my side.

"Yeah. It's just . . . to say it takes a lot out of me when someone borrows my power like that would be an understatement of ridiculous proportions."

In the battle for the demon throne, pretty much all of the fighting was done using each demon's power-essence, which is why my protection was so important to the demoness. This battle is apparently going to be a bit more down and dirty. Meaning, in addition to the inner demony magic strength, they're going to be using their physical strength as well.

The two demons (we'll consider Mr. Gabriel and his brother one demon for our current purposes, since, physically at least, they are) circle each other a few times, looking each other over. They're about the same size, although if you count all the legs, I think Mr. Gabriel's brother might be a little bit bigger overall. Their auras seem to be about the same intensity, but I can't be sure anymore that I'm really seeing all there is to see in that regard. For all I know, Mr. Gabriel is masking part of his energy to make me think he's weaker than he is. I can see that Peter's demon aura coats his outer edges, and I'm guessing that's to help protect against the spider's delayed poison thing that laid Peter out the first time they faced each other.

It's all up to Peter now. Until he gives me the signal that Mr. Gabriel is on the run, all I can do is watch, and wait.

And worry.

Peter lifts one of his front hooves toward the other demon. "You," Peter says in a deeper, less-human version of his regular voice, "are going to pay for what you did to Hector, you spidery bastard. Can you hear me in there, Little Brother? I'm going to tear you apart."

With a roar, Mr. Gabriel throws himself forward, leaping into the air and grasping at Peter with all of his many disgusting limbs. Peter slashes at the other demon with his hooves and tail, and after a moment Mr. Gabriel backs off again. Peter makes the next advance, striking out with all his sharp appendages, but Mr. Gabriel encircles him with his legs again, effectively wrapping Peter too tightly in enemy body parts to get enough leverage to do any damage. They struggle against each other and then pull apart yet again.

It continues this way, one or the other leaping forward, attacking with limbs, teeth, pincers, and/or antlers as well as the red energy that flows from both of them at every extremity. Mr. Gabriel howls in pain as Peter manages to completely slice off the tip of one of his legs, but a few minutes later Peter screams as Mr. Gabriel's teeth sink deeply into his shoulder.

It's excruciating to watch and not be able to do anything. They seem evenly matched, even with all the extra strength that the demoness gave Peter and with my extra protection. I remind myself that Peter is not by nature a fighter. Not this kind of fighter, anyway. He hates this kind of thing. Whereas Mr. Gabriel and his misguided but very deadly little brother live for it. They love to hurt and maim and kill. They probably don't even mind all the pain that comes with it. Mr. Gabriel is completely in his element here and enjoying every minute. And it starts to become clear that he's winning.

I look at Ryan, and I can see he's thinking the same thing.

Peter is giving it everything he has, but I don't think it's going to be enough. With each new clashing of bodies, Peter comes away a little slower, a little less bright with red power. Mr. Gabriel barely seems diminished at all. He throws himself at Peter again and again, becoming more and more exuberant, and Peter falls back and falls back, clearly beginning to focus more on defending himself against Mr. Gabriel's attacks than launching attacks of his own.

As I watch, Peter shoots me an agonized glance. He knows he's not going to win.

Annie reaches over and grips my shoulder tightly. William is beside her, an arm around her shoulders. I think seeing Mr. Gabriel in his brother's body helped her let go of whatever lingering revulsion she was feeling from having seen her evil demon stalker inside her sweet human boyfriend. Leticia and Diane are holding each other's hands tightly, staring silently at the ongoing battle before them. Jules sits grimly on the other side of Ryan, watching along with the rest of us.

This isn't going to work. We have to do something. I look at my fan, but it's useless until Mr. Gabriel is out of his brother's body. I see Ryan's eyes flick down to the shears, and I poke him in the side and shake my head at him. Attacking Mr. Gabriel with those would barely hurt him and would almost certainly get Ryan killed. And that's not something that is allowed to happen. It's true that my months-ago deal with Mr. Gabriel required him to promise he wouldn't hurt or kill Ryan or let any other demons do so, either. But I have no idea what effect Mr. Gabriel's mostly-death might have had on the terms of the deal, or whether he's still bound by it when he's using some- one else's body. I'm not about to let Ryan chance it. Especially not when the shears can't possibly make a difference, anyway.

If only Peter were just a little stronger, a little more of a fighter, a little more of the type of demon who liked this kind of thing. As much as I appreciate his theatrical leanings and his incredible talent as a writer and composer, right now none of that is doing us any good at all. He can't even really draw strength from the few injuries he's managing to inflict upon his opponent, because that's just not the sort of power he feeds upon.

I sit up suddenly, seized by an idea.

Peter doesn't feed upon pain and killing and torture. He feeds upon drama. Which means, if we could somehow deliver some of that to him right now, it could give him the strength he needs.

Peter said real-life drama is better than fictional drama. Which is maybe good, since I don't think staging an impromptu performance of *The King and I* is really a valid option right now. But I know of a little ready-to-hand real-life drama that won't take long to access at all. If I'm willing to go there.

And . . . I have to be. Because if Peter doesn't win this fight, then nothing else is going to matter, anyway.

But I still really, really don't want to. Not now, not after everything Ryan said about building back trust and how long it might be before we're really, really okay again.

Too bad, Old Cyn says in the back of my brain. *Get on with it, you hussy.*

Old Cyn has turned into someone's aged grandmother when I wasn't looking, apparently.

Stop stalling, I tell myself in my own present-Cyn inner voice. *It's now or never.*

Right. Okay.

Showtime.

I take a deep breath and speak as loudly as I can, making

sure my voice will carry to where Peter is still valiantly but increasingly hopelessly toiling away.

"I kissed Peter!"

Everyone turns to look at me. Even, for a moment, the two demons, who freeze mid-grapple on the grass.

Ryan is staring at me like I've sprouted some demon appendages of my own. *"What?"* he manages finally.

"That night I came back from the demon world." I get down from the bleachers and step out a few paces onto the field, calling back to him. "You had left with Jules and you weren't talking to me, even though I really could have used your support right about then, you know, and instead you walked off with her, holding hands, and Peter said he wanted to thank me properly for helping him break the tether, and then he kissed me. And . . . and I let him. And I kissed him back."

Ryan is still staring at me, open-mouthed. So is Jules. So are Annie and Leticia and Diane and William.

"And I liked it!" I shout. "It was amazing!"

Ryan jumps down and comes over and grabs my hands like he's trying to capture my sudden explosion of crazy and keep it contained. "Why are you saying this?" he asks. "Cyn, what are you doing?"

Dimly, I am aware of the demons fighting each other again. I want to turn to look and see if Peter seems any stronger, if this feeding-on-drama thing really works like that, only I'm a little too caught up now in what I created. I can't look away from Ryan's shocked and deeply unhappy face.

"You said no more secrets, well . . . there you go. My final secret revealed. I'm attracted to Peter, and I kissed him, and sometimes, in my dreams, we do other things that I'm not going to go into detail about right now. I don't want to be with him, I want to be with *you,* but . . ."

"But you kissed him," Ryan says flatly. "And you liked it. And you think now is a good time to tell me all about it."

"You were holding her hand!" I scream at him, and I realize this part is not coming out solely for Peter's benefit. This part has been lying in wait inside me like an infection, silently growing and festering, and I didn't have any idea how big and painful it had gotten until this moment. "She's been your best friend for practically your whole life and *you never even mentioned her to me!* Why would you do that? Why would you keep her a secret unless you had something to hide? And then I *saw* you, I saw you turn your back on me and walk away with her, *holding her hand,* like you were together, like it was the most natural thing in the world, just like everyone has been saying to me since I got here . . ."

"Cyn, stop it! You're being crazy! Jules and I are just friends, I don't know how many times I have to tell you that!"

"We are *not!*" Jules shouts suddenly, and Peter makes a sound of near ecstasy off to my right, and this time I can tell without even looking that he is indeed taking all of this in and that it is working.

"What?" Ryan says, turning now to stare at her.

She jumps down from the bleachers to join us. "Do you not remember what happened at the end of last summer? The last night, when we stayed up until dawn behind the seats in the theater? Something changed that night, you know it did. I've liked you for so long, struggled through so many summers of waiting, and finally, finally you were starting to like me back. . . . You kissed me good night, right outside my bunk before I went inside. You stood there, with your arms around me, kissing me, and I thought, this is it, finally . . ."

"Jules . . . that was . . . it didn't mean . . . it was late, and we'd been up all night, and of course, of course, I care about you, but I don't . . . I'm not . . ."

"No," she says in the same sort of flat voice Ryan used just a few minutes earlier. "It did mean something. It doesn't now, I know. It's too late. But it did. You were finally starting to let me in, to think of me in the way I had wanted you to for so long. I couldn't wait for this summer, to see what would happen, to see you, and then you get off the bus and casually introduce me to your *girlfriend,* who you never mentioned to me, either, not in any of your texts or e-mails or anything . . ."

It makes me nauseous to think of Ryan texting and e-mailing Jules all year long, and never saying a word. Especially if what she's saying is true, and he kissed her . . .

Suddenly there is a scream of anguish from the field, and we all whip our heads around to look. Peter is driving his spiked hooves into Mr. Gabriel's brother's abdomen over and over, and the flailing spider legs are starting to slow and fall still.

"Cyn!" Peter shouts. "Now, Cyn! He's out! He's trying to run!"

I pull my hands from Ryan's grip and stumble forward,

yanking my ridiculous fan from my waistband and beginning to fan at the weakened demon body like a maniac.

"I can't see him!" I shout at Peter. "Am I even fanning the right place?"

"Yes! Keep going!"

So I do. I try to channel my churned-up emotions into the muscles of my arms. I try to focus on the motion of the fan and not on my all-too-vivid mental image of Ryan and Jules standing in the middle of the path with their arms around each other and their mouths pressed together. I realize that at some point I have started crying, but I'm using both hands on the fan for maximum intensity, and I'm afraid to take a second to wipe my eyes. I'm getting tired already, but Peter is staring intently at . . . something . . . which I take to mean that Mr. Gabriel is not gone yet and I have to keep going.

I sense someone coming up behind me, and I hear Annie's voice. "Hey," she says. That's all, just *Hey,* but she stands behind me and puts her arms around me and I feel like I can fan for a little longer, so I do. I stand there, taking comfort in my best friend's silent presence, silent and so much stronger than I ever realized, and I move the fan up and down and up and down, and I try not to think about anything else at all.

Finally, Peter reaches out a hoof to stop me.

"It's okay," he says. "It's done."

I let my hands drop. My arm muscles are burning. I know it's just a fan, not a kettlebell or anything, but you try fanning with that much effort and intensity for that long and see how your arms feel afterward.

Then I see one of the spider legs move and I leap backward, pulling Annie with me. "Peter! He's not dead!"

"No," Peter agrees. "I couldn't . . . once Mr. Gabriel was gone, I had to stop. I didn't want to kill him."

"Why not?" Annie says, flabbergasted. "He's a monster. He deserves to die."

Peter just shakes his head.

"That's not his thing," I tell Annie. "Let it go."

Then I look back down at the barely alive demon. "But what are we going to do with him?"

Before anyone can make a suggestion, there's a flash of light, and then Aaron is standing there. He's bloody and disheveled, but he grins widely at us all the same. His shoulder fins are waving in excitement.

"Hey, nice job, you guys! We were getting a little worried there for a while, but finally we felt him come through the tether. My mistress was ready for him on the other side, and now all of him is safely contained once again."

"Contained?" I ask. "Why didn't she just kill him?"

"She wasn't exactly at full strength anymore," he says defensively. "And he still has a lot of supporters down there. She thought it might be wise to keep him alive for now, as a bargaining chip if nothing else. Plus, I know she wishes to . . . have some words with him. And perhaps discuss some possible methods of punishment for his behavior. But don't worry—he can't come up here and bother you again."

"How do you know?" Annie demands. "Last time we all thought he was dead, and he managed to come back. Now we know he's not. What's to stop him from trying again? And again?"

"Now that we know about him, we can keep him safely locked away," Aaron says. "I swear. He has a lot to answer for, and my mistress is going to see that he does. Which he can't do if he's up here gallivanting around. She'll make it so that he cannot possibly escape the demon realm. Really. It's going to be okay."

Annie still looks doubtful, and I can't say I blame her. Plus, it's Aaron. Who, granted, has been fairly forthcoming and helpful over the past several days, but still . . . you never really know with him.

"What about this one?" I ask, giving Little Brother a kick in the leg with my sneaker. It comes back sticky with some sort of goo, and I scrape it frantically against the grass. Ick.

"I will take him off your hands," Aaron says briskly. "This is good-bye for now, since there's a lot of cleanup and stuff that needs to happen down there." He winks at me. "Not good-bye forever, though, of course. See you next time!"

He vanishes, and Mr. Gabriel's brother vanishes with him.

Peter coughs delicately. "If you all don't mind, I'm going to go change back somewhere a little more private." He heads for the trees at the far end of the field.

"Why did he want to change back in private?" Annie asks. "He changed the first time right in front of us."

"I think when he changes back, he'll be naked," I say. "Just a hunch, but it makes sense. His clothes do seem to have evaporated somewhere along the line."

"Oh." She sounds a little disappointed and glances over her shoulder at where Peter is walking away from us.

"Quit it," I say, elbowing her. "You have a boyfriend now. No peeking at other naked men."

"Screw that," she says. "Looking is totally allowed. Back off, relationship police."

We go back to the bleachers, where the others are waiting. Most of the others. "Where's Jules?" I ask.

"She . . . left," Ryan says.

"Speaking of leaving," Leticia says, "I think it's time we went back to our hotel. I need to sleep for about ten hours. You ready to go, Annie?"

"Yes," Annie says definitively. She goes over to William, who slips an arm around her waist.

Sweet, sweet William. I really like that guy.

"Okay, then," Diane says. "See you two tomorrow, yeah?"

I nod, and they head back toward the main campus and the parking lot.

And then it's just me and Ryan standing alone in the empty moonlit soccer field.

"Was that true, what you said?" he asks. "Did you really kiss him? I . . . got the sense you were saying it for Peter's benefit somehow, but . . ."

"Peter feeds on drama," I explain, not sure how this had failed to come up before now. I guess Ryan and I were always just talking about other things. Or not talking at all. "Like most demons feed on souls or pain or fear or death."

"Really?" He looks at me hopefully. "So you were just . . . ?"

For one teeny second, I am tempted to lie to him. To

258

pretend it was all made up, and to maybe even express shock and dismay that he could possibly believe that it was true.

But just for a teeny second.

"Fake drama wouldn't have worked," I say. "It was true. I really did kiss him. Or at least, I really kissed him back. For a second. But then I told him to stop and said that it could never happen again. And it has not."

He gives me a sad smile. "Except in your dreams."

"I can't help that. And it doesn't mean anything except probably that I feel guilty about it and my subconscious is trying to work through it." I pause and then ask, "What about what Jules said? Was that true?"

Ryan goes over and sits down on the bleachers. I follow and sit beside him.

"Yes," he says. "And she's right . . . something did happen that night. Things felt like they'd changed between us. But when I kissed her, I didn't . . . I thought I would feel differently than I did. I guess I convinced myself that she felt the same way, that we were still just friends. She didn't bring it up all year, and I didn't, either, and so I thought maybe we could just let it go and pretend it never happened."

"But you didn't really think that," I say gently. "Or you would have told her about me."

"Yeah," he says. "I guess that's true."

I make myself ask the next question. "Are you sure you don't want to be with her?"

"Yes! I really do just want to be her friend." He reaches out and pulls me closer to him. "I want to be with you."

"Even after I kissed Peter?"

He makes a show of thinking about this for a minute. "Yes," he says finally. "But please do not ever do that again. And also try to stop dreaming about him. What exactly happens in these dreams, anyway?"

"That is between me and my subconscious," I say firmly.

"Hmm."

I take a breath. "Ryan . . . you know we are always going to have some things we don't tell each other. I don't mean secrets like the kind I kept from you before. No more of those, for real. I mean little things, stupid things . . . I am never again going to tell you when I have a sexy dream about someone other than you, for example. And just so you know, I do not want to hear about it if you have a sexy dream about someone else, either. But also you should just never do that."

"I'll do my best."

"Hmm."

He's quiet for a moment, and I rest my head on his shoulder while I wait for his response. He smells good. Like soap and that stuff he uses in his hair and the underlying Ryan-scent that I love, that always makes me think of rugby and theater and his leg-weakening smile and of curling up together in his bedroom, his arms wrapped around me and my face tucked safely against his chest.

His arm snakes more tightly around my waist and gives me a squeeze. "I guess I can live with that. But . . . do try to share all the important things, okay? Even the things you're not totally sure are important but might be. Also anything demon-related that happens outside of your dreams."

"Deal," I say.

"Deal," he agrees, kissing the top of my head.

"So kissing Jules wasn't nearly as good as kissing me, then?"

"I'm not sure I remember clearly enough. Let me check." He tilts my face up to his and kisses me nice and slow, just like the first time, only without the having-to-be-careful-about-the-stage-makeup part. "Yup," he says when he pulls away. "Kissing you is definitely better." He hesitates, and then asks in a voice that makes me think he's not entirely kidding, "Is kissing me better than kissing Peter?"

"I *think* so," I say. "But I should probably make sure." Now it's my turn to lean in. I kiss him less gently. And for a lot longer.

He doesn't seem to mind.

Chapter | 15

For the first time pretty much since I got here, camp life becomes somewhat normal.

Of course, *normal* for the few days before opening night is kind of a relative term, but even the craziness of squeezing most of tech week into one long day and getting all the finishing touches squared away on the set and the scene changes and everything else seems blessedly routine when there are no evil demons trying to kill and/or abduct anyone. That's one thing about demons: they really put things in perspective.

And finally the shows go up, and they are amazing.

I think the offstage drama between Ryan and Jules made their performances even better. The tension between them works so perfectly with their characters and the story . . . they are both really excellent. Really, really excellent. I can't even bring myself to hate Jules for anything. I mean, it's Ryan. *Of course* she secretly fell in love with him after all those summers together. And it sounds like he was not entirely forthright in how he dealt with what happened, which could not have made things easy for her. I'm not saying I want to be her best friend. Or even her friend at all. But I can watch her onstage and admire and respect her, and be civil to her, and even feel some empathy for her, which is more than I would have expected to be capable of after learning she'd kissed my boyfriend. I mean, before he was my boyfriend. But still.

And yes, I know that makes me a raging hypocrite, since I kissed Peter while Ryan *was* my boyfriend. But in the end, that turned out to be useful, and so I'm not going to keep beating myself up about it. But I do hope the dreams stop happening eventually. They are very . . . disconcerting. Peter and I have done things in my dreams that I've not gotten close to doing with Ryan yet. And I always wake up feeling confused and unsettled and . . . sweaty.

Moving on.

Our own show, of course, was the best of all. I mean, it really was — that's not just my opinion. Everyone said so. Well, not the official camp Tony Award committees, not yet. But they *will*. And, okay, Jules didn't exactly say it, but she didn't say any other show was better, either. Annie and Leticia and Diane and William started a standing ovation on our opening night, and every single person in the theater stood up. I was really proud of Peter. He was so happy, and he totally deserved it. He's really talented, that one. And he went through quite a lot to get to be here. I know he's going to go on to do great things.

We broke the tether again later that night after the fight in the soccer field, so Peter is no longer connected to me in any physical or demon-energetical way. He does want to keep in touch, though. Which is good, because I can use that kind of connection when I graduate from college and am looking for real theater jobs. He'll probably have at least three popular and critically acclaimed musicals going by then.

Annie and William and Leticia and Diane go home the day after *Scarlet Pimpernel*'s opening night.

Annie and William seem to be okay again. I take Annie aside when they come over to say good-bye.

"How are you doing?" I ask her. "I know this was not the fun camp visit you were imagining."

"No, it was not," Annie agrees. "But I'm doing okay. Still nightmares, but William helps with those." She can't help smiling whenever she says his name. It's super adorable. "I hate knowing Mr. Gabriel is still alive, though. Even if he's trapped somewhere, even if he's being tortured and punished by the demoness . . . I wish he were dead. Totally and completely dead. I don't know how I can ever really relax while he's still out there. Down there. Whatever. You know what I mean."

I do. "Yeah. I hate knowing that he's going to be there the next time the demoness summons me."

"Well, he won't be there, like, like standing right there. He'll be locked away somewhere."

"I know." I have to believe that will be true, or I will not be able to function. "But still. I hate the idea of being in the same place as he is. Even if it's only for a short time."

"Well, at least the next time she summons you will be the last time, right?"

"Right." For some reason, saying this out loud makes me nervous. But that's dumb. A deal's a deal, and I've got one more trip and that's it. Forever.

"I wish you were coming home with us," Annie says.

"I know. But there's still two more sessions. Two more shows! Although there won't be another original show in the next group. They only do that once a summer."

"I guess you wouldn't really want to leave Ryan up here with Jules for the next six weeks anyway."

"Definitely not. I believe him that he's not interested in her that way, but . . . better to stick around and keep an eye on things, just in case."

"Okay, you two," Leticia calls. "Time to say good-bye so we can get on the road. My mom will freak out if we don't get home before it's dark."

There are hugs all around, and Annie and I both get a little weepy. Leticia rolls her eyes at us. "You already know we're going to come up for the next show," she says. "It's not going to be that long."

"Just promise to give us a heads-up if there are any more demon things happening this time, okay?" Diane adds. "I might pack some knives or halberds or something."

"Strobe lights," I say. "We should all stock up on strobe lights."

Annie looks thoughtful; half remembering, I guess. Leticia and Diane look at me like I'm crazy. At some point I'll have to fill in all the details for them of what happened in the fall.

Then they all pile into the car. Annie snuggles in against William in the backseat. Diane honks once in farewell before she pulls away from the curb.

I watch them go, and I think about what Annie said. About not being able to ever relax, knowing Mr. Gabriel is still out there. Down there. Whatever.

Obviously I know exactly what she means.

He's going to be waiting for me the next time I respond to the demoness's call. She may think she has him safely locked away . . . but I've stopped him from getting what he wants twice now. He already wanted to kill me before. Now I think . . . I think he's going to be waiting down there, nursing his rage. Making some plans. His brother might still be alive and willing to help him. I would hope that his brother would grow a backbone and realize that Mr. Gabriel is not worth helping. But I doubt that's going to happen. Little Brother didn't really seem the backbone-growing type.

I can go back to hoping that the summons won't come for a very long time. And maybe it won't. Maybe this time it will be years before I hear from Aaron or the demoness again.

But somehow I have a feeling it will be sooner than that.

Our next two performances are later that day, and then everyone in the show helps to take apart the set and clean everything up and put the costumes and props back in central storage. Peter and I hang out backstage after strike, doing a final sweep of backstage. It makes me sad to know our flats are going to be painted over by the next crew, and everything we created was only for these three performances. But that's part of the beauty of theater, too, of course. Every show is its own unique work of art, and every run is temporary and ephemeral.

But it's still sad when a good show is over.

Especially when not everyone is sticking around for the next one.

"So, are you really just going to go on pretending you're a seventeen-year-old?" I ask him. "Go to high school somewhere, then college, then get a job?"

"Pretty much," he says. "Although not a *job*. I mean . . . please. I'm going to be a phenomenal international superstar. People are going to be falling all over themselves to work with me. It's not really the same thing as having a *job*."

"Noted," I say. "That sense of humility is going to serve you well at the real Tonys."

"Maybe we'll be there together," he says. "I would love to work with you again, Cyn."

"Likewise," I say, and I mean it. "I just hope you remember me when you're a phenomenal international superstar."

"I promise to really, really try."

"Thanks."

We're both quiet for a minute.

"Maybe I should transfer to your high school," he says. "What's the story with Diane anyway? Are she and Leticia super serious or what?"

"Yes," I say firmly. "And anyway, I would like you to consider all of my friends off-limits, please. Demon relationships are too complicated."

Peter looks slightly wounded at this but lets it go. He's

holding one of the apocalypse-blackened street signs from our show, turning it over and over in his hands.

"I could still transfer, though," he says, eyes flicking up to meet mine and then darting away again. "I could write next fall's musical. We could work together again."

"No." I say it quickly before I can be tempted to reconsider. I did love working with him. And he really has become a friend. But he's too . . . distracting. And more important: I just don't think I should be encouraging demons of any kind, even the non-evil ones, to come to my school. They seem to attract one another. I would really, really, really like my senior year to be demon free.

"But—"

"No."

"Oh, all right." He turns the street sign over a few more times. "I'm going to miss you, though."

"I'll miss you, too, Peter." I hesitate, then add, "You could stay for the rest of the summer, you know. I'm sure they'd let you." I laugh, because I keep forgetting that he can just make those things happen if he wants to. "Or you could just arrange it, or whatever."

"Nah," he says. "I want to get started on writing something new, and I think staying here might be too"—he glances at me—"distracting. Besides, now that I can go wherever I want, I feel like I should do that. Explore the world! See dinner theater in Ohio! Okay, maybe not that. But I could go anywhere. For as long as I want. Without worrying about being dragged back to a place I don't belong."

"You *should* travel the world," I say. "An international theater tour. Gather some inspiration."

"That's a great idea," he says, his expression brightening significantly. "I'll spend the rest of the summer traveling, then find somewhere to have a senior year of high school, then use my summer experiences to write the best college entrance essay ever."

I laugh again. "I'm sure you will."

He looks at me again, and his adorable grin sneaks slowly across his face. "One more kiss for the road?"

"Don't make me hurt you, pony boy."

The camp Tony Award ceremony happens that night.

Steven starts off by making a speech about how we're all winners, blah-blah-blah, but no one is listening, because we just want him to get on with it. Different counselors and staff begin coming up to announce each award. The winner for Best Actor in a Featured Role in a Musical, Lower Camp, is announced (Draymond Johnson, who played Wolf in *Shrek*), then the same categories for Middle and Upper. They switch to Best Actress in a Featured Role in a Musical next, and Maria's little sister, Lucia, wins in the Lower Camp category for her part as Ursula in *Bye Bye Birdie*. Maria stands up and cheers as Lucia takes the stage to accept her award, beaming and waving. Sasha wins for her supporting role in *Aftermass*, which makes me super happy, although I'm also slightly concerned about the glares she gets from both Darleen and Celia, who were both vying for that award themselves.

There aren't any nominees; everyone is considered eligible for their categories. All the official Tony categories are represented, except things like "best revival," which makes sense, since technically all of the shows are revivals except for Peter's, and there are also some additional categories, like Musical Chorus Member MVP. I get more and more nervous, waiting. Ryan notices and takes my hand and then starts to pet it soothingly. I had been a little worried at first that maybe the whole ceremony would be kind of silly, but everyone takes it really seriously. Ryan told me there are often tears, both from winners and non-winners, and that the feeling of going up there and receiving the award, even though you know it's just camp, and not, like, Broadway or anything, is beyond amazing.

"You'll see," he told me, sliding a welcome arm around my waist.

I really hope he's right. I knew I wanted to win from the moment I found out the awards existed, but sitting here now with all the other campers, I am *desperate* to win. I want the recognition. I want the confirmation, from this group of mostly strangers whom I didn't really get a chance to know because I was too busy dealing with demons. I don't even know who half the members of the awards committee are. If they give me an award, it won't be because they like me . . . it will be because they think I really deserve it. *I* think I really deserve it, but there's something about outside validation that just . . . makes it feel more real. I suppose I shouldn't put that much importance on what a group of summer camp counselors thinks. I know I shouldn't. But, right now . . . I do.

I also made Peter swear to me that he would not do

anything to influence the results in any way. I believe that he won't; he was so insistent about proving himself without using demon magic. There's no actual award for best book and score, since none of the other musicals are originals, but he will get to go up to accept a recognition award for his work. And, of course, all of the other awards won by his cast and crew will reflect back on what he gave us to work with. I know he's going to be savoring every single win.

Of the categories I'm most interested in, Best Actress in a Leading Role in a Musical comes up first. I'm not surprised when Jules's name is announced for the Upper Camp award, and the resounding cheer from the audience indicates that most people agree that she deserves it. I try not to mind when Ryan leaps up to hug her before she takes the stage. Things are . . . strained between them since the other night, but they obviously still care about each other. Ryan warned me that they're probably going to have to have some long talks to get past what happened. I promised him I wouldn't give him a hard time about it. As long as all they did was talk. I feel Old Cyn getting all squinty-eyed and jealous at the thought of them spending any time alone together (*he's* your *boyfriend!* she reminds me for the zillionth time), but I stuff her back down in the back of my brain, where she belongs. Ryan's right about the importance of being able to trust each other. I've got to trust him if I expect him to trust me in return.

Best Actor in a Leading Role in a Musical is next, and of course Ryan wins for Upper Camp. Jules and I both jump up to hug him, but without hesitation he turns to me first. I close my eyes so I don't have to watch the expression on her face at being second in line. I think it might take longer than Ryan realizes for them to be okay again.

We both stay standing as he bounds sexily up to the stage to accept his award. There aren't any speeches; that would take forever, and would be a little over the top in any case. The winners just get to stand there for a moment on the stage with their award and take a bow before heading back to their seats. Ryan bows with a flourish, and all of his friends are whistling and catcalling as he makes his way back to us. He wins a Tony almost every summer, so this is far from his first time, but he still looks radiantly happy as he walks back down the aisle.

When they announce the category for Best Scenic Design, I grab Ryan's hand so tightly that I am probably hurting his beautiful fingers, but he is a sweetheart and lets me. "It's going to be you," he whispers. "No question."

And it is. There is barely a second to register hearing my name before Ryan pulls me into the tightest, best hug ever. It's hard to let it end, but I have to, because I have to go up there to get my award.

I walk quickly down the aisle, getting a few high fives from some of the bunk 6 girls and a few of Ryan's friends who are sitting close enough to reach out to me as I go by. The cheering is nothing like what Ryan and Jules received, but I don't care about that. They have been coming here forever and know pretty much everyone, after all. Still, even kids I've never met are clapping with more than just polite effort; people really did seem to love the look of the set, and everyone's been talking nonstop about Peter's show since it opened.

I climb the stairs, and Steven hands me the award. "Congratulations, Cynthia," he says. "Well deserved!"

I thank him and turn to the audience to take my bow. I see Peter sitting a few rows back, surrounded by some of his many admirers, and he gives me a glowing smile and an energetic double thumbs-up, which makes me laugh.

And then it's done, and I head back down the stairs and back to my seat. Ryan is standing up and still clapping, and I get another tight hug when I squeeze past him. "I'm so proud of you!" he says. "But not at all surprised."

"Right back atcha," I say. I feel like I'll never be able to stop smiling. I sit and look down at the award in my hands. It's heavier than I expected, and nicely crafted; they really do this whole awards thing right. Again, I know it's just camp, but . . . this is the first award I've ever won for theater. That makes it really special. I keep glancing down at it and smiling all over again.

There are a few more awards before the big ones, Best Play and Best Musical. Michael wins for Best Director, which I'm not sure is deserved, but it counts as another win for Peter's show, and so I'm happy on that score. Michael takes the longest, slowest bow I've ever seen.

And then Best Play is announced (*The Adventures of Tom Sawyer* for Lower Camp, *Arsenic and Old Lace* for Middle, and *The Odd Couple* for Upper), and then it's time for Best Musical.

Everyone falls silent, waiting for this one.

It's not really a given that Peter's show will win. All of the Upper Camp shows were really, really good. Even the ones without Ryan in them. And *The Scarlet Pimpernel* did have Ryan, *and* got the leading actor and actress awards, as well as best costumes. . . . I mean it wouldn't be unreasonable for it to win. But I would feel awful for Peter if it did. He really, really wants this.

And I really want it, too. For him and also for me. And for Sasha and everyone else who worked so hard to make it as good as it was. Even Darleen and Celia, who, when they are not busy fighting, are both really talented.

Steven tortures us by drawing out the Lower and Middle Camp awards as much as possible.

Finally, he brings out the last envelope.

"And the Tony for Best Musical, Upper Camp, goes to . . ."

There is a collective intake and holding of breath.

"*Aftermass,* book and score by Peter Franco!"

The applause is overpowering. Peter's admirers include pretty much everyone in the entire camp at this point, and even the directors and casts of the other shows are clearly excited for him to have won. It takes him a full five minutes to get up to the stage because of all the hugs and high fives and fist bumps he gets along the way. As I watch, I realize I hadn't known what last name he'd chosen for himself until now. He doesn't look like a Franco to me, but I'm sure he had his reasons.

When he gets up there and Steven hands him the Tony, Peter looks down at it with the happiest expression I have ever seen on anyone's face ever. I know he's thinking about it being the first of many, that this is his first step toward the life he has dreamed about for so very, very long. He faces the crowd, and he's forgotten about his demon aura in his excitement, and so there's an extra glow about him for my eyes in addition to the one that everyone can see. His eyes find mine across the theater, and he adds a special personal thank-you smile before bowing deeply with the perfect blend of pride and humility and gratitude. People start getting to their feet, and before long, the entire audience is standing, and everyone keeps clapping and cheering until Steven finally has to break in and tell us that if we don't stop soon, all the ice cream at the reception is going to melt before we get there.

This gets a dutiful laugh, but it also does the trick. Peter heads back down from the stage, and the standing ovation becomes a general exodus to Hines Hall, which is where the reception is being held. There is indeed ice cream, as well as an assortment of other desserts and nonalcoholic beverages.

Ryan and Jules and I meet up with Toby and Maria and a bunch of Ryan's other friends. I guess they're starting to become my friends, too. Sasha and Lisa R. join us after a while, as does Craig, who immediately brings the conversation around to what we think the next set of shows might be, and what the chances are that this time they will include *Candide.* Everyone makes their obligatory, teasing no-one-likes-*Candide*-but-you comment and goes on with their other conversations. Except Lisa R., who says she doesn't know *Candide,* at which point Craig drags her over to the bleachers to sit down so he can tell her all about it.

Peter is on the other side of the room, surrounded by even more admirers than usual, soaking in the congratulations and accolades and gently fending off adorable Lower Campers who seem to be trying to bring him more desserts. He'll be heading out in the morning along with the other single-session campers, and then a fresh group of kids will arrive in the afternoon. I'm sure I'll talk to him again sometime during the evening or tomorrow before he leaves, but whatever else happens, I feel like Peter and I have already said our real good-bye.

Although I also feel certain it's not good-bye forever.

I look around at all these people, some I've come to know, some who are still strangers, all of them here because they love theater and want to spend their summer immersed in it with other theater-loving types. I'm still amazed that this kind of miraculous wonderland exists, and that I somehow never knew about it for so long. I guess I just didn't have friends who went to sleepaway camp, and my parents didn't really know about it, and so I never had a reason to investigate. Thank goodness for Ryan. Well, not just for this reason, obviously. It's just one more reason in the already very long list of reasons why I am grateful for him.

As I'm looking around, I notice Susan loitering suspiciously near a corner. I peer at her, trying to figure out what she's up to. Ryan sees me peering and joins me. "Is that your friend Susan?"

"Yes."

"What's she doing?"

"I think," I say slowly, noting who is approaching her position from the other side of the corner, "that she is about to pounce on that cute oboe player currently heading in her direction."

"Ah," Ryan says. "Should we . . . try to stop her?"

I think about this for a second. "No. I think we should let her go for it. And see what happens."

"Where did she even get this idea?" He is giving me one of those delicious lopsided smiles now. Which makes me smile back uncontrollably. Still. Always.

"I may have said something. As a joke. About how to break the ice when you have a crush on a boy." His grin widens, and I hasten to add, "But I totally did not tackle you on purpose that time. You know that, right? I was running to try to find Annie and you just happened to be in the way."

"Sure," he says. "Whatever you say, Cyn."

"Ryan, I'm serious!"

"Okay."

"Say you believe me."

"I . . . don't believe you. Sorry."

I kiss him to make him shut up. And then I keep kissing him, because . . . well, it's Ryan. It's hard to stop.

But then a thought occurs to me.

I pull back a little. "Do you say things to annoy me just to get me to kiss you to shut you up?"

"Of course not," he says. "Hey, do you want to hear about this sexy dream I had last night about someone else?"

"Watch it, mister."

"Make me."

I do.

Acknowledgments

As usual, many lovely people helped me along the way as I wrote this novel. Special thanks to Brent Felker and Bridey Flynn, who read drafts and asked good questions and noticed very important things. Thanks also to Melissa Posten for *Scarlet Pimpernel* reference; Suzanne Fine, Andi Fleisch, Evan Levy, Jennifer Rosenkrantz, and Eliot Sirota for helping me remember things about theater camp; Alan Florendo and Jessica Hillman-McCord for musical theater recommendations (past, present, and future); Adi Rule and John Rule for eleventh-hour physics assistance; and Kristin Cartee, Tina McIntyre, Jennifer Rosenkrantz, Stephanie Santoriello, and Jenny Weiss for very-much-appreciated general support and encouragement, book-related and otherwise. Finally, none of this would be possible without my amazing agent, Jodi Reamer, and my wonderful editor, Sarah Ketchersid — thank you both for continuing to put up with me and for believing in my books!